SHALLOW DEPTHS

INSPIRED BY TRUE EVENTS

WRITTEN BY MILAN SKRECEK

HARDCOVER ISBN: 9798342252997
PAPERBACK ISBN: 9798342464895

Printed in the United States of America
POD

This book is dedicated to Laura, my incredible wife, whom I had the fortune to meet in an unlikely setting that feels straight out of a fairy tale–a cruise ship.

Amidst the vast ocean and under the expansive sky, our paths crossed, sparking a connection that has profoundly enriched my life. Laura, your unwavering support and love have been my anchor through storms and calm seas alike. Our journey began amidst the backdrop of breathtaking sunsets and the rhythmic sounds of the waves, a fitting start to our 'Legendary' adventure together.

This dedication is but a small token of my gratitude for the laughter, insights, and companionship you've shared with me since that serendipitous encounter. Here's to all our days, from the spectacular to the everyday, as we navigate this beautiful life together.

Chapter 1

TAXI, TEARS, AND TINY ESCAPES

The taxi ride from Miami Airport to South Beach was about as pleasant as getting kicked in the gut, which, ironically, is what my life has felt like for the past week. Between my dad's funeral, the alcohol coursing through my veins, and the pile of debt I didn't ask to inherit, I was in a mood. A "what the hell am I doing?" kind of mood.

I shifted in the backseat of the beat-up yellow taxi, glancing at the Cuban driver up front, who seemed completely uninterested in me. Which was fine. I wasn't in the mood for chit-chat, and I had more pressing concerns, like sneaking a sip from the tiny bottle of Jim Beam I smuggled off the plane. A relic from the in-flight "comfort kit" I shamelessly abused. Daddy would've laughed if he knew–he always loved a good hustle.

Except, he wouldn't know now, because he was dead. Just like his good advice and charm. And, apparently, any savings he might have left me because *surprise*, my gambling-loving father left me nothing but bills and broken promises.

I uncapped another tiny bottle, the small sound masked by the whoosh of cars and the endless traffic that seemed to define Miami at sunset. Cars honked at each other in a weird symphony of frustration. Bright neon signs glowed from the countless strip malls and restaurants lining the 836 highway, casting colorful reflections on the glossy hoods of luxury cars. Meanwhile, the dull roar of the city and the humidity creeping into the taxi's cracked window gave the whole scene a sticky, dreamlike quality. Why do old men like to drive with the window slightly cracked open? Sheesh!

I took a quick swig and tucked the bottle away before the driver noticed. He didn't need to, though. This wasn't his problem. Hell, it wasn't even my problem until it suddenly was. I was supposed to be living the dream, right?

Traveling the world as a "shopping guide" on luxury cruise ships, helping tourists blow their money on diamonds, jewelry, and watches they didn't need–sounds glamorous, right? The brochures sell it like a dream: the open sea, exotic destinations, and a front-row seat to high-end shopping sprees. From the outside, it seems enchanting, even noble. Us shopping guides are seen as the custodians of commerce, the middlemen who connect eager tourists with the best local deals. Yet, beneath this shimmering veneer of service, there exists a darker reality, one they don't mention at orientation or in the recruiting pamphlets.

The stores on the islands, where I shepherd wide-eyed tourists, are managed by a tight-knit group of corrupt players. It's an exclusive club of power brokers who make sure every dollar leaves the guests' wallets and ends up in theirs. These people don't care about the "local culture" or "authentic shopping experiences" they market so heavily. Heck, 95% of them weren't even born in the Caribbean. No, they care about one thing–control.

They run the island shops like a well-oiled machine, and they've made it clear, over the past three years of being a shopping guide, that I'm just another cog in their wheel. To them, the tourists are walking ATM machines, and I'm the one with the PIN code.

The cruise lines themselves are no better. They play innocent, acting like they're just offering a convenient service to their passengers, but they're somewhat complicit.

They rake in kickbacks, payments, whatever you want to call it–a classic payola scheme, really. They push tourists into overpriced, shiny stores where they drop ridiculous sums of money on what amounts to polished rocks. All the while, I'm standing there, smiling, pretending this is the "deal of a lifetime" when I know damn well it's not.

This life isn't the *Love Boat*, that cheesy, feel-good image of cruise life we grew up watching. No, this is real, gritty ship life, far removed from the cheerful, sunny decks shown in glossy ads. People think working on a cruise ship is about seeing the world and living the high life, but the truth is, most of us are running. Some of us from home, some from responsibilities, others–like me–from debt or heartbreak.

In my case, it's both.

I ghosted the best thing to happen to me since getting the job as shopping guide. My girlfriend, I mean. It wasn't even like a conscious decision at first–it just kind of happened. After Dad died, everything went numb. Like, I couldn't even *feel* anymore, and I didn't have the energy to explain that to anyone, my brother or sister, or even my annoying mom, which is how my siblings feel Dad got into his mess.

So, I just... vanished. Stopped responding to texts, ignored her calls, let the whole thing fade out like a song on the radio you're not really listening to anyway. It seemed easier that way. She was on a ship and I was on land.

And then the drinking started. Not that I hadn't been drinking before–because let's be real, a good buzz is practically mandatory when you work on a cruise ship–but after the funeral, it became less about unwinding after a shift and more about drowning everything I didn't want to think about.

I'd sit in my Dad's now vacant house, a bottle of bourbon in one hand and the other scrolling through old photos of Dad and me. He was my hero, my constant, and suddenly he was gone. It hit me like a freight train. The kind of blow you can't recover from with a few days off work. And instead of dealing with it, instead of facing my girlfriend, my grief, and my life, I just... disappeared into the bottle. Nights blurred into mornings, and the pain stayed muted, but it was always there, lurking under the surface. I couldn't face calling her because I couldn't even face myself. How could I explain that the girl she fell for–the girl who was all charm and sass–was now just a hollow shell, barely keeping it together?

The worst part is, she didn't deserve it. I know that. She deserved an explanation, a conversation, something. But every time I thought about reaching out, I'd pour another drink instead. It was easier to be numb, to let the alcohol smooth over the jagged edges of reality.

I kept telling myself I'd deal with it all *tomorrow*. But tomorrow never came. And so, she moved on, I guess. Or maybe she's still wondering what the hell happened to me. Either way, I'm too far gone now to fix it.

I take the tiny bottle out of my purse again and slowly twist the cap, trying to be discreet. My head is pounding, and I just need something to take the edge off–the edge of grief, guilt, and everything else I've been carrying since Dad's funeral.

The taxi driver swerves suddenly, missing a seagull by inches, and the liquor sloshes out of the bottle, spilling on my shirt.

"¿Qué diablos?" I spit, my voice sharper than I intended, as I wipe at the liquid soaking into my clothes. Great, now I'm going to smell like cheap booze. I shoot a look at the driver, who's too busy cursing in rapid-fire Spanish to notice. I try to tuck the tiny bottle back into my purse without drawing any more attention to myself, my fingers fumbling as I awkwardly hide the evidence.

The driver glances in the rearview mirror, his eyes narrowing like he knows I'm up to something but is too polite– or maybe just too disinterested–to say anything. I raise my eyebrows and give him a quick smile, hoping to deflect his curiosity, and lean back into the cracked leather seat, clutching the bottle tight in my hand like it's a lifeline.

I used to believe in my job, believe in the dream of traveling and making good money. In the beginning, it wasn't all bad.

There were times I felt like I was making people happy. You see the smiles when someone buys a luxury watch or finds the "perfect" piece of jewelry for their anniversary.

But then, as the years went by, I started noticing the cracks. The guests who'd leave disappointed when they realized they'd been overcharged for polished rocks. The way the stores played with their emotions, and how I—me, Christina Delgado —was their willing accomplice.

It's a life where the enchantment of travel meets the harsh reality of aggressive sales tactics and ethical compromises. And here's where it gets complicated: part of me *hates* it. I hate knowing that I'm pushing overpriced trinkets on people who are just looking for a piece of paradise to take home with them. I hate that the "local flavor" I talk up is all part of a calculated script provided during our yearly sales training retreats.

But the other part? The other part of me gets it. This job, this life, it's an escape for me, too. A way out of Charleston, a way to forget about Dad's gambling debts and my family falling apart. I used to be Daddy's girl, and now he's gone, leaving me with nothing but unpaid bills and the weight of bad decisions.

And honestly, the ship, with all its glittering fakery, feels like a safe distance from all that. Out here, I can pretend for a little while that I'm in control, that I'm not sinking under the weight of everything I've inherited—his debt, his love of the hustle, his inability to say no to temptation.

The driver makes a sharp turn, nearly throwing me across the backseat, and I curse under my breath. He's taking one of those sketchy shortcuts locals always seem to know, weaving between narrow streets lined with pastel-colored buildings that hadn't seen a fresh coat of paint since the '80s.

Laundry flaps from balconies, and kids play in the street while their parents watch from folding chairs on the sidewalk. It was like a scene out of a movie, except I wasn't paying attention to the plot.

I don't know if I'm more disgusted with myself for playing along or impressed that I've managed to keep doing it for this long. Three years is a long time to be a shopping guide, to be in that world. It's the ultimate contradiction–being the one to sell dreams while knowing that most of those dreams are built on half-truths, kickbacks, and overpriced baubles.

But then again, who am I to judge? I'm just as complicit. I need the commissions, the kickbacks, to keep going. Every sale brings me a little closer to keeping my head above water, and as long as that's the case, I'll keep doing what I do best: selling the fantasy.

But that's where the conflict now gnaws at me, late at night, while on vacation, off the ship, back at my Dad's old house. Do I keep going? Do I keep pretending that this is enough, that the travel and the pay check will somehow fill the growing void left by everything I've lost? Or do I walk away, knowing that what lies ahead is even more uncertain than the seas I've been sailing?

It's like I'm stuck in a loop–traveling, selling, drinking, repeating. And I can't tell if I'm doing it to survive or if I'm too scared to find out what happens if I stop.

Dad used to say I had a way with people. That I could sell ice to an Eskimo. And, honestly? He wasn't wrong. I'm good at this–too good. The problem is, I don't know if I even like it anymore.

I leaned back into the musty seat, trying to find a comfortable spot. The leather was cracked, and I could feel the sticky heat clinging to my skin. The sky was turning that perfect shade of dusky pink, a Miami sunset to die for. Yet, all I could think about was the long list of unpaid bills I now needed to pay. Dad's bills. Or, more accurately, Dad's gambling debts that had somehow become *my* problem.

Right before the funeral, and after dealing with my my brother and sister not showing up, my phone buzzed, the screen flashing with a number I don't recognize. I answered thinking it was a friend of Dad's asking for directions to the church, only to be greeted by a voice that instantly makes my stomach drop. It was one of Dad's loan sharks–a guy named Carlos, with a voice as slimy as a doorknob at Diddy's house.

"I'm sure you know why I'm calling," he said, his words dripped with menace. My mind raced–*How the hell did he get my number?* I haven't even been back long enough to sort through Dad's mess, and now this? Carlos went on, reminding me of the debt Dad left behind, the one I didn't even know existed until recently, and now it was apparently mine to deal with. Great. Just what I needed.

Being Daddy's girl was great when he was alive. He had charm, that man. He could walk into a room and light it up. But he also had a love for blackjack and poker, and, well, that's where it all went sideways. As it turns out, charisma doesn't pay the bills, and charm doesn't keep creditors, or loan sharks at bay. Now I'm stuck with his mess, and I have no idea how to get out from under it.

I glanced at the meter, watching the numbers climb as we inched closer to South Beach. Miami was loud, colorful, and chaotic–a far cry from the quiet, suffocating atmosphere back in Charleston. God, Charleston. The funeral. The cemetery. The endless string of military friends offering their "thoughts and prayers" while I just stood there, numb. A hollow shell of myself. And, as usual, I was the only one left to deal with the aftermath. My siblings had disappeared into their own lives, leaving me to clean up the mess. Typical.

I shook my head and focused on the here and now, wiping the tears that well-up periodically whenever I think of my Dad.

Miami was a city that never stopped, never slowed down, and maybe that's why I felt like I belonged here. Or maybe it was just the bourbon making me feel like I could handle this madness. The city was alive, buzzing with people who probably had their own problems, but at least they weren't dealing with a dead father's gambling debts.

"¿Todo bien, señorita?" the driver asked, glancing at me through the rearview mirror.

I forced a smile. "Sí, gracias, lo siento, estoy tan callado, pensando demasiado en mis elecciones de vida," I say letting the driver know I'm overthinking my life choices. He nods, seemingly satisfied with my half-assed answer.

"No somos todos." he says, and goes back to focusing on the road–or whatever Miami's version of road etiquette was. It seemed like chaos to me, but hey, I wasn't the one behind the wheel.

I stared out the window, watching the ships leave the port as we drive along MacArthur Causeway. Passed Star Island, and into the South Beach District with their glittering hotels, high-end boutiques, and neon-lit bars. South Beach was a playground for the rich and the reckless, and here I was, stuck somewhere in between. My job as a shopping guide wasn't exactly the ticket to wealth and fame, but it was decent enough to keep me afloat. For now.

But how long could I keep doing this? Hustling tourists to buy overpriced jewelry while pretending it was the "deal of a lifetime" had lost its sparkle. The kickbacks were nice, sure, but the guilt was starting to outweigh the commission checks. And now, with Dad gone, the idea of continuing felt even more pointless.

I reached into my purse, feeling for the other mini bottle, but stopped short. Maybe I didn't need another drink. Maybe I just needed to figure out what the hell I was doing with my life. I quickly apply some cherry chapstick before taking some cash out. Gotta keep them lips looking soft and juicy.

"Pagaré en efectivo," I said abruptly wanting to pay the driver in cash, leaning forward and handing the driver a few crumpled bills.

He nodded without comment, pulling up to the curb outside my hotel. The neon sign above the entrance flickered slightly, casting a faint glow over the street. Tourists milled about, some dragging their suitcases behind them, eager to explore South Beach or check into their overpriced rooms and begin their week of excess.

"Gracias," the driver said as he took the cash, giving me a quick glance that made me feel like he knew way more about my life than he should.

I grabbed my bag and slid out of the taxi, stepping into the warm, sticky night air. Miami had a way of wrapping itself around you, suffocating and exhilarating all at once. I stood there for a moment, taking it all in–the sounds, the smells, the college kids on Spring Break.

This was my life now. Numb. Somewhat lost. Unsure of where I was heading but still moving forward because, really, what other choice did I have? I couldn't go back to Charleston. Not now, not yet anyway. So, I'd keep going, for now. Keep hustling, keep selling, keep pretending everything was fine.

But deep down, I knew something had to change. I just didn't know what, or how, or when.

With a sigh, I walked into the hotel, the door closing behind me with a soft whoosh. Another night in another city, another step forward into the unknown. And for now, that was enough.

Chapter 2

THE HOT MESS EXPRESS

So, there I was, standing at the check-in desk at my hotel in South Beach, trying to hold it together while everything was falling apart. Sadly, the Jim Beam I had during the car ride to the hotel was already wearing off. My credit card had just been declined–not once, but twice. The front desk clerk, a perky little thing with a plastic smile, handed it back to me like it was contaminated.

"You can cover the security deposit with cash if needed. Heaven knows most of these college kids needed to do that. Spring break is always a zoo," she said, voice dripping with that fake concern that made my skin crawl.

"How much is it?" I asked, already knowing this wasn't going to go my way.

She double-checked her screen, probably enjoying this way too much. "It's two hundred and fifty dollars." If only I could slap that shitty smile off her face.

I fished around in my wallet and came up with a grand total of a hundred and eighty bucks. I leaned in, flashing her what I hoped was a sheepish grin, but let's be honest, it probably looked more like a grimace. The line behind me started to get restless, and I could feel their impatient glares burning into the back of my head. This was not how I envisioned my night to go.

"I only have, uh, a hundred and, uh, eighty to my name," I admitted, feeling like a total idiot.

The clerk just stood there, her silence more damning than any lecture. Realizing I was getting nowhere, I shoved the bills back into my wallet. "Ok, give me a sec."

I stepped to the side, pulled out my phone, and saw a sea of missed calls. Great. As if things couldn't get any worse, I noticed my nails were a mess, and there was a drink stain on my sleeve. So, that's where the bourbon landed. Perfect.

Desperate, I called my brother, Eric–my go-to guy when life decides to slap me across the face, which lately has been pretty often. Eric's 27, a firefighter, and my biggest cheerleader, even when I don't deserve it. He answered on the first ring, wrestling with tin foil that refused to cooperate with his potatoes.

"Ola, Pollita," he greeted me, his voice laced with that big brother sarcasm I knew too well.

"Hey bro, I'm in South Beach and need some help," I said, trying to keep the panic out of my voice.

"You looking for bail money?" he shot back, probably grinning like an idiot.

"Did the police call you already?" I deadpanned, hoping a little humor might lighten the mood.

Eric yelped as he burned his fingers on the potatoes. "¡Chinga tu madre!" he cursed, making me laugh despite everything.

"Well fuck you, too, brother," I shot back, unable to resist.

"Nah, these potatoes are hot, and I burnt myself. What's up?" He says in a more focussed, helpful tone.

"My credit cards were declined at check-in. Can I use your card number?" I asked, absentmindedly trying to rub the bourbon stain off my sleeve. No luck.

"You not paying your bills anymore? I thought you 'cruise ship shopping guides' made bank?" Eric quipped, clearly enjoying my misery. I exhale.

"My last two ships were a grind. Hence the demotion to the ship I join tomorrow," I confessed, hating how small I felt.

There was a pause, and I could almost hear him gearing up for his favorite lecture. "I don't want to tell you what to do…"

"Oh, here it comes," I muttered, rolling my eyes even though he couldn't see me.

"...but don't you think it's time you came home? Call it quits. You can find a job here, live with me for a bit. Or Dads house until they take it away. Go back to school. What are you running from? Is it Mom? Was it Dad?" he asked, cutting right to the heart of it, like always.

I sighed, pulling out my cherry chapstick and slathering it on. I'm beginning to think this cherry chapstick is a coping mechanism or some kinda tick. "I'm not running from anything. I don't want to go home a failure."

"A failure in whose eyes?" he pressed, softer now, the way only a brother can.

"Mine," I admitted, my voice barely above a whisper. "Look, I appreciate my big brother always looking out for me. I really do."

"Money's not everything..." Eric started, but I cut him off.

"I just need to be here, for now. I'll come home when I'm ready."

There was a long pause. I knew he was trying to figure out what to say next without making me bolt.

"Familia es todo!" he finally said, and I felt that familiar pang in my chest.

"In an ideal world, maybe," I replied, my voice a little sharper than I meant. "I've learned the hard way that blood doesn't always equal unconditional love or support."

Eric let that sink in for a couple of seconds, and I could almost hear the wheels turning in his head.

"Hope I'm not clumped into the issues you have with mom. Just don't get too lost at sea. I'm here whenever you need. Now, pass the phone over to the clerk, and I'll give her my card number," he said, all business now.

"Thanks, bro," I said, grateful but still feeling like a mess.

"Speak with you... when I speak with you, I guess."

"Te amo, mi pollito," he said, his voice softening again.

"I love you too," I replied, smiling despite myself. I handed the phone to the clerk and watched as she took down Eric's card info. At least that crisis was averted. For now.

Later, I dragged my suitcase through the busy hotel lobby, dodging drunk college-age girls taking selfies, frat boys sneaking booze, and cops who were too busy ogling the spring break crowd to do much else. I noticed a group of tipsy women on, what looked like, their bachelorette party, and overheard the women reading the bride-to-be, in a veil, a "Dare List". They all oooooh, in unison, at their her latest mission.

My phone rang again, a distinct "Mom" ringtone I added so I know it's her calling, but I hit ignore without a second thought. I wasn't in the mood to deal with her tonight. She was a bit of a handful at the funeral, something I wasn't ready for or needing to take on.

I stepped into the elevator dragging my roll-away case, clutching my phone. The elevator was packed with a bunch of rowdy frat boys, one of them blocking the button side of the elevator. What happened to chivalry these days? The door begins to close as I reached past to select my floor but the door slid open and the loud music, from the lounge, filled the elevator.

Just as the doors were about to close, trapped in a sea of sweaty frat boys in this cramped elevator, the door slides open again and the loud music, from the lounge in the lobby, enters the elevator.

Out of nowhere, this whirlwind of a woman in a bridal veil pushed her way in and up to me. Before I could even process what was happening, she leans in and kissed me.

No warning, no introduction, just bam! Like, really kissed me. The kind of kiss that makes you forget your own name. This girl is a walking fire hazard, a blow torch burning–with lipstick, and I'm pretty sure she just melted half my brain cells.

The kiss was long and hot. Seriously hot. I haven't been kissed like *that* for fuck knows how long. The frat boys went dead silent, in complete awe watching two hot girls kiss. Only the music from the lounge in the lobby was heard. Then the bachelorette party started cheering, which got the frat guys cheering too.

When she finally finished and pulled back, I was left dazed, trying to figure out what the hell just happened. My head still cocked to the side, mouth slightly open, arms up by my side. The frat guys cheer. She stepped backwards out of the elevator.

Just as I'm trying to process the fact that I was just kissed by a girl in a veil, my phone rings. That distinctive ringtone set for my moms' calls cut through the chaos like a knife, but when I glanced at my left hand, it was empty.

I snapped my head back toward the lobby, and there she was—the veiled temptress—slipping my damn phone into her purse like it was a party favor. The elevator doors slid shut, and I was left staring at my own reflection, in the polished metal elevator door panel, cursing under my breath as we started our slow, awkward ascent.

"Motherfucker," I snapped, shoving one of the frat boys aside and hitting every button on the panel like a crazy person. The elevator stopped on the second floor mezzanine, and I bolted out, dragging my suitcase behind me like it was the ball and chain to my hot mess express. From the mezzanine, I spotted her—the veiled thief—entering the lobby lounge below with her bachelorette party friends.

I raced downstairs, stopping only to ask the two Miami-Dade officers standing at the doorway for help.

"Officer, a girl in a wedding veil stole my iPhone. I'm traveling for work, and it has all my work contacts. Can you help me find her?"

The cops, who were too busy ogling the college girls to care, reluctantly agreed. "In a veil? Sure. Can't be that hard. We'll do a lap."

I pushed through the crowd in the lounge until I found the bachelorette party, and there she was—the veiled thief, laughing it up like she hadn't just committed grand theft iPhone. I marched up to her, grabbed her arm, and spun her around.

"What the fuck? Where's my phone?" I demanded, not even trying to hide my fury.

She blinked at me, all wide-eyed innocence.

"Hey, cherry chapstick, you getting rough with me?" she teased, but there was a flicker of fear in her eyes. Her bridesmaids started to circle, but she waved them off.

"Give me my phone back!" I hissed, motioning toward the cops who were slowly making their way over. Her bravado crumbled, and genuine fear replaced it.

"Wait, what? No. Listen, I was so swept up in our kiss, I didn't realize I grabbed your phone. I'm sorry. No need for cops. I'm out with workmates, and I can't get in trouble, again." she admits.

"You should have thought of that sooner," I shot back, not letting her off the hook that easily.

"I'll do anything, just don't tell the cops," she blurts out frantically. I stare at her, stunned by her demeanor.

The two Miami-Dade police officers finally reached us and start their questioning. Her bachelorette friends somehow scatter like cockroaches hit by kitchen lights.

"Is this the girl that stole your phone?" one of them asked, looking slightly bothered by the request.

I glanced at her, then around the room, weighing my options. I look back at her, giving her a look that could silence an entire room. The tough-girl act was gone, and now she was just a deer in headlights, caught between her pride and the trouble that was slowly making its way over in the form of two uniformed officers.

"No, wrong girl in a veil," I finally said, watching the relief flood her face as the cops moved on.

"Thank you," she whispered, looking at me like I was her hero. But I wasn't done yet.

"You fuckin' owe me, big-time. Gimme my phone," I demanded, holding out my hand.

She pulled it out of her designer handbag, and I snatched it back, immediately checking the screen. Multiple notifications lit up, including one from Mom that read:

"Thanks for organizing the funeral. I hope you arrived to Miami safe. I'm tired and off to bed."

I glanced back at her, half expecting her to bolt, but she just stood there, biting her lip.

"I'm a clinically certified kleptomaniac, so I have no control over what happens when I'm nervous. For what it's worth, we did share an absolutely amazing kiss, so you can't be that pissed at me. Right?" she said trying to lighten the tension.

I looked at her, then up at the veil she wore. She continues to tell me way too much information, her words spilling out in a nervous, rapid-fire monologue. I could practically see the panic bubbling beneath the surface as she rambled on, her voice calm and collected, as if the more she talked, the less likely I was to notice the real problem.

"My workmates are escorts and get all the attention when I go out with them. I wear this veil to at least get *some* attention...and get free drinks. They like to play "Dare" games to keep themselves entertained because standing around doesn't get them free drinks." she says, her voice trailing off, clearly hoping I'll find the excuse as reasonable as she does.

Her hands fidget nervously with the edge of her dress, like she's waiting for me to either call her out or let her off the hook. It's the kind of explanation that's equal parts oversharing and deflection, and I can tell she's just grasping at anything to keep herself from looking guilty.

"Great. You're a klepto and a liar." I chirp.

Emily's expression softened, her shoulders slumping a little as if the weight of the situation was finally starting to hit her. She fiddled with the big gold bangles on her wrist, and played with her golden-blonde locks, and for the first time since this whole mess started, she actually looked... human. Not the sly, scheming type I'd been ready to deck for stealing my phone.

"I said I'm sorry," she repeated, her voice quieter, more sincere this time. "Can I make it up to you? Maybe buy you a drink?"

I narrowed my eyes at her. "No," I said firmly, my patience long gone. "I'm not in the mood to deal with any more of your bullshit."

She bit her lip and nodded, not even trying to argue this time. For a second, I thought that was the end of it–finally, I could move on from this disaster of a day–but then she spoke again, her voice a little too honest for comfort.

"Look, I know I messed up. I didn't even realize I had grabbed your phone until you called me out on it. I steal when I'm nervous and, I swear, I wasn't trying to steal from you. I was just–" She hesitated, her eyes darting away as if she was trying to find the right words, looking over at her girlfriends who returned after the cops left. "I don't fit in with them, you know? The girls at work. They're all escorts, and when they go out, I'm invisible, *they* get all the attention. Guys flock to them, and I'm just... there. The odd one out."

I raised an eyebrow, still skeptical because to me, she is no slouch. "So, you put on a veil and pretend you're getting married?"

She let out a sad little laugh, shaking her head.

"I guess so. It's stupid, I know. But I don't even care about the attention as much as just... trying to feel like I belong." She looks over at her gaggle of escorts, points out the stunning asian, and adds "One of them is my roommate, Becca, and she invites me out to make me feel like part of the group, but deep down, I know I'm not. I'm just the girl who schedules their appointments, not the one making the big bucks."

I stared at her for a moment, trying to decide if I should feel sorry for her or still be pissed off. Honestly, it was a toss-up.

"So why keep doing it?" She shrugged, her eyes finally meeting mine again.

"I don't know," she reluctantly answers. "It's better than sitting at home alone, I guess. And I'm working on it. I'm taking online law classes. I want out, you know? I don't want to be a part of this forever. I'm trying to better myself. Maybe one day I'll be on the other side of the law instead of skirting around it."

There was something in her voice–genuine, maybe even a little hopeful–that made me pause. I hated to admit it, but I kind of got it. Not the whole "stealing my phone" part, but the rest? Feeling out of place, trying to find your footing, figuring out what to do when I grow up? Yeah, that hit home a little. And my Dad always taught me to look for the best in every situation.

Emily smiled, and noticed I was thinking too much. "Can still buy you that drink?"

I gave her a small smirk and let out a sigh, the tension easing just a bit. "Alright, fine. But don't think I'm letting you off the hook that easy. You're not as slick as you think. And you still owe me. You're lucky I'm thirsty."

Emily's smile widened just a bit, like she was genuinely surprised I didn't tell her to get lost. She pushed her hair behind her ear, looking more like a shy schoolgirl than someone who schedules appointments for high-class escorts. It was strange seeing this side of her–vulnerable, almost like she was letting her guard down for the first time.

"Okay, cool," she said softly. "Let's go to the bar, we'll never get served over here. They do a killer mojito." She grabbed my hand and pulled me through the crowd, my case hitting the backs of peoples legs and we made our way.

Along the way I couldn't help but think, *Mojitos, huh*? The night had taken a turn I wasn't expecting, but maybe a drink would help clear my head–or at least blur the mess of thoughts swirling around. Heaven knows I love to drink.

Chapter 3

MOJITOS AND MIXED SIGNALS

The bar area was packed with college kids, all drinking way too much, their loud, slurred conversations blending into a chaotic symphony of youthful debauchery. Everywhere I looked, there were neon-colored drinks in plastic cups, girls in tiny outfits dancing, and guys trying–and failing miserably–to look cool while downing shots of tequila.

Emily and I squeezed through the crowd, avoiding a group of college guys who were chanting something incoherent, probably on their fifth round of drinks, judging by the glazed looks in their eyes. The smell of cheap beer and rum was heavy in the air, mixing with adolescent angst and desperation. It was the kind of atmosphere where you could feel the collective bad decisions being made in real-time.

"Spring breakers," I complain under my breath, shaking my head as I dodged a girl who almost stumbled into me with an oversized margarita. "Just what I needed."

Emily gave a small laugh, holding my hand like it was the only thing keeping her sane in the middle of this chaos. "It's a scene, that's for sure," she said, her voice barely cutting through the noise.

I couldn't help but roll my eyes at the whole situation. I mean, I've seen my fair share of drunken tourists on vacation, but spring break in South Florida? That's a whole different beast. These kids had zero self-control, and you could tell they were all living for the Instagram stories they'd barely remember the next day.

We finally managed to find a spot at the far end of the bar, a little less chaotic but still surrounded by the inevitable backdrop of screaming twenty-somethings trying to hook up with strangers.

Emily waved down a bartender and leaned onto the bar to tell him our order, her movements smooth and confident despite the chaos around us. The bartender worked quickly, muddling the mint leaves with expert hands. I watched her as she fidgeted slightly, nervously drumming her fingers against the bar top.

I glanced at her, my eyes briefly taking in the way her tight dress hugged her curves–perfectly fitted, almost too perfect for this place full of sloppy spring-breakers. The dress was that deep red, the kind that practically screamed for attention, and on her, it worked. She had that effortless grace, the kind that could make heads turn, even when she wasn't trying.

Her long, blonde hair cascaded over her shoulders, framing her face in a way that highlighted her sharp features. There was something magnetic about the way she carried herself, and I couldn't help but wonder how someone who felt so out of place in her own life could still exude so much confidence in moments like this.

Emily flashed the bartender a polite smile, but there was a hint of weariness in her eyes, like she was used to this–used to being looked at, used to playing the part.

As Emily continued to lean up on the bar, I couldn't help but take another quick glance at her, my eyes drifting over the way that red dress clung to her body, perfectly tailored in all the right places. It was instinctual, one of those moments where you're not even thinking, just appreciating the view. But of course, in my luck, she caught me.

Through the loud music, her eyes met mine, and a slow, playful smile crept onto her lips. She didn't look annoyed or embarrassed–quite the opposite, actually. She seemed to like it, the attention. I could see the spark in her gaze as she caught me red-handed, and suddenly, I felt the heat rise to my cheeks.

"Enjoying the view, cherry chapstick?" Emily teased, raising one eyebrow, her voice smooth like she'd been waiting for this moment.

I rolled my eyes, trying to play it cool, but I could feel my pulse quicken. "Don't flatter yourself," I shot back, though the smirk tugging at the corner of my lips probably didn't help my case.

Emily chuckled, hoping off the foot rail at the Base of the bar, leaning in a little closer to me, her voice lowering just enough to make my heart skip a beat. "Oh, I'm not. But I don't mind if *you* do."

The bartender came back with our drinks, but the air between us was suddenly charged, like an invisible line had been crossed, and neither of us seemed eager to step back.

I took a long sip of my drink, letting the cool mint hit my throat, doing my best to drown out the madness around me.

Emily took a slow sip of her drink too, her eyes still locked on mine, that playful smirk not going anywhere. "So, what do you do, cherry chapstick?" she asked, casually leaning back against the bar like she was ready for whatever story I was about to spin.

I raised an eyebrow at her, a little surprised by the sudden interest. "I'm a shopping guide," I said, taking a sip of my mojito, trying to keep my tone light. "You know, one of those people who tell cruise passengers where to shop in all the overpriced jewelry stores at every port."

Emily's eyes lit up with curiosity. "Really? So, you're like, the person who knows where all the diamonds and luxury watches are hiding?"

"Pretty much," I said, shrugging. "I join a new ship tomorrow morning–the Ocean Seduction."

Emily let out a low whistle. "Ocean Seduction? Sounds fancy. Is that like, the name of some secret luxury shopping experience or something?"

I laughed, shaking my head. "No, that's just the ship's name. But hey, I wouldn't mind if it doubled as my sales pitch. 'Ask for the "Ocean Seduction" collection, and get exclusive discounts on a unique collection of jewelry.' I should add that to my spiel."

She grinned, clearly amused. "I'd buy something from you just for the tagline."

I smirked. "I'll keep that in mind when I'm trying to meet my sales quota. But honestly, it's a hustle. I spend my days convincing people to drop money they don't have on things they probably don't need."

Emily tilted her head, watching me closely. "It sounds… exhausting, honestly. But kinda fun too. You meet a lot of people, right?"

"Oh yeah, more than I care to, sometimes," I said, swirling the ice in my glass. "But every now and then, you get someone who's actually looking for something meaningful. You get to help them make a memory. That part's not so bad."

She took another sip, her eyes never leaving mine. "So, what's it like working on these ships? Seems glamorous from the outside."

I laughed, a little louder this time. "Glamorous? Hardly. Sure, it can be fun, but most of the time, you're surrounded by thousands of people, and yet, somehow, you feel more alone than you would in an empty room."

Emily's expression softened, and for a moment, the playful banter fell away. "I get that," she said quietly. "Being surrounded by people but still feeling like you're on your own." We pause and drink at the same time.

"I used to go out with my friends like this back in Cincinnati," she said, glancing at a group of girls who were drunkenly laughing and hanging off each other. "They'd always be the life of the party, and I'd just be there, tagging along, hoping I didn't stick out too much."

"You stick out now?" I asked, leaning against the bar, raising an eyebrow.

Emily shrugged. "Sometimes. I mean, it's different now with my job. The girls I work with are... well, you saw what happened with me today. They don't really see me as one of them, but they invite me out so I don't feel left out. It's like a pity invite, you know?"

I looked at her, seeing the cracks in her cool exterior for the first time. Beneath the bravado, the stealing-my-phone nonsense, and the veil of her job, there was someone who just wanted to belong. And even here, surrounded by a sea of people, she seemed more alone than ever.

"Yeah," I said after a pause, "I get it. More than you know."

Emily met my eyes, and for a brief second, we were two people lost in the middle of this neon jungle, both trying to find a place where we fit.

I glanced at her again. She didn't look like someone who worked at an escort agency. I guess that's the point, right? But still, it was hard to reconcile this girl who looked so normal with what I imagined her job to be.

"You know," I started, my voice lower now, "I'm not sure I get it. You're working at an escort agency, taking online law classes, trying to get out... so why are you still doing it? You could leave, right?"

Emily sighed, glancing around before answering, like she was afraid someone would overhear. "It's complicated," she admitted. "The money is... decent. Not escort-level, but enough to keep me going while I study. I've thought about quitting, but I owe a lot–my University of Cincinnati student loans, Goooooo Bearcats!" Emily brings her hands up and imitates a cheerleader. I smile. She continues " Them there's my Miami rent, and, you know, living in Miami is not cheap. I put on a brave face for my family. They don't even know what I do. I tell them I'm working for some fancy office downtown." she finishes.

That hit me in a way I didn't expect. The secrets, the lies. It was like we were both carrying around this weight, doing whatever we had to just to keep the people we cared about in the dark. Maybe we were more alike than I realized.

"Law school, huh?" I said, trying to keep it light. "You know you're not supposed to break the law if you wanna be a lawyer, right?"

Emily chuckled, looking down at her feet for a second before meeting my eyes again. "Yeah, I know. But I'm trying. I really am. It's just… hard. This job, the people, the lifestyle–it's not me. But I'm stuck in it for now."

"Thanks for not completely hating me," she said, raising her glass for a toast.

I smirked and clinked my glass against hers. "Don't push your luck. You still owe me for the whole stealing-my-phone thing."

Emily grinned sheepishly. "Fair enough. I'll make it up to you on day, I swear."

I finished my drink, letting the cool, minty flavor wash over me. For the first time since this whole mess started, I didn't feel like I had to keep my guard up. Maybe Emily wasn't so bad after all. Just a girl trying to find her way, like the rest of us. Just then another text came in from my mom, the buzzing snapping me back to reality.

"Listen, I got to go." I said firmly, too tired to deal with this bar any longer. "My mom keeps texting me and I need to get some sleep before work tomorrow" I groan, knowing I have to deal with my mothers texts. I place my empty plastic cup in the bar and grab my roll-away case to go.

But as I turned to leave, she grabbed my arm again, this time with a hint of something more playful–maybe even a little hopeful.

"Can I at least get your number?"

I paused, biting back the smile tugging at the corners of my mouth. I didn't even try to hide the curiosity in my eyes.

"What, you want my number now?" I asked, my tone teasing, like I was testing her.

She grinned, that same mischievous sparkle lighting up her face. "Because you said I owe you, and let's face it, that kiss was fire. Duh."

I shook my head, pretending to be exasperated, but there was no hiding the amusement creeping into my voice. "You really know how to work a moment, don't you?"

Instead of rolling my eyes like I would have, I pulled out my phone. "Fine," I said, as Emily handed me her phone. "But just so you know, I'm not into games." I dialed my number on her phone and handed it back to her.

Emily's smile only widened as my phone rang in my hand, I showed her my screen as proof. I add Emily's name and number into my contacts, and pocket my phone.

"I'm curious on how you'd like me to pay you back," she teased. "Will it include a kiss that you'll ready for?"

I laughed, unable to stop myself from leaning into the flirtation. "Alright, enough with the teasing. But, just so you know, I've got my eye on you. Try not to steal anything else from me, okay?"

She tucked her phone back in her bag, giving me one last playful look. "I'll try to behave... but if if you don't expect too much from me, you might not be let down."

I smirked, shaking my head at her audacity. "Wow, you might not want to say those type of things to people if you ever want people to trust you. Stick to the law classes."

Emily winked, and as I walked away, I couldn't help but feel a flutter of excitement in my chest. There was something about her–something messy and complicated, but also maybe exactly what I needed. This wasn't just a random encounter. It was the start of something unexpected, and for the first time in a long time, I found myself curious to see where it might lead.

Chapter 4

THE OCEAN SEDUCTION

The scent of humid sea salt and diesel fumes hit me like a wave as I dragged my suitcase up the gangway onto the Ocean Seduction. The Ocean Seduction was the kind of ship that had once been the talk of the high seas–a luxury liner that probably dazzled with its grandeur when it first set sail.

Now, though, it was more like that aging socialite who used to turn heads at every party but had since fallen out of grace. You know the type: once the epitome of sophistication, now barely hanging on to her old charm, clinging to the past with an array of cosmetic fixes that couldn't quite mask the ravages of time.

The ship's exterior was a tired white, streaked with age and salt. She had the elegance of a bygone era, but now the paint was chipped, and the metal railings bore the scars of countless storms. If you looked close enough, you'd find rust creeping up like invasive ivy on a crumbling mansion. It was clear this was a vessel that had seen better days, much like a wealthy woman whose opulent gowns now lay hidden beneath a threadbare shawl.

Once aboard, the illusion of grandeur fell apart like an old Hollywood movie set. The corridors, lined with patterned carpets and gold-plated trim, looked like they had once been lavish but now were just a shadow of their former selves. The carpets were worn thin in places, their original splendor overshadowed by stains and scuffs. The walls had a few too many cracks for comfort, and the lighting fixtures, though ornate, flickered with the occasional ghost of their former brilliance.

In the grand dining hall, the once-majestic chandeliers hung a bit crooked, their crystals dusty and dull, like gaudy jewelry that hadn't been cleaned in decades. The furniture, once plush and inviting, now had the saggy demeanor of an overused armchair, and the upholstery was faded, bearing the colors of an era long past.

Even the staff, bless their hearts, seemed to be an extension of the ship's weary soul. They worked tirelessly, maintaining what could be maintained, but there was a palpable sense of fatigue in their movements. The ship had the sort of charm that only those who had lived through better times could remember fondly, and it clung to every corner, every creak of the floorboards, like a faded photograph in a forgotten album.

The Ocean Seduction was that grand old dame of the sea, clinging desperately to its last vestiges of opulence. It was the kind of place where you'd expect to find the remnants of past glory glinting under the surface, still striving to remind everyone of the elegance that had once defined her, even as the passage of time and the demands of the modern world pulled her further into the realm of nostalgia.

The crew entrance was this noisy, chaotic mess, with workers hustling to load the ship with all the food and supplies needed for the next however-many weeks. And there I was, wrestling my suitcase up the ramp like it was filled with bricks –or my emotional baggage, more like.

Just as I was cursing my life choices again, a chunky guy overdressed in an ill-fitting Men's Warehouse suit appeared beside me. He took one look at my struggling self and stepped in to help.

"You got a body in here?" he asked, lifting the suitcase with an ease that made me almost hate him.

"Is this not where people go to disappear?" I shot back, raising an eyebrow. He chuckled.

"For all intents and purposes, yah."

Finally inside the ship, I was greeted by a blast of air conditioning that almost made me forget the mini workout I'd just done. Almost. There's this thing about air conditioning. You don't really notice it until you step in from the heat, and then it hits you–crisp, cold, and unmistakable. It's not just the chill in the air that makes you breathe easier; it's that smell. That sterile, mechanical scent of freon and cool air rushing through vents. The kind of smell that makes you feel like you've crossed some invisible line from the chaos of the outside world into a place where things are a little more under control. But then you notice it's anything but controlled.

The main hallway, famously called the "I-95," a tip of the cap to the famous Interstate highway that ran from Northern Maine to Southern Florida, was a maze of crew members buzzing around like ants in a colony, each with their own mission. The smell of poorly cooked international food wafted through the cool air, reminding me that ship life was far from glamorous.

The guy, who was still helping me with my suitcase, sticks out his hand. "I'm Charles, the Spa Manager. Call me Chuck!"

The voice next to me was warm and friendly, the kind you'd hear from someone who's used to dealing with people day in and day out.

I turned to take a better look at this big, friendly-looking guy standing beside me in line. Chunky, sure, but solid, with the kind of smile that made you want to trust him. His skin gleamed under the harsh fluorescent lights of the ships crew area, and despite the slight glisten of sweat on his forehead, there was an ease about him, like he was used to just rolling with whatever came his way.

"Christina," I replied, shaking his hand. "shopping guide."

Chuck smiled, but there was something behind it. I'd seen that look before–the kind that says life's been a bit of a mess, but you're trying to keep your head up. We were waiting in line for the crew pursers office and as the line moved slowly forward, we started talking. There was something easy about the conversation, like he needed to tell someone his story, and I just happened to be there.

Chuck was from San Diego. He told me he'd worked at Costco for years, managing one of their busiest locations. It wasn't glamorous, but it paid the bills. He had a house in the suburbs, a wife–LaToya–and a daughter, Aniyah, who was about to turn twelve. Life had been stable, predictable. Until it wasn't.

"It was one of those things you never see coming," he said, shaking his head, his voice carrying that mixture of disbelief and anger. "I come home early from work one day, and there's LaToya... smashing the landscaping guy."

I blinked. "The landscaping guy?"

"Yeah," he said, with a humorless laugh. "I'm standing there, just trying to make sure people get their 20-pack of toilet paper, and my wife's in the backyard with the guy who trims our hedges."

I could hear the bitterness in his voice, but also that strange calmness that comes after you've had time to process something truly devastating. The anger wasn't fresh anymore; it was something he'd been sitting with for a while.

"What did you do?" I asked, curious.

He shrugged. "What could I do? Threw him out, threw her out. Told her I wanted a divorce. But man, it wasn't that simple. We'd been together for fifteen years. Aniyah is just a kid. It tore me up. She tried to explain it away, like it was just one of those things that happened because we'd grown distant. But distant doesn't give you a pass to cheat on someone."

He paused, looking ahead as the line moved forward. "So yeah, after that, things fell apart pretty quick. Divorce was messy, obviously. LaToya moved out, took Aniyah with her. I couldn't stay in that house anymore. Everything there just reminded me of what I'd lost."

"So, you came to the ships?" I asked, trying to piece together how he went from manager of a big box store to spa manager on a cruise line.

"Yeah, after the divorce, I needed a fresh start. I'd been working at Costco for years, but my heart wasn't in it anymore. I was just going through the motions. Then one day, I saw an ad for spa manager positions on cruise ships. I thought, why not? I'd been working out for years, knew a little about fitness and wellness, so I figured I could make the jump. Plus, getting away from everything back home sounded like exactly what I needed."

He let out a deep sigh, rubbing the back of his neck as he spoke. "It's been tough, though. Leaving Aniyah behind? That's been the hardest part. I FaceTime her when I can, but it's not the same. She doesn't get why I had to leave. Hell, I don't even know if I fully understand it myself. But I had to do something. I couldn't stay there, you know? Watching my life fall apart from the inside out."

The line shuffled forward, and we followed, but Chuck's mind was still somewhere else, probably back in San Diego with the pieces of his old life. I could tell this gig was more than just a job for him—it was an escape.

"Do you miss it?" I asked.

"What, Costco?" he laughed, shaking his head. "It's a great place to work, but no, not even a little. But Aniyah? Every damn day. She's a good kid, smart. I hope she gets that this isn't about her. That I didn't leave because of her. It's just... I needed space. Space to figure out who I am outside of being a husband and a dad."

I nodded, understanding more than I wanted to admit. Life had a way of ripping the rug out from under you when you least expected it.

"So now I'm here," Chuck said, looking around the tight crew purser line up with a mixture of excitement and anxiety. "It's weird, starting over at my age. But maybe this ship will be good for me. I need something new, something different. I've been lost for a while, but maybe out here, I can start figuring things out again."

I smiled at him, appreciating his honesty. "I hope you do, Chuck."

As we approached the crew purser's office, the line moved forward once more, and I could see him relax just a little. Maybe this ship was exactly the fresh start he needed.

"Talking to my friends before making the jump to ships, I hear about becoming a shopping guide," Chuck said as we moved up the pursers line, "but I heard it was super tough to get that job and even tougher to keep it."

I smirked. "Everybody wants to be a diamond, but very few are willing to get cut." Then, with a sigh, I added, "My debts drove me here."

Chuck leaned in closer, lowering his voice like we were sharing some kind of conspiracy. "Isn't that why we're all really here?" looking down the line at the other crew members signing on.

Before I could respond, the remaining person ahead of me left and I stepped up the Dutch door that separated us from the crew purser.

"Christina Delgado, shopping guide." I state, handing the purser my passport. The Filipino crew purser was exactly the kind of guy you wanted handling your sign-on process– friendly, chatty, and with this soft, almost feminine charm that put you at ease the second you stepped up to his desk.

His smile was wide, and his voice had this lilting quality that made everything he said sound a little like a song. "Welcome aboard, Christina Delgado, shopping guide," he cooed as he handed me the paperwork, his perfectly manicured fingers sliding a manila envelope across the counter. He had this way of making the tedious process of signing on feel like catching up with an old friend.

Even the way he said, "Make sure you meet in the main lounge at 1:00pm for lifeboat training, sweetheart," felt like he genuinely cared. It was impossible not to like the guy.

"Shopping guides live in passenger areas on this ship, due to crew cabin space." he says jealously as he hands me my room key and magnetic name tag.

I snap on my name magnetic name badge, take the old plastic room key card and just as I was about to thank Chuck for the help, a tall, stoic Russian guy bounced up to us like he was auditioning for a Bond villain role.

"I'm Victor, in dance cast. You shopping guide? I'm your assistant on Ocean Seduction. Let me help with bag," he said, his thick accent, and broken English, adding to the whole Eastern European vibe.

"Wait, no, it's heavy..." I protested, but Victor didn't even flinch. He'd already hoisted my suitcase up like it weighed nothing and was heading down the hallway, his strides quick and determined. I barely had time to wave a quick goodbye to Charles, who gave me a sympathetic look as I rushed off after my assistant. Victor moved like a man on a mission, and it was all I could do to keep up.

We were weaving down the I-95, the main artery of the ship, where crew members darted back and forth to get to their destination. The hallway was loud, a constant hum of chatter in different languages mixed with the clanking of metal trays and the whoosh of laundry carts being pushed at full speed. It had that distinct smell of industrial-strength cleaning supplies, fried food, and just a hint of the ocean air that somehow managed to sneak in, even this far inside the ship.

Victor, always seemingly on a mission, barely slowed down, expertly dodging a group of housekeeping staff who were chatting animatedly by crew mess doors. They all say hi to Victor and I get the sense he is well liked on this ship. I, on the other hand, wasn't so graceful, muttering apologies as I sidestepped everyone left in Victor's wake.

"Victor, slow down!" I called after him, but he was already halfway down the I-95, barely turning his head to acknowledge me. Typical Victor–efficient, but never much for conversation unless it was absolutely necessary.

As I hurried to catch up, I took in the sights of the I-95–the nerve center of the ship that most passengers never saw. It was all fluorescent lighting and metal walls, the complete opposite of the plush, polished guest areas above.

This was the real ship, where everything happened behind the scenes, where the crew worked around the clock to keep the ship running smoothly. You could feel the energy here– fast-paced, chaotic, but somehow organized in its own way.

By the time I finally caught up to Victor, we were standing in front of the aft crew elevators. He stood there patiently, still holding my suitcase like it was no big deal, his face expressionless as always. I took a deep breath, feeling the mix of humid heat, coming in through the open shell doors as fork lifts load items onto the ship, and the cold blast of air from the AC vent above us. Utter chaos. Loud content beeping from the forklifts fill the area.

My heart was still racing from the quick dash down the hall. Victor glanced over at me, finally acknowledging my existence with a slight raise of his eyebrow.

"You okay?" he asked over the forklift noise, his thick Russian accent making the words sound clipped.

I gave him a half-smile, trying to catch my breath. "Just... keeping up."

The elevator dinged and the doors slid open with a faint metallic squeak. Victor stepped in first, pulling my suitcase in effortlessly, and I followed, grateful for the brief moment of stillness and quiet. Inside the elevator, the scent of bleach mingled with the cold, sterile air, a stark contrast to the bustling chaos we'd just left behind. The cold metal of the walls pressed against my back as I leaned against them, and for a second, it reminded me of Dad. Funny, how the smallest things can drag up memories you've buried.

He worked on ships too, back in the day–before everything fell apart. The Navy was his life. He'd always smelled of metal and saltwater when he came home, his uniform crisp and his eyes hard but kind. I guess that's where I got my weird obsession with ships, though mine's a little less noble. While he was out there serving his country, I was just here selling overpriced diamonds to tourists. *Good job, Christina*, I thought sarcastically.

I sighed, glancing over at Victor, who stood like a statue, staring straight ahead. He didn't know any of this, of course. To him, I was just another shopping guide who barely scraped by, not the daughter of a man who used to command fleets. The irony hit me like a punch to the gut. Here I was, standing in the same cold metal box that felt like home, but now it was a prison, a reminder of how far I'd strayed.

"Next stop," I muttered to myself as the elevator shuddered to life, climbing slowly. It was like the universe mocking me, dragging me up, but never quite letting me reach the surface. As the doors slid open again, we stepped out into the tiny area between the crew quarters and the guest areas. A place that wasn't quite either. Just like me–stuck between worlds, never really belonging to one or the other.

I let out another sigh, shaking off the nostalgia as I followed Victor. There was no point dwelling on it.

Chapter 5

VODKA AND VICTORY

Victor and I stepped out of a nondescript, industrial door from the crew area into the world of the passengers, and the contrast was like night and day. One second, we were in the cold, sterile maze of the I-95, all harsh fluorescent lights and metal walls, and the next, we were in the overly polished, but somehow still outdated, passenger hallways.

The décor screamed "luxury from a decade ago"–shiny brass fixtures that had lost their shine, tacky patterned carpet with swirls of reds and golds that had clearly seen better days, and framed photos of generic seascapes lining the walls. It felt like stepping into a time capsule that hadn't quite caught up with the modern world. The lighting was softer here, but not in a flattering way–more like the dim glow of a once-grand hotel that's now trying to cover up its age.

The hallway was a hive of activity, with excited passengers milling about, dragging their suitcases and chattering loudly as they tried to figure out where their cabins were. It was that first-day-on-board vibe–people buzzing with anticipation, still wearing their travel clothes, not quite ready to relax but eager to start their vacation. Some were looking down at their keycards, others flipping through the ship's deck plans, clearly trying to get their bearings.

The cabin stewards, dressed in their outdated uniforms and polite smiles, were scattered throughout the long hallway, assisting passengers who looked completely lost.

They moved with that calm, patient energy that only comes from dealing with the same questions over and over again. I caught snippets of conversations as we walked by.

"Excuse me, where's cabin 8227?"

"Do these stairs go up or down?"

"Do all you crew sleep onboard?"

"What time is the midnight buffet?"

And there were kids—so many kids—racing around with no sense of direction, already hyped up from the excitement of being on a cruise ship. Parents tried to wrangle them, but it was a losing battle. You could just tell.

The sunlight streamed in from the open cabin doors, giving everything this golden glow that made even the outdated décor look almost charming. Almost. The sun bounced off the shiny brass railings, the light making the faded carpets look a little less sad, and for a moment, it almost felt serene. But that was quickly drowned out by the noise of families hauling their luggage inside, the scraping of suitcase wheels, and the occasional excited shriek from someone who'd just laid eyes on their balcony for the first time.

We were only a couple of doors away from my cabin, and I could already feel that mix of relief and exhaustion setting in. I couldn't wait to drop my bags and just breathe for a second.

Victor, still carrying my suitcase like it was nothing, didn't break his stride. "Not far," he muttered, glancing back at me briefly before resuming his brisk pace. He didn't seem fazed by the commotion around us, but I took it all in—the energy, the chaos, the sense that everyone here was ready for something new, something fun.

As we passed cabin after cabin, I couldn't help but notice the little details: the way some passengers had already flung open their balcony doors to let in the sea breeze, the smell of the ocean and excitement hanging in the air. This was the start of their adventure, and for a moment, it almost felt contagious. Almost.

Then I remembered I wasn't here for vacation—I was here to work.

When I finally caught up to Victor at my cabin, he was already placing my suitcase on the bed. The room was tiny, maybe 80 square feet, but at that moment, it felt like a palace compared to the chaos outside.

"Your shopping guide desk is on Promenade Deck Seven by Casino," Victor explained, pointing out all the important things I'd need to know.

"I stocked fridge for you. I have to call wife back home in Thailand. I'll be up to stock your desk after. I go now."

I narrowed my eyes at him, determined to set some boundaries.

"Just so you know next time, I don't need help with my suitcase. Got it?"

Victor responded with a smile that screamed "FUCK YOU" louder than words ever could, then turned and walked out without another word. I closed the door and, in the silence, I could hear my ears ring.

Victor Treblinenko. I haven't worked with him before, but I'd heard of him even before stepping on the Ocean Seduction. The other shopping guides, who've worked on this ship before, always talk about Victor like he's some kind of legend. Tall, built like a Greek statue, and with that typical Russian stoicism that makes it hard to tell if he's about to crack a smile or break a boulder in half with his bare hands. He's not just another dancer, though; his story's something else entirely. And, as I've come to learn, the man's full of surprises.

Victor grew up in Basmanny, one of those trendy parts of Moscow where old Soviet buildings sit side by side with hipster cafes. His dad, from what I've heard, had some serious connections—worked at the Kremlin, no less. I always imagined him as this tough-as-nails guy, the kind who could make things happen with a single phone call, even though he probably never had to raise his voice. And then there was his mom, a classically trained ballerina. Yeah, that's where Victor gets it.

Now, in most places, you might have a choice about what you want to do with your life. But Russia? Especially back then? Let's just say it wasn't uncommon for your parents to decide for you. So while little Victor probably had dreams of being, I don't know, an astronaut or maybe something totally different, his mom had other plans. She wanted a dancer in the family. And not just any dancer–a classically trained one, like her. Victor was tall even as a kid, lean and strong, and that's all she needed to push him in the direction of the stage.

So, ballet it was.

Victor didn't hate it–at least, that's the impression I get–but I'm sure he didn't exactly dream of pirouettes and tights when he was growing up. Still, he did it, and he did it extremely well.

His parents were always there for him, despite their stoic Russian way of showing affection. I'm not sure they ever had a "We're so proud of you, son" moment, but they were solid, always present in his life, showing their love in quiet, unspoken ways.

Now, here's where things get even more interesting. In Russia, it's mandatory for all males aged 18 to 27 to complete one year of active-duty military service. Most guys dread it, try to find ways around it, but not Victor. He saw it as another performance, another stage. So what did he do? He joined a military dance troupe.

Yeah, that's right–while most guys were out there doing drills and crawling through mud, Victor was entertaining the troops with carefully choreographed routines. But don't think for a second that it was some soft option. You've got to be strong to keep up with that kind of physical demand, and Victor's 6'3" frame and ridiculous strength made him stand out. He wasn't just any dancer; he was a powerhouse.

After completing his mandatory service, Victor could have gone back to Moscow, maybe found a comfortable job in one of those prestigious theaters his mother ran, but that wasn't his style. One night, while surfing the internet–like we all do when we're looking for something more–he stumbled upon an audition notice for cruise ship dancers in Bucharest, Romania.

He figured, why not? It wasn't long before he was packing his bags and heading for the auditions.

Turns out, that 6'3" frame and ballet-trained muscles impressed the hell out of the casting directors. He got the job and started traveling the world, performing on the high seas. But, like anyone who spends months at a time on a ship, the cruising life gets old fast. Victor, though? He found a way to make it work for him.

While most dancers hit the crew bar during their off-hours, Victor found extra gigs–side hustles, you could say. One of them? Assisting the shopping guide. The guy's a machine– unloading stock, setting up presentations, even running errands when things get hectic. He does it all with the same blank expression, never a complaint, never a word out of place. And why? To earn more cash, of course.

You see, while Victor's busting his ass at sea, his wife Aranya–whom he met in Thailand during one of his vacations –is busy enjoying the life of a cruise ship wife. And by that, I mean she's living it up, spending his hard-earned money like it's going out of style. Victor doesn't mind, though. That's the thing about him–he's cool with it. Maybe even relieved. Aranya loves that he's away for six months at a time. She gets her freedom, he gets his peace, and when they're together, well... it works.

They have their arrangement, and Victor's more than okay with it. He knows the deal. Aranya is stunning, from what I've heard from the other shopping guides–tiny, gorgeous, and full of life. She loves to shop, travel, and live the kind of carefree life most people only dream about.

Victor, on the other hand, thrives in routine and structure. Maybe it's the Russian in him, maybe it's just who he is. Either way, the two of them have this unspoken understanding: he's the provider, she's the spender, and neither of them seems to mind.

But that doesn't mean Victor's not saving up for something bigger. From what I've gathered, he's not going to dance forever. He's planning. You don't bust your ass at extra gigs on a cruise ship just to blow all your money. No, Victor's smarter than that. He's got a goal in mind, though he keeps it to himself, like everything else. He's playing the long game, whether it's building a future for himself and Aranya or setting up a comfortable life back in Thailand someday.

And while most people crack under the strain of ship life– months away from home, surrounded by the same faces, the same routine–Victor handles it like a pro. Nothing rattles him. Not the tight schedules, not the constant travel, and certainly not the crew drama that always seems to bubble up. He just keeps his head down, does his job, and makes sure he's earning every penny he can while he's out here.

So, when he signed up for the Ocean Seduction, it wasn't just another contract for him. It was another step toward whatever future he's planning. He's not one to complain or share too much, but you can tell there's something going on beneath that stoic exterior. Victor's a guy who's seen a lot, done a lot, and isn't about to let anything–be it ship life, his past, or even the complicated relationship with his wife–get in the way of his endgame.

Left alone in my shoebox of a room, I took a moment to absorb my new surroundings. My eyes landed on the tiny fridge, and I made a beeline for it, hoping for some kind of relief. Opening it up, I found it stocked with Heineken beers and water. Thank you, Victor.

I grabbed a beer, cracked it open, and pounded it like it was the first drink I'd had in days. As I kicked the fridge door shut, my purse toppled off the top and spilled onto the floor. Of course, out popped a crumpled funeral obituary program.

Great.

It read: "In loving memory of ERIC DELGADO." I picked it up, trying to smooth out the wrinkles, and placed it on the shelf like it was some kind of shrine.

My Dad, Eric Delgado, was one of those old-school Navy admirals who commanded respect just by walking into a room. His uniform was always pressed, his stance always straight, and his gaze always so intense that you felt it even when he wasn't looking directly at you.

He was decorated, for sure–one of those guys who's got more medals than most people have apps on their iPhones. But behind that hard exterior, he was our dad, doing his best to keep the family together.

He was a great dad in his own way, but he was also as heavy-handed as they come. I guess when you're in the military, you get used to being in charge, and that didn't change just because he was home. My brother Eric, my sister Laura, and I knew better than to step out of line. He was strict, and he didn't sugarcoat things. We grew up under his watchful eye, always knowing that if we messed up, the consequences wouldn't be pretty.

But as tough as he was, his love for Mom, Martina, was the one thing that softened his edges–just a little. He adored her, and even though his love for gambling was legendary (in a not-so-great way), it never quite eclipsed how much he loved her. There were nights when he'd be deep in poker games or hitting the slots, but the way his eyes lit up when he talked about her–well, that was something different. I want a love like that.

It was clear that, even if his bets sometimes got the best of him, his heart was always tethered to her.

Despite his flaws, and maybe because of them, he did his best for us. We all knew that his strictness came from a place of wanting us to be strong and successful. He had his demons, no doubt, everyone does, but his gambling was a never-ending source of trouble. Through it all, he was a man who gave everything he had to his family, even if it meant putting on a tough front and battling his own personal vices.

So yeah, he was a stern, decorated admiral who could intimidate just by breathing, but there was a side to him that softened whenever he was with Mom. And maybe, just maybe, that's where all his love that didn't go into gambling found its way.

Then, I pulled out an old photo of Mom and Dad, leaning against one of his classic cars–back when things were simple, back when I still believed in happy endings. They were smiling, arm in arm, looking like they didn't have a care in the world. Dad's arm casually slung over Mom's shoulders, his proud grin making him look ten feet tall. I pinned it to the corkboard above my desk, my hands trembling just a little.

Without thinking, I kissed my fingertips and touched the image, a little ritual I'd picked up along the way. A pointless gesture, but one that made me feel close to him, even though he was gone. Permanently gone.

My throat tightened as I stared at the photo, the edges of my vision blurring as tears threatened to spill over.

I blinked them back, hard, biting the inside of my cheek. I couldn't cry right now. Not here, not when I had so much else to deal with. But the guilt started to creep in anyway, slow and heavy. I wasn't there when he passed. I wasn't by his side, holding his hand, telling him everything was going to be okay. Instead, I was out here, chasing commissions, selling overpriced jewelry to people who didn't need it.

I could've been there. I should've been there.

But no, I had to be on a ship, in the middle of the Caribbean, too wrapped up in my own life to even say goodbye. I swallowed the lump in my throat, forcing the guilt back down where it belonged. Buried, deep inside, where it couldn't interfere with my day-to-day. That's how I survived– ramming those feelings down, pretending they didn't exist. It's easier that way, right?

I wiped my eyes quickly, before anything could spill over, and took a deep breath. No use in dwelling on it. What's done is done.

I finished up my beer and checked my look in the mirror. Out the door and down the long passenger hallway I went. The once colourful carpet which has seen better days leading me to the atrium, middle grand staircase area of the ship. Remember, it's a *ship*, not a *boat*. Climbing the grand staircase I weave through excited guests as they explore this ship, even if it's tired looking.

The Miami heat hits me harder than a slap from Will Smith as I stepped onto the open Promenade Deck. Guests were everywhere, enjoying the view, snapping photos, and generally being the happy vacationers I was supposed to cater to.

As I weaved through the crowd, a couple with a young child stopped me, asking for a photo. The little girl, clearly terrified of being on board, clung to her mom like a lifeline.

"Hey there, sunshine," I said, crouching down to her level. "What's your name?"

"My name is Hana and I'm six years old," she replied, her voice trembling.

"Hi Hana, nice to meet you. My name is Christina. You know, the first time I came on a ship, I was terrified too. I'm not a great swimmer, and I thought the ship was going to sink."

Hana's eyes widened. "My Dad says it won't happen, but I'm so scared."

I smiled, "You know what helped? A good friend of mine gave me this magic bracelet. It's the exact one my friend gave to me years ago, and I want to give it to you. But only if your Mom and Dad are okay with it." pulling a small charm bracelet from my pocket.

The charms were all shaped as ocean and ship-themed baubles, perfect for a six-year-old. The little girl looked up at her parents, who nodded in approval. I winked at them as I secured the bracelet around Hana's tiny wrist. Her fear melted away, replaced by a big, beaming smile.

Just as I was Basking in my good deed, my phone rang. The display read: "Unknown number." Great, now what?

"If you ever feel scared and need a little extra courage, just rub the charms to activate the magic," I told Hana, leaning down to her level, my voice soft and secretive.

"But here's the real magic–always love your mom and dad, because no matter what, they'll be there for you. Love them with all your heart, trust them even when things get tough, and always make sure you're being true to yourself."

With that, I answered the call feeling the tears well up again thinking about my Dad, already dreading the phone conversation.

"This is Christina," I said, trying hard to hold back tears. I walked along the Promenade Deck and looked out at downtown Miami. The sun and salty air made me smile. It always has and always will. I did my best to listen, to the phone call, but lately, I could care less about these type of calls. I answered with enthusiasm, alluding I'll do my best to right my wrong.

"Thanks for the reminder. I'm going to make a payment on that card later today," I continued, slipping into my best responsible-adult voice.

"I'm heading to the bank now," I lied, hoping they wouldn't catch on.

"Listen, you're breaking up. Trust me when I say..." I trailed off, purposely omitting every second word to make it sound like the connection was terrible. "...I'll...that...paid...today..."

Finally, I made a static noise with my mouth and hung up. Sometimes, you just have to fake it till you make it.

Darting back inside by the front of the ship, the air conditioning was refreshing. That Miami humidity is nice but the cool air is nicer. I arrived at my desk on Promenade Deck

Seven, only to find Victor already there, stocking it with brochures and luxury brand stickers.

The guy was living up to his legendary status. I opened the top drawer, revealing about a hundred individually packaged magic bracelets, a shopping guide staple freebie giveaway, just like the one I gave the terrified young girl outside. I grabbed another and slipped it into my pocket, just in case I need to spin some lies later.

Adjusting the brochures and luxury brand stickers with Victor, and mentally preparing myself for the day, a voice from behind me sliced through my thoughts a train wreck .

"You are proof that God has a sense of humor," said Camila Gonzalez, strutting up to my desk like she owned the place. See, Camila and I have history and it's not the good kind. We were good until we weren't. I can already tell by her glare this is not going to be good.

"Ah. Hi, Camila," I replied, awkwardly hugging her trying to smooth things over. She does not hug back. As I pull away, I glanced at her name tag. "You're a CRUISE DIRECTOR now. Congrats!" She shoots me a half smile and looks at Victor. "Can you come with me for a second?" Camila didn't wait for an answer, just grabbed one of the brand stickers and started walking away toward an exit back to the crew areas.

I followed her through a staff door into a private stairwell, trying to figure out what the hell was going on. Before the heavy fire door slammed shut behind us, Camila peeled the sticker off, stepped up on a railing to get higher and slapped it over a security camera. Before I could even ask what she was doing, and after the door closed, she unleashed a flurry of slaps that caught me completely off guard.

I threw up my arms, trying to block the blows. "Um, I can explain." The slaps finally stop, but the verbal assault begins.

"Fuck you," Camila hissed, her voice low and venomous. "I'm your supervisor now, and mark my words, I'm going to make your time here a living hell."

With that, she stepped up again, peeled the sticker off the camera and stormed out, leaving me standing there, stunned and slightly bruised.

Well, this was going to be fun. I fixed my hair, and my jacket collar, in the mirror by the exit door. Wouldn't want to look like I got the shit slapped out of me when I get back to my desk.

I gently rub the red welt on my right cheek in hopes the redness will fade. The throbbing keeps time with my heartbeat as I use all of my body weight to pull the heavy fire-door open and step back into the passenger area. Making it back to my desk, Victor glances over and immediately notices the welt on my cheek. He tries hard to hide his smile.

"Trouble in paradise, already?" Victor questions, putting the relationship pieces together in his head instantaneously. Anyone who's ever worked on ships will tell you it's like a college dorm. Relationships start and end extremely quickly and since all the staff live and work together, it's like speed dating in a pressure cooker. I do my best to show zero emotion which is pretty easy because I've been told I'm a wiz at that. I switch the subject.

"Thanks for organizing the brochure rack. It looks great!" I add. Victor smiles as he realizes I don't want to talk about what just happened to me.

To me, Russians seem socially awkward at the best of times. It's a cultural thing. Victor is a tall and lanky strawberry-blonde haired dancer in the ships cast.

Most dancers on ships love their life onboard. They do 5 to 7 production shows, for guests, per week and work a lot on a 3 and 4 day cruise schedule. A 3 and 4 day run is hectic, not just for dancer, but for cleaners, waiters and everyone in this big flotel–floating hotel.

Also, the production dancers are expected to assist the cruise staff with early morning tenders, Bingo (which is BIG business onboard cruise ships), and other cruise related duties. Granted, dancers earn five times more than a cabin steward or ten times more than a cleaner, but they also have highly specialized talents, so it's a pretty good life. Some dancers, like Victor, see the value in earning more money and take on extra duties to make extra cash.

Oh yeah, EVERYONE get's paid in *cash* on ships. That is one of the biggest perks of life at sea. Your income is not subject to tax in international waters. As the shopping guide, I pay Victor for the help he provides setting everything up for my desk hours, the shows, the gang-way map brochures.

The more he does, the less I need to worry about. I can focus my efforts on finding the 20 percent of people on board that will make up 80 percent of my sales.

As the shopping guide on this floating relic, my job is to play the friendly insider, steering passengers towards the "best" luxury shopping store in the Caribbean.

By 'best' I mean the ones that slip me a little something, on the side, for every big spender I send their way. I earn a commission on all sales, made by this ship, in the store shown on the "Shopping Map" I hand out, for free, to guests. It's a classic payola scheme. Diamonds might be a girl's best friend, but kickbacks are MY best friend.

My desk, nestled in the hustle of the Promenade Deck, was a little kingdom. It had all the essentials: brochures, informative shopping maps, and a drawer full of "magic" charm bracelets I hand out to sweeten the deal. The charm bracelets were my secret weapon, especially with the moms and kids. Nothing says "trust me" like a shiny trinket.

Chapter 6

DIAMONDS AND DEALS

Debarkation day sets the tone of the entire cruise. The Ocean Seduction is on a 3 and 4 day itinerary, which make up the week. The 3 day usually starts on a Friday and guests come onboard with the sole purpose to get smashed all weekend, parting til Monday morning. The shorter the cruise, the younger the clientele.

My job is to sway those guests into shopping instead of spending time at the beach, spending all their money at the bar or in the casino on board.

The 4 day cruise runs Monday to Friday and these guests don't necessarily want to party as much as they want to relax. I have a limited amount of time to convince these guests to shop on their cruise. I'm not proud of this, but I have to add that I was demoted down to this "class" of ship due to poor sales numbers. As a shopping guide, the more sales you clock for store, the better ship you are assigned. When I say "better" I mean newer, bigger, and more expensive for guests to book a vacation.

The higher the net-worth of the clientele, the easier it is to separate them from their hard-earned money. Conversely, the lower your sales number get, the worse ship you are assigned. Hence why I'm here on the oldest, slowest, cheapest ship in the fleet - the Ocean Seduction.

"I must go get ready for show." Victor states.

"Thanks for your help. I'll record the hours for you." Victor walks off and I sit at my taller, bar height desk and wait for the madness to begin.

My first visitor was a woman in her forties, doing a great job hanging on to her youth, decked out in designer resort wear, the kind of outfit that screams, "I paid too much for this." She steps up to me and speaks to me in a southern drawler.

"Hi there! Can you help me find something special this cruise?" Her voice as sweet as sugarcane.

"Oh, absolutely!" I answer trying hard to hide my excitement. I stand and fix my tight pencil skirt. The woman's eyes outlining my shape. She smiles.

"There's a great place in Nassau where guests can get amazing deals on diamonds. You can get up to 80% off." I lean over and start writing the name, of the store, on a Shopping Card with my big fat sharpie. I can feel the woman look down my top. Hey, I'll do anything for a big sale...well, almost anything. I finish and hand the card to my Southern Peach.

"You've come to the right person," I said, leaning in like I was sharing a secret. "There's a little spot called Caribbean Diamonds and Gemstones. They have a stunning selection, and if you mention my name, and give them this card, you'll get the VIP treatment. Trust me, they'll roll out the red carpet for you."

What I didn't mention was that Caribbean Diamonds and Gemstones would be sliding a nice little bonus my way for every purchase. And judging by the size of the rock she was already sporting on her ring finger, I was potentially going to have a very good cruise.

"Thanks for the tip, scrumptious. My husband and I are looking for a little fun, other than shopping, this cruise." She lofts like a easy to hit tennis ball to hit. I clue in immediately, and finally notice the upside-down pineapple icons on her top. "You look like a fun unicorn," her smile widening.

"Awe, thanks for the offer, but I'm taken." Leaning in so my answer doesn't stop her from shopping at CDG.

"Suit yourself." she utters disappointedly.

As she walked away, hopefully mentally spending her husband's money, I couldn't help but smirk. This job was all about knowing how to play the game, and honey, I was a pro. Well, I use to be a pro.

But not everyone was as easy to charm as Mrs. Southern Peach. I pushed the thoughts aside and focused on the next passenger approaching my desk. There was always someone new, someone ready to be charmed, and someone ready to spend. And as long as they kept coming, I'd keep smiling and playing the game.

Because on the Ocean Seduction, you either keep up or get left behind. And trust me, there is no lower than this.

Two hours later I finished up my desk hours with plenty of leads and hope springing eternal in my heart. I needed to feel like a pro again. Being demoted to this class of ship was a devastating blow to not only my ego, but my bank account. Looking at my watch I see that I missed the dinner meal hours in the staff mess down in the crew area. So, what's a girl to do to but enjoy a liquid dinner.

I clean up my desk, restock the brochure display and make my way over to the Martini lounge for a well deserved drink.

The moment I stepped into the Martini Lounge, I could feel the day's stress starting to melt away. The soft lighting, the gentle hum of conversation, and the tinkling of piano keys in the background all whispered promises of a much-needed escape.

I made my way to the bar, standing beside a sleek, cushioned stool. The bartender, a tall, distinguished Romanian with salt-and-pepper hair, immediately nodded in my direction. I scan is name badge.

"Dirty Martini, please, Radu" I state, barley getting the words out of my mouth before he acknowledges my order. There's something comforting about being served by a professional bartender, even in the middle of the ocean.

As I waited for my drink, a forgettable drunk guy–who I'm sure thought his Hawaiian shirt was charming–stumbled up behind me. Before I could even glance over my shoulder, he trips and crashes into the back of my legs, sending both of us tumbling to the floor in a tangle of limbs and bad decisions.

"Oh my goodness, I'm so sorry," he slurred, laying on the floor laughing like it was the funniest thing he'd ever done. "I bought these shoes from a drug dealer. I don't know what he laced them with, but I've been tripping all day."

I stared up at him, flat on my back with his cheap cologne assaulting my senses. This is what I get for trying to enjoy a quiet drink. His meaty hand, adorned with a Hublot Big Bang watch that screamed "I'm compensating for something," hovered in front of my face.

"I'm good, I don't need help," I said, waving him off and getting to my feet awkwardly in my tight skirt. Because if there's one thing I don't need, it's a drunken fool trying to play hero. I don't need help.

Once I was standing, I brushed myself off and gave him a quick once-over. "Big Bang. Nice watch," I remarked, raising an eyebrow.

"Huh? Oh, yeah," he replied, clearly not catching the hint that I was not impressed.

As if on cue, a group of cruise ship dancers glided by, their toned bodies, in their tight dresses, practically glowing in the dim light.

Drunky McStumblepants swayed as he openly leered at them, like he was trying to mentally undress them faster than his eyes could scan.

"Ahh, see, that's all I want," he declared, sounding like a heartbroken man-child. "A beautiful girl like that. What I wouldn't give to feel wanted again. That would make me so happy."

There it was, the sound of genuine heartache mixed with just the right amount of self-pity. I'd heard it a thousand times before, and it never failed to tug at something in me. Maybe it was the curse of empathy, or maybe it was just the way my dad had drilled the concept of duty into me, but I couldn't help but offer some advice.

"I know what it's like to see disappointment in the eyes of others," I said, my voice softening just a touch. "But being happy starts within you. Do whatever makes you happy...and if that includes getting another expensive watch, then I'm here to help. I'm the shopping guide on board."

He looked at me, and for a second, I thought I saw a flicker of hope. But then, just as quickly, it faded into a familiar kind of desperation. "I don't need another watch, I need to feel alive and fuck something tight and tanned again!" he pleaded, like he was confessing his sins like a guilty minister. "Listen, I've been on a hundred cruises, and all of them have beautiful women looking for excitement."

Before I could respond, he slipped from his chair, catching himself before landing on the floor again as another attractive girl walked by. He was tipsy, and clearly had too many wobbly-pops.

"If there was a way to get with one of the dancers, bar waitresses, or even a cabin steward during the cruise...I'd do it!" he proclaimed, his eyes lighting up with an idea he clearly thought was brilliant.

I sighed inwardly, wishing I had finished that martini a few minutes earlier. "Crew fraternizing with guests results in an immediate dismissal," I reminded him, trying to keep my tone firm but not harsh. No point in crushing the poor guy completely.

He wasn't listening, though. "No, I mean if I could PAY for it, like it's part of a cruise package, then it would be OK," he said, his voice dropping to a conspiratorial whisper. "I'd pay A LOT for one that looked just like that."

He pointed, albeit wobbly, at the approaching figure of Camila, her curves and confident stride making her the kind of woman men like this could only dream about. Instinct kicked in, and I sprang out of my chair, stepping directly into his line of sight before he could even think about trying something.

"Come on, Big Bang, let me help you back to your cabin," I said, grabbing his arm and guiding him away from what was sure to be a very bad decision.

Camila's sharp voice cut through the chatter and music of the lounge. "What's going on here?"

"Nothing, no help needed. Just assisting this friendly drunk guest back to his cabin," I said quickly, shooting her a reassuring smile. The last thing I needed was her stepping in and complicating things.

I managed to haul him up off the barstool, which, let me tell you, was no easy feat. The guy's built like a linebacker, and here I was, trying to keep him upright with what felt like the strength of a paper clip. He swayed as I draped his arm over my shoulder, and I instantly regretted every decision that had led me to this moment.

The walk to the elevator felt like trying to steer a ship through a hurricane. Patrick was wobbling from side to side, and I was doing my best to steer him through the crowd of well-dressed, very sober guests who, of course, were all staring. I could feel their judgy little eyes burning into me, like they were thinking, Look at this girl, can't even handle her drunk date. News flash, he's not my date, but whatever.

We finally made it to the elevators, but of course, the universe was against me, and only the fancy glass ones—the ones that take you all the way up to the top deck where the rich folks stay—were available. I pressed the button and prayed the thing would get there fast, all while Patrick leaned his weight more and more on me. At this point, I was Basically holding him up entirely. My back was killing me.

When the doors finally opened, I shoved him inside, hitting the button for the top floor. I'm not saying I was hoping no one else would get in, but I definitely shot a death glare at anyone even thinking of joining us in that elevator.

Patrick leaned against the glass, staring out at the lights of the ship like he was seeing stars for the first time. "This ship is amazing, you know?"

"Uh-huh," I replied, catching my breath. "And so is your suite. Why don't we focus on getting there? What's your deck number?" I question to make this process as quick and painless as possible.

"Eleven" he slurs.

The ride felt like it took forever, and the higher we went, the more I started thinking about just ditching Patrick somewhere along the way. I mean, who would notice, right? But then I imagined him stumbling around, probably face-planting into a potted plant or falling down a flight of stairs, and I sighed. No, ditching Patrick wasn't in the cards today. Of course, I'm the one who's gotta have a conscience.

The elevator dinged, and we reached the top floor. Of course, we did. Naturally, Big Bang Patrick would have the biggest, most expensive suite on the ship. The kind of cabin with more square footage than my entire life savings. Even on the old Ocean Seduction, the Ocean Suites were impressive. I nudged Patrick out of the elevator, and we started the drunken shuffle down the hallway, his arm still draped over my shoulders like I was some kind of human crutch.

As we wobbled toward his suite, something strange happened. I got this weird pang–something that hit me deep, like an unexpected punch to the gut. Out of nowhere, a memory of my dad flashed in my mind. Why now? What the hell?

I tried to shake it off, but it stuck. I thought about the nights Dad used to come home late, after he and mom divorced, smelling like whiskey and cigarettes after a long day or, hell, maybe after winning–or losing–another round of poker. He'd stagger in, and no matter how tired I was, I'd always help him to bed. He was always too proud to ask for help, but I'd be there anyway, guiding him down the hall, just like I was doing with Patrick now.

Why was this memory bubbling up with this drunk stranger leaning on me? I mean, Patrick wasn't my dad. Far from it. But something about the helplessness, the weight of another person depending on me to just get them back in one piece–it triggered something. It pissed me off, too. I didn't ask to be reminded of Dad right now. Especially not in this context, with some random, entitled drunk.

I bit my lip, trying to hold back whatever the hell was clawing its way up from the pit of my stomach. I didn't need to feel this right now. Not here, not on this stupid cruise ship, with this stupid man drooling on my shoulder. But memories, they don't wait for the right time, do they? They just hit you when you least expect it, and suddenly you're drowning in them.

"Come on, Patrick, keep it together," I muttered under my breath, more to myself than him. Maybe if I focused on getting him to his suite, I could stop my brain from wandering back to Dad, to that stupid guilt that always lingered in the back of my mind.

Up on deck 11 the carpet in the hall was that thick, fancy kind that makes it impossible to drag someone along, and I was practically dragging him at this point. His size 13 feet were barely moving, and my legs were ready to give out. "Almost there," I huffed, more to myself than to him.

"11023 is the suite for me," he sang over and over again. Nothing like a drunk fool singing in your ear.

Outside Patrick's cabin, I fumbled with the keycard he'd somehow managed to dig out of his pocket. I felt a lump forming in my throat, that familiar knot I used to feel every time I saw Dad in one of his weak moments. But I swallowed it down. No time for that. Not tonight..

He started slurring something about being a director at a pharmaceutical company, and how his products could make men "HARD in two minutes."

"That's a weird flex," I declare, holding him against the wall so he doesn't topple on top of me.

"I'd pay a lot for someone to make me feel desired again. My wife only thinks of me as a walking paycheck," he confessed, his voice a mix of sadness and regret.

"Listen, drink lots of water, get plenty of rest, and if you need help with shopping, I'm here for you," I said, more out of a sense of duty than actual concern. I turned to leave, fully intending to ignore whatever nonsense came out of his mouth next.

"Hey, since you're the shopping guide, you could be the one who gets all the girls for guys like me," he called after me, his voice hopeful in the worst way. "Think about it. Guys like me will pay a lot for some sweet action on vacation."

I didn't even bother responding. Some people were beyond saving, and I had no intention of playing matchmaker for drunken, self-pitying men who thought money could buy them anything, even affection.

As the elevator doors slid shut with a soft whoosh, I leaned against the cool metal wall, feeling the weight of the world–or at least the weight of this massive cruise ship–on my shoulders. It was just another day in paradise, right? If paradise included ex-girlfriends who could turn a polite conversation into a UFC match, old ships that were as easy to navigate as a maze blindfolded, and the constant worry about mom's nursing home bills piling up like a high-stakes poker bet.

I let out a long breath, trying to center myself. The elevator hummed softly, a soothing counterpoint to the chaos of my thoughts. I couldn't help but laugh, a short, sharp sound that echoed slightly in the confined space. "So this is my new ship, huh?" I muttered to myself. "Fuck me."

The violence from the encounter with Camila lingered in my mind like the aftertaste of a shot of cheap liquor–bitter and unwelcome. Camila hadn't always been a hurricane, beautifully predictably would be a better way to describe her. Our relationship might have been over, but the aftershocks were still hitting me when I least expected it. At least the thoughts of Camila replaced the thoughts of my father. I don't know which is better.

As the elevator continued its descent, I thought about this new ship assignment. It was supposed to be a fresh start, a smaller vessel that would magically make all my problems, or me, disappear.

Instead, it felt like I'd traded a rowboat for the Titanic. "Maybe this ship will also hit an iceberg," I joked to myself, the irony not lost on me. Navigating through the endless corridors and getting used to the new faces and routines was more stressful than any of the ports we stopped at.

Then there was the ever-looming issue of money. Besides my Dad's gambling debts, my Mom's nursing home wasn't exactly the Ritz-Carlton, but the bills could make you think it was. Each payment was a reminder of the promises I'd made to keep her comfortable and cared for, promises that were getting harder to keep with every passing day.

As the elevator dinged, announcing my arrival back to the deck by the Martini lounge, I straightened up, fixing a smile on my face. The doors slid open, revealing the bustling, vibrant atmosphere outside the lounge. The air was thick with the sound of laughter, clinking glasses, and the soft undertones of a jazz piano. It was showtime again.

Back in the Martini Lounge, I slid back into my seat, grateful to see my half-finished drink waiting for me. The bartender had kept it safe, like a loyal friend. I took a sip, savoring the way the alcohol warmed my throat.

Camila appeared beside me, her expression unreadable. "You're not going to slap me around again, are you?" I asked, half-joking, but not entirely sure.

"Explain to me how you ended up on this ship," she said, her tone cutting through any attempt at humor. "Is the knot slipping? Weren't you the highest-rated shopping guide last year? How does one fuck everything up so quickly?"

I took a long, slow sip of my martini, letting the silence hang between us for a moment. "Still teaching your sorrows to swim?" she pressed, her eyes narrowing.

"I know you're hurt, and I know it's my fault," I admitted, the weight of my own guilt pressing down on me. "I'm sorry for ghosting you."

Her eyes softened, just for a moment, before hardening again. "Do you know how long I waited for a text? Email? You went dark on social media. How many nights I stayed up stressed because I didn't know anything? You were everything to me. And then, you weren't."

I reached for her hand, but she pulled away, the distance between us growing in that small gesture. I finished my drink in silence, the taste suddenly bitter, and walked out of the lounge, leaving the ghosts of the past behind me.

Chapter 7

LYDIA'S CHILL TO NASSAU'S THRILL

The sun was already in full blast mode as I strolled along the pier in Nassau, feeling the heat and humidity rising off the water like an invisible force field. I could practically taste the salty air on my lips, which was a nice distraction from the sweat trickling down the back of my neck.

I followed behind an already rowdy group of spring-breakers making their way to the Cruise Terminal at the street-side of the pier. Ah, to be young and on vacation, without a care or worry. What am I saying? I have the best job in the world even if my current assignment didn't reflect my love for the job.

The college kids carry a small bluetooth speaker with the 80s hit "Simply Irresistible" blasting as they sing along. I'm more than certain none of them know that classic was produced at Compass Point Studios on this same island. I'm a wealth of useless music trivia that only serves me well in my drunken stupor or when I'm watching Jeopardy.

The cruise ships, those behemoths of the sea, loomed majestically, casting long shadows that made me feel like a tiny ant in a tropical paradise. I loved this place, with its vibrant colors, the sound of calypso music drifting from the market, and the scent of freshly grilled seafood in the air.

I weirdly feel at home in the Caribbean. But today, my mind was elsewhere, not quite in sync with the cheerful vibe of this beautiful, but dangerous, island.

Just as I was about to take a deep breath and enjoy the moment, my phone rang. The obnoxious ringtone I'd set for work-related calls echoed off the pier. I glanced at the screen– Evergreen Manor. My stomach sank. I moved to one of the benches on the dock, sitting down heavily as I swiped to answer.

"Hello?" I said, trying to keep my voice steady.

"Good morning, Christina. It's Lidia from Evergreen Nursing Home." The voice on the other end was that perfect blend of fake concern and underlying annoyance that only a true 'Karen' could master.

Lidia Walker, the director, could be best described as someone who 'weaponized' their position, her career a testament to every bad customer service review you've ever read. Her path to becoming the director of Evergreen Nursing Home was less about career aspiration and more about a series of bad choices and shadier dealings that somehow landed her at the helm.

Lidia wasn't always set on a path of managerial tyranny. In her early years, she had floated through various jobs, never quite finding her niche but always sure she deserved a better position than the one she was in. Her sense of entitlement grew with every job, feeding into her belief that she was meant for greater things. This belief, however distorted, was the driving force behind her eventual career in elder care–a field she entered not out of a desire to help others but as a last resort after numerous professional failures.

As an intern at Evergreen Nursing Home years ago, Lidia was immediately out of her depth, but she masked her incompetence with a domineering attitude that compensated for lack of knowledge with sheer audacity. Her early days at the facility were marked by a rapid understanding that in the world of elder care, particularly in homes not known for their stellar standards, oversight was minimal and opportunities to ascend through the ranks were ripe for the taking–if one knew how to manipulate the system.

Lidia's ascent to director was not earned through dedication or care but engineered through underhanded tactics and the exploitation of every loophole and weak link in the administration. She learned early on that in a system burdened by bureaucracy and cost-cutting, being aggressive and assertive often got you further than competence and kindness. Her knack for sidestepping protocols, coupled with a talent for placing blame elsewhere, quickly made her a central figure in the nursing home's hierarchy.

Once in the position of director, Lidia's true colors shone through even more starkly. She ran Evergreen with an iron fist, her policies more focused on budget cuts and personal power plays than on the welfare of the residents. Her managerial style was authoritarian, to say the least, with a heavy dose of favoritisms that ensured only her allies prospered while others suffered under her reign.

For Lidia, the residents and staff were mere pawns in her continual game of power. She thrived on the small daily tyrannies that reminded everyone of her authority. Complaints from family members were met with bureaucratic gibberish designed to exhaust and confuse, ensuring that few pursued their grievances to any meaningful conclusion.

This approach made Evergreen not just a nursing home but a silent battleground where morale was low, tensions were high, and compassion was often the first casualty.

The residents, including my mom, Martina, found themselves navigating a facility where care was inconsistent and often conditional, depending on Lidia's mood or the staff's ability to avoid her wrath. It was common knowledge among the residents that staying under the radar was the best way to ensure a peaceful day.

Lidia's reputation for being ruthless and unapproachable was well-known beyond the walls of Evergreen. In the community, she was often spoken of in hushed, wary tones, as someone to avoid crossing unless absolutely necessary. Her network within the elder care industry was built not on respect but on the fear and influence she wielded, a testament to her skill in leveraging power dynamics to her advantage.

Despite her success in climbing the career ladder, Lidia's personal life mirrored the chaos and control she exerted at work. Relationships were transactional, friends were few, and her life outside of Evergreen was marked by isolation—a self-imposed exile from any genuine human connection that might threaten her carefully curated façade of control.

In essence, Lidia Walker's life and career at Evergreen Nursing Home were a stark reminder of how ambition, when untethered from ethics and compassion, could create a life devoid of true success or happiness. Her reign at the nursing home, while marked by apparent professional achievement, was ultimately a lonely, hollow victory—a life filled with power but devoid of real purpose or joy.

"Were you able to find alternate arrangements for your mother?" Lidia pressed.

My heart skipped a beat. Alternate arrangements? Sure, because finding a nursing home that doesn't want all your money upfront was as easy as finding a four-leaf clover in a desert.

"Right. Not yet. I'm trying my best to find funding," I replied, trying not to let the panic seep into my voice.

"These are challenging times for all of us," Lidia said, her tone dripping with insincerity. I could almost see her pursing her lips, probably tapping those perfectly manicured nails on her desk.

"If we don't receive payment by the end of the week, she will be evicted."

Evicted. The word sliced through my thoughts like a shark through calm water, sending waves of anxiety crashing into me. I rubbed my eyebrows, trying to push back the headache that was already forming.

"You can't just throw her out on the street. Where would she go?" I questioned sincerely.

"As the primary caregiver on her account, you are responsible for her care," Lidia said, her voice taking on that condescending tone that made me want to scream. "We'll make arrangements to get her to you."

"That is not an option. I work on a cruise ship," I said, my voice rising slightly in desperation.

"We're not heartless here, Christina," Lidia continued, as if she were some saint. "We haven't informed her that her account is in serious arrears. It's just business, I trust you understand. This is your final notice."

Click. The call ended. I stared at the phone, the screen now blank, reflecting my own troubled expression back at me. I felt like the ground had been pulled from under my feet, and for a moment, I couldn't move. My mother, the woman who'd sacrificed so much for us, was on the brink of getting evicted, and there I was, thousands of miles away, hawking jewelry to tourists. It wasn't right. But what could I do? I didn't have the money to pay her bills, and time was running out.

A quick glance at the time snapped me back to reality. I didn't have the luxury of dwelling on this. I had a job to do, and I couldn't afford to lose it–not with everything that was at stake. I quickly collected my messenger bag and made my way toward the exit of the pier, the Cruise Terminal.

Prince George Wharf was buzzing–and by buzzing, I mean it was a full-blown carnival of commerce with a side of conch shells. The air was thick with the smell of tourist sweat, sunscreen, and the occasional whiff of coffee. And let me tell you, coffee is a godsend when you're dealing with the hustle and bustle of a cruise terminal at midmorning. Not that I was in the mood to savor it–I had bigger fish to fry. But first, let me enlighten you on the colorful chaos that is this place.

Walking through Prince George Wharf is like stepping into a vibrant postcard, only the postcard is trying to sell you something, or braid your hair, at every turn. On my left, there's a stall with a display of conch shells so artfully arranged, you'd think they were diamonds.

The guy behind the counter, a smooth-talking Bahamian in a straw hat, was busy convincing a sunburnt tourist couple that these were the finest conch shells in the Caribbean. The husband looked skeptical, but the wife? She was all in, nodding like he was offering her a deal of a lifetime.

"Ma'am, dis conch shell bring good luck, you hear? And only twenty-five dollars. Special price just for you!" The guy's voice was a silky blend of charm and salesmanship that could probably convince me to buy a conch shell–if I didn't already purchased three, for friends, back home. More than likely all collecting dust on their shelves.

Up ahead, I spotted a small cluster of stalls selling tie-dye shirts that looked like they were straight out of a 70s hippie commune.

Bright splashes of color, the kind that could probably be seen from space. I've always wondered who buys those. I mean, unless you're planning to start a jam band on your next cruise, what exactly is the end game here? But, to each their own, right? The stall owner, a wiry old man with a wicked smile, had a line of eager tourists waving cash at him. Go figure.

Then there was the coffee stand. Oh, the coffee stand. Now, this is where I slowed my roll a little. The aroma hit me like a wave, and suddenly, I didn't care that I was supposed to be rushing. I needed that jolt. The barista was a young Bahamian girl, maybe in her early twenties, with a grin that could light up the darkest depths of the ocean. I ordered a black coffee, no frills–because let's be honest, when you're running on fumes, you need the pure stuff. She handed it over with a wink.

"Don't burn yourself, pretty lady," she said, her accent giving the words a musical lilt.

"Thanks, darling. I'm pretty fireproof these days," I shot back, taking a careful sip.

Further down, the real fun began. Tour guides. Now, these guys are a different breed. They're like friendly sharks circling a school of clueless fish, waiting for the perfect moment to pounce. I saw one of them–a big guy with a belly that announced he'd enjoyed one too many plates of fried conch– eyeing a group of tourists who had just disembarked. He ambled over with the confidence of a man who's done this a thousand times.

"Welcome to Nassau, my friends! Lookin' for the best tour on the island? I'll show you the real Bahamas. You won't get this experience anywhere else, trust me," he boomed, throwing an arm around one of the men in the group like they were old pals.

I almost pitied them. Almost. But then again, if you're in Nassau and you don't expect to be offered an overpriced tour by a guy who makes it sound like he's your long-lost cousin, you're not paying attention.

The tourists exchanged glances, clearly overwhelmed. I could practically see the wheels turning in their heads–should we go? Should we trust this guy? And just like that, they were being shepherded toward a minivan that looked like it had seen better days. Good luck, folks. Enjoy the ride.

As I continued through the cruise port, I couldn't help but notice the groups of women–Bahamian women with a no-nonsense attitude and hands that moved faster than you could say "cornrows." They were everywhere, armed with beads and combs, and they had one goal: to braid your hair. And trust me, they didn't take no for an answer.

"Come here, sweetheart, let me braid dat pretty hair of yours," one called out to me as I passed by, her voice full of confidence. She was a large woman, probably in her late fifties, with a floral muumuu that matched the bright flowers in her hair. Her fingers were already twiddling a few strands of beads.

"Oh, honey, these latin curls don't do braids," I replied with a grin, patting my hair like it was a sacred artifact. "But I appreciate the offer."

She shook her head and produced that distinctive 'suck-teeth' sound; the act of sharply inhaling through the teeth to create a loud, sucking sound, often used to convey a mix of disgust, defiance, disapproval, disappointment, frustration, or impatience. A very common colloquialism in the Caribbean.

"One day, you'll come around. And when you do, I'll be right here."

She winked and turned her attention to a little girl with wide eyes and a head full of blonde curls, who was next in line for the braiding extravaganza.

The pier was a riot of colors and sounds, with every shop and stall trying to outshine the other. From the sun-bleached postcards to the rainbow assortment of straw bags and hats, it was a sensory overload in the best possible way. Everywhere I looked, there was something–or someone–trying to catch my attention.

As I passed a stand selling freshly cut coconut, the vendor caught my eye and held up a machete. "Coconut water? Best way to cool down, miss!" he hollered.

I raised my coffee cup in response. "I'm good, thanks. Already cooling down with some liquid energy."

He laughed, a deep, hearty sound that made me smile despite myself. There was something infectious about the Bahamian spirit–their ability to make you feel like you're part of some grand, never-ending party.

Finally, as I neared the end of the terminal, the crowds began to thin out. I exit and the shops were replaced by a view of the turquoise waters that were so stunning they almost didn't look real. I took a deep breath, feeling the heat and salty air fill my lungs. For all its chaos, Prince George Wharf had its moments of serenity.

But I couldn't stay here forever, no matter how much I wanted to. I had work to do, places to be, and sales to make. With one last look at the bustling pier behind me, I squared my shoulders, ready to dive back into the fray.

Chapter 8

THE HUSTLE ON BAY STREET

Bay Street was everything you'd expect from a Caribbean shopping hub–loud, colorful, and teeming with tourists clutching shopping bags like trophies. As I climbed the polished granite steps leading to CDG–Caribbean Diamonds and Gemstones–I couldn't help but admire the store's facade.

It was the most impressive jewelry store chain in the in the Bahamas, with its towering glass windows and ornate gold lettering. Inside, it was like stepping into a world of glittering opulence.

The place was packed with tourists, all eager to drop some serious cash on shiny baubles they'd probably forget about once they got home.

The first order of business, with any shopping guide, was to check in with Artem Hadad, the man who directed this place with an authoritarian presence.

Artem Hadad loomed like a specter over the Caribbean's luxury jewelry market, his presence as imposing as his physical stature. Standing at an impressive six feet five inches and tipping the scales at 350 plus pounds, his size was matched only by his ruthless ambition and relentless drive to dominate the industry.

He wasn't built from muscle but from a lifetime of hard deals and harder choices, his figure a testament to a life of excess and power.

Born into one of Israel's wealthiest families, deeply entrenched in the global diamond industry, I learned quickly that Artem's cradle was practically lined with diamonds and deceit. The Hadads were not just wealthy; they were a dynasty, with tentacles stretching from the bustling markets of Tel Aviv to the glittering stores of the New York diamond district.

From a young age, Artem was groomed not only to inherit this empire but to expand it ruthlessly. The diamond industry, cloaked in luxury and allure, was often a front for some of the shadier dealings of the trade, including inflating the value of diamonds under the guise of rarity–a concept Artem exploited with a keen sense of profit.

In his world, diamonds were not rare; they were just expertly marketed to be perceived as such, allowing traders like him to swindle millions of customers worldwide. Artem knew the power of perception all too well and wielded it with the precision of a maestro, ensuring every piece that glittered in his 75 Caribbean Diamonds and Gems stores was both a token of desire and a trap for the unwary.

Moving through the Caribbean, Artem Hadad became a name synonymous with luxury and fear. As a "top level" player in what was colloquially known as the Caribbean Duty-Free jewelry mafia, he governed with ruthless discipline, ensuring that his stores and their products were the top choice for every tourist and local with money to spend.

His network wasn't just a business; it was an empire, with each store a stronghold over which he reigned supreme.

Artem's attitude toward his employees was tyrannical, particularly toward the shopping guides on the cruise ships. He viewed these individuals not as people but as pawns in his grand scheme to maximize profits. To him, they were either assets or liabilities, nothing in between. If a shopping guide like me didn't adhere strictly to promoting his stores above all others, I wasn't just a disappointment; I was a target.

Artem's philosophy was simple and brutal: sell relentlessly or be removed. His methods for ensuring loyalty were underhanded and fear-inducing, involving everything from severe financial penalties to outright threats of dismissal or worse.

He operated under a belief that fear was a better motivator than any commission plan could ever be. In his eyes, the ideal shopping guide was one who pushed Caribbean Diamonds and Gems relentlessly, who could convince any passenger stepping off a cruise liner that not visiting one of Artem's stores was a missed opportunity of a lifetime. Under his directive, us shopping guides were expected to manipulate, charm, and coerce guests into purchasing as much as possible. The pressure was immense, and many buckled under it, but Artem never cared to ease it; instead, he thrived on it, feeding off the desperate energy it created.

Despite his success, Artem's personal life was a series of strategic alliances and calculated relationships. He was known to say that he'd sell his own grandmother if the price was right, a statement that those close to him knew was not just hyperbole.

Loyalty in Artem's world was bought and paid for, never given freely, and always had a price tag attached.

His involvement in the Caribbean islands had also earned him a notorious reputation. Local business owners either feared or despised him, but none could deny the power he wielded. To cross Artem was to jeopardize not just your business but your very well-being. He was known to retaliate against those other store who defied him with a vindictiveness that was both cold and calculated.

Despite the glitter and glam that surrounded the diamond industry, Artem Hadad was a stark reminder of its darker side– the greed, the manipulation, and the sheer force of will required to remain on top. He was a titan in a world where brilliance was often just a facade for brutality, a man who believed that the ends always justified the means, no matter the cost to others.

I made my way to the back office, a fortress-like secure area hidden behind an enormous magnetically locking steel door. It felt like entering the vault of some high-security bank or secret bunker, where only the privileged few were allowed access. The air inside was cool, sterile, and thick with the tension of deals being made and numbers crunched. As the door clicked shut behind me, I couldn't shake the feeling that once you were in, there was no easy way out.

"Good morning, Artem," I said as I stepped inside.

Artem didn't even bother looking at me. He was too busy staring at a wall of security camera monitors, his beady eyes scanning the screens for any sign of trouble.

"Christina, you're back," he said, his voice as abrasive as ever. "Will we be seeing some big sales numbers this week?"

"The guests this week look promising. I feel–"

"You feel? You feel?" Artem interrupted, finally turning his gaze toward me. His eyes were cold, calculating. "Don't tell me how you feel. Tell me you have hundreds of people convinced to purchase something expensive at my stores this cruise."

He moved around his desk and sat on the edge, leaning in and using his hands to talk to convey his message. "Let me remind you that I've built 75 stores in the Caribbean and do over 10 billion dollars a year in sales thanks to my contracts with SHIPBOARD MEDIA and their amazing shopping guides."

I forced a smile. "Thank you."

"I don't include you in those *amazing* shopping guides," Artem continued, his voice dripping with disdain.

"I don't like you because you don't sell enough for me anymore. I spoke with your boss, Kevin, yesterday and I know you're on your way out, back to whatever shit-hole you grew up in."

"Charleston has its quirks, but it's far from a shit-hole," I shot back, refusing to let him see me sweat.

"If it was up to me, you'd already be gone. Now, get out there and sell some fucking diamonds!" he barked, dismissing me with a wave of his hand. I swallow my pride, smile politely and exit.

Out on the CDG retail floor, I was *in* my element. The air was thick with the scent of perfume and the clink of fine jewelry being laid out on velvet trays. The store was like a glittering paradise–diamonds, emeralds, sapphires, and rubies all catching the light like they were made to seduce, to sparkle just enough to loosen even the tightest wallets.

Diamonds, gold and platinum gleamed under the spotlights, and I could almost feel the weight of people's expectations in the air. They weren't just here to buy shiny rocks; they were here to feel important, to indulge in something they couldn't get back home. And me? I was their guide through this treasure trove.

I moved from customer to customer, slipping into my role as the friendly, knowledgeable shopping guide like I was born for this. And let's be real–I kind of was.

The hustle, the charm, the game of making someone feel like this was the thing they couldn't leave without. It was an art form. I mean, I could sell ice to a polar bear, and today? I was on fire.

An older woman caught my eye as she hesitated near a display of necklaces. Her hand hovered over a diamond-encrusted piece, but she didn't quite have the courage to try it on. I swooped in, all warm smiles and gentle encouragement.

"Oh honey, you need to *try* this one. It's *so* you," I said, reaching for the necklace and slipping it around her neck before she had a chance to object. She caught her reflection in the mirror and smiled, her eyes lighting up like she'd just seen herself in a whole new way. "Isn't it beautiful?" I leaned in a little closer, my voice soft but insistent. "You deserve something this special."

She blinked at herself, hand resting delicately on the diamonds, and I knew I had her. Another sale locked and loaded.

A young couple hovered nearby, clearly nervous but in that sweet, just-about-to-get-engaged way. The guy kept looking at the engagement rings but didn't seem to have a clue what he was doing. I swooped in like a shopping angel, plucking a diamond solitaire from the case. "This one," I said, holding it up like it was the Holy Grail. "Timeless. Classic. Just like your love." They both blushed, and I couldn't help but smirk a little. Hook, line, and sinker.

Then there was the guy by the luxury watches. Middle-aged, a little sweaty, torn between a sleek, understated design and the kind of watch that screams 'Look at me, I'm a big deal.'

I sauntered over, flashing my best 'I know exactly what you're going through' smile. "This one," I said, tapping the classic design, "says you're confident. But," and here's where I pointed to the Audemars Piguet Royal Oak 15450, "if you want to make a subtle statement, and piss off all your rich guy friends, go with this one. This one shows you're a baller without the mid-life crisis corvette." He looked at me, then back at the watch, and I could see the gears turning. Sure enough, two minutes later, he was handing over his credit card.

The register dinged again and again, the sound of those sales going through was sweeter than anything they could've piped through the store speakers.

Each sale? Another victory.

Another tick closer to keeping my job, keeping my mother in that nursing home. The pressure was always there, but out on the floor, I could handle it.

But the grind didn't stop at CDG. Bay Street was lined with 25 stores I had to visit–each one a potential jackpot for me. It's mandatory that shopping guides make an appearance at all the shops on the shopping map, no exceptions. So, with my trusty messenger bag slung over my shoulder, I stepped out into the humid Nassau air. The sun beat down, and the street was alive with tourists who had no idea where they were going but were ready to spend.

I ducked into a local Caribbean souvenir shop, and the moment I walked in, I spotted a customer laughing as he tried on a dreadlock wig. "Oh, that's definitely the look for you," I joked, joining in. He laughed, handing me a steel drum mallet, and I tapped out a quick rhythm on one of the displays. We both laughed, and just like that, I'd made a new friend—and maybe a new sale later on.

Stepping back onto the street, I spotted a couple looking helplessly lost, map in hand. I couldn't help myself. "You're here," I said, pulling out my own map and pointing to where we were standing. "And you want to go there," I pointed toward the jewelry stores down the street. "Best deals on the island, trust me. And if you want a local tip, check out the café around the corner for lunch—it's quiet and has the best conch fritters in town."

They looked at me like I was a lifesaver, thanking me as they hurried off in the direction I pointed.

I ducked into a narrow alley between two stores, the kind of place you wouldn't find unless you knew it was there. The perfect spot for a little... personal moment. I reached into my bag, pulled out a mini bottle of bourbon, and snapped it open. The burn was exactly what I needed. Just a few seconds to breathe, to reset before I dove back into the chaos.

With that little pick-me-up, I was ready to hit my favorite shop on my map: The Jewelry Box.

The sign was simple, almost too simple for a place with such a killer collection. But sometimes, the real gems are hidden where you least expect them. The day wasn't over, and neither was my hustle.

Chapter 9

THE JEWELRY BOX

The Jewelry Box is a cute little shop that is doing it's best to hold on to it's glory but has seen better days, and honestly, so have I. It's right across from that famous Hard Rock-themed cafe on Charlotte Street. After weaving around tourist getting their bearings in this crazy port town, the moment I step inside the faint scent of stale air mixed with cheap cologne hits me.

My eyes take a second to adjust from the brightness outside to the the lighting that make the display cases look electric. The jewelry cases aren't new, and bare some scratch marks on the glass, but they are filled with wonderful pieces that tourist buy every week.

SUNNY KAPOOR. The name alone could make you smile, and not just because it sounds like a Bollywood heartthrob in an old romance movie. Sunny is flamboyant with a capital F. His outfits scream for attention–today is no exception. He's rocking a bright pink shirt, white pants that should be illegal after Labor Day, and enough gold chains to weigh down a small yacht.

Sunny is the manager of The Jewelry Box and a character and a half, let me tell you. At 35, he's this whirlwind of energy, always dressed in colors that beg "look at me!" His Pakistani accent is thick, but it's the kind of thick that adds character, like a rich, creamy coconut sauce over a boring piece of chicken.

But the real story of Sunny is a lot darker than his bubbly exterior lets on. He grew up in a small town in Pakistan, and let's just say his childhood was anything but pleasant. His dad was a real piece of work–abusive, controlling, the kind of man who could turn a sunny day into a storm in seconds. And his mom? Well, she was barely there, more like a ghost who drifted in and out of his life, leaving him to deal with his father's cruelty all on his own. I don't blame her.

Sunny had to learn how to survive, and boy, did he learn. He figured out early that life was just one big stage, and if he played his cards right, he could manipulate it to suit his needs. That's where the flamboyance comes in. The whole over-the-top, possibly-gay persona? It's all part of his act.

Sunny discovered that if people—especially women—thought he was gay, they'd let their guard down, trust him more, and sometimes even fall for his charm. It's his way of staying in control, of hiding the scars from a childhood that could've destroyed him. And then there's me. I know Sunny's got a thing for me—he tries to hide it behind all that flash, but I can see it. It's like he's torn between keeping up the act and letting someone in, and honestly? It's kind of sweet, in a complicated, messed-up way.

The moment he spots me, his face lights up like I'm the sun after a week of rain.

"OMG sweetie, you're back!" Sunny exclaims, practically tripping over his own feet as he scurries over to me.

"Sunny, I missed you," I reply with a smirk. The truth is, I didn't miss him as much as I missed the easy commissions he brings in, but I'm not heartless.

There's something endearing about the way he fawns over me like I'm his long-lost love.

"Hello, my beautiful rainbow. Come in, would you like a water?" Sunny asks, his voice dipping into that sugary-sweet tone he reserves for special customers—or in this case, special acquaintances. He doesn't wait for my answer before comically shouting over his shoulder, "Surjeet, water water water!"

Surjeet, Sunny's long-suffering Pakistani assistant, bursts out of the back office like a rabbit out of a hat. He's clutching an ice-cold bottle of water like it's a lifeline, which, in this heat, it probably is. Sunny grabs the bottle and quickly wraps it in a paper towel before handing it to me with a flourish.

"Thanks, Sunny. How are sales?" I ask, opening open the bottle and taking a sip. The cool liquid is a relief, just like that shot of Bourbon earlier, but it does little to quench the thirst of my real problem.

Sunny's face splits into a grin as wide as the ocean. "Yes, Christina, your sales are on fire. The owner is beyond happy."

I can't help but notice the way he says "beyond happy" as if the owner's happiness is somehow an anomaly. But before I can dwell on it, Sunny's eyes narrow, and he gives me a look that could pierce steel.

"Why so glum, chum? Is everything OK, sweetheart? Tell me what's up, you know daddy will do anything to help," he says, digging for answers like a prospector after gold.

I sigh, leaning against the counter. "It's just work stuff. If I don't increase my sales at CDG, Artem will force my company to fire me."

His flamboyant demeanor falters for a second, replaced by genuine concern. "Artem is a greedy dirt-bag. You always sell enough of *our* goods. Isn't that enough for your bosses?" Sunny's voice drips with disdain at the mention of Artem, as if saying his name leaves a bad taste in his mouth.

"Nope. Artem signed a new contract guaranteeing we hit our crazy-high sales targets for their stores. If I don't hit my targets, I'm fired and the financial support I give my mom ends and she'll be kicked out of her nursing home," I explain, feeling the weight of the world pressing down on me like an anchor.

Sunny's expression softens, and he reaches out to pat my hand. "Sweetie, the banks have plenty of money to lend. And, the BOX can always provide a loan, if needed."

My heart skips a beat. This isn't the first time Sunny has offered financial help, but I've always managed to brush it off. Today, though, I know I need the help. The desperation in my voice must have tipped him off because he's watching me with the intensity of a hawk.

"Tell me more, how much could I borrow?" I ask, trying to sound casual, but failing miserably.

Sunny smile slightly, his eyes gleam with excitement, like a cat that's just caught sight of a mouse. "That depends on how long you need it for?"

"A couple of cruises," I reply, already feeling the noose tightening around my neck.

Sunny leans both elbows on the glass counter, his chin resting on his knuckles like he's ready to tell me a juicy secret.

"How about this, you send guests from your ship here next cruise. Make them ask for the, I don't know, the 'Ocean Seduction'. Keep the products vague, we'll choose the products once they get here. Any sales commissions, for the Ocean Seduction Collection, will be credited against the principal amount. Interest is eight points a week."

I lean back, scoffing at the terms. "Eight points? Holy shit, those terms are steep. No offence."

Sunny leans back too, a sly smile playing on his lips.

"None taken, girl, but..." He snaps his fingers, the sound sharp as a whip, and Surjeet appears again like a genie summoned from a lamp.

"Bring me thirty thousand," Sunny says in Urdu, Pakistans main language, and Surjeet nods, disappearing into the back office.

My heart pounds in my chest as I swivel in my chair, watching Surjeet return with a weathered Adidas shoe box, held together by an elastic band. He hands it to Sunny with a deferential bow, and Sunny places it on the counter between us.

"At The Jewelry Box, unlike the bank, there is no paperwork, forms, or credit approvals needed" Sunny says, lifting the lid to reveal stacks of $100 USD bills. The sight of that much cash makes my head spin. It's one thing to think about borrowing money; it's another to see it laid out in front of you like a buffet of bad decisions.

I quickly shut the lid and push the box back. "I can't take this!"

Sunny shakes his head, his smile never faltering. "Sweetie. You can and you will. This is a one-time offer only available to the loyal. You did say your mom needs help, right? Ah, the things we do for family..." He reaches out to stroke my hand, his touch as smooth as his words.

"Do the right thing, help your mom, send guests here to shop, pay off your loan. Nothing has ever been so easy," Sunny continues, his eyes closing as he slowly pushes the shoe box back across the counter. I push the weathered Adidas shoe box back to Sunny.

The weight of his words presses down on me, and I know I'm trapped. I've danced around the edge of this decision for weeks, but now, there's no more room to dance. I have to jump.

Sunny hands me a business card, his fingers lingering on mine for just a moment too long. "Take it now, or my boss will get very angry. And, you wouldn't like it if my boss got angry. If you ever need more..." He slides the box back across the counter with the same practiced ease as a magician performing a trick.

I put the card down, take the box and shove it into my messenger bag, the weight of the money making it sag heavily on my shoulder. After picking up the business card, and without another word, I turn and walk out of the store, the sound of the door chime ringing in my ears like a death knell.

The sunlight blinds me for a moment as I step outside, and I blink rapidly, trying to adjust. The heat and humidity feeling a little more intense now. My mind is racing, trying to process what just happened. Did I really just borrow thirty thousand dollars from Sunny? Did I really just agree to that? How did I get into this mess?

I'm so lost in thought that I don't notice two other shopping guides until I plow straight into them, my body crashing to the ground with an unceremonious thud.

My messenger bag spills open, and Sunny's business card flutters to the pavement like a guilty secret exposed.

"Well, well, well, what do we have here?" a voice drawls above me. I look up to see fellow shopping guides Craig Long–an arrogant Australian with a smirk that could curdle milk–standing over me. Beside him, Tyson Henderson, a Texan with shaggy blonde hair and teeth too big for his mouth, is grinning like a Cheshire cat.

Craig and Tyson work for the same company I do, Shipboard Media, but they are on better ships due to their sales and, more-so, their ass-kissing. Shipboard Media hires many shopping guides from the US, UK, Australia and Canada.

Any country where the citizens speak English as their first language is the only mandatory requirement of the position. Preference are given to individuals with positive personalities and attitudes during the hiring process.

Craig snatches up my messenger bag and the card, holding them out of my reach like a naughty brother teasing his sister. "Look, Tyson, a free messenger bag," Craig says, scanning the card with feigned interest.

"Christina is more interested in getting dudes' phone numbers than selling diamonds."

I scramble to my feet, trying to grab my bag back, but Craig holds it out of reach, laughing as I lunge for it. Before I can react, a third figure steps in–Victor, a towering presence with a no-nonsense attitude.

Victor's hand shoots out, snatching the messenger bag and card back from Craig in one smooth motion. "You looking for arm to be broken?" Victor asks, his accent thick, voice low and dangerous. His eyes fixed on Craig, almost nose to nose.

Craig's smirk falters, and he steps back, clearly not wanting to push his luck. Victor slowly hands my bag and card back to me without looking, his eyes narrowing at Craig and Tyson.

"Here's some advice," Craig sneers as he backs away. "Don't focus on getting dudes' numbers or helping these shitty stores." He jerks his thumb toward The Jewelry Box sign. "Only push CDG stores. I hardly even mention these dumpy little stores to guests."

Craig flips Victor the bird before swaggering off with Tyson in tow. Victor puckers his lips in a mocking kiss, then turns to me, pulling his sunglasses down to peer at me over the rim.

"Don't need help, huh?" Victor chuckles, his voice tinged with amusement.

I force a smile, still rattled from the encounter.

"Thanks, Victor," I mumble, clutching my bag like it's a lifeline. Victor just shakes his head, a knowing look in his eyes. "Watch yourself, Christina. Not everyone's as nice as me," he says before walking off, leaving me standing alone on the sidewalk.

Chapter 10

BLACKMAIL AND BAD DECISIONS

Before I can fully process what just happened, another voice cuts through the haze of my thoughts. "Oh hey, Christina, right?" I turn to see Patrick–the forgettable drunk guy, who crashed into my legs, from last night.

He's dressed well and sports a charming smile that probably gets him out of trouble more often than not. Today, he looks the kind of guy who could sweet-talk his way out of a speeding ticket, and I can't help but be wary.

"I didn't get a chance to thank you for your help last night," Patrick says, his tone casual, but there's something in his eyes that makes me uneasy.

"Big Bang," I reply, giving him a nickname that just slipped out. "Did your wife give you any trouble?"

Patrick laughs, but it's a laugh that doesn't quite reach his eyes. "Nothing I can't handle. I'm Patrick, by the way."

I dig into my bag, pulling out a shopping map and handing it to him. The weight of the money in the shoebox is a constant reminder of the mistake I just made.

"Be nice to your wife. Today is the best day for shopping. Every store on the map has discounted duty-free goods," I say, trying to steer the conversation back to safer waters.

Patrick takes the map, flips it over and scans the back. He shoots me a look, one dripping with disappointment. "Aren't you forgetting something?"

I blink, confusion momentarily clouding my mind.

"Did you find someone for me yet?"

"Someone?" I say confused, but in the back of mind it all comes rushing back to me.

Patrick presses, his tone just a little too insistent.

The realization dawns on me like a cold slap to the face. "I wasn't kidding," he continues, his voice dropping to a conspiratorial whisper. "I'd really appreciate, you know, something nice, this or even next cruise. We're sailing again next cruise. Help a brother out."

I stare at him, incredulously.

"You know that's NOT what I do on the ship, right?" Patrick nods, his smile never faltering.

"Yeah, but I see who you work with. All these beautiful girls might want to make some extra cash."

My blood runs cold. Is he serious?

"Are you for real? I already said I can't and won't help you. Prostitution is illegal. Everywhere. Even on cruise ships. Have fun shopping," I snap, turning on to walk away.

But Patrick isn't done. He grabs my messenger bag strap, pulling me back toward him. Before I can react, he pushes a huge wad of $100 bills into my ribs, his grip firm and unyielding. He get's right in my face.

"Here's half up front, twenty thousand. Find me someone hot or I'll say you kissed me when you helped me back to my cabin," Patrick threatens, his voice low and menacing.

My heart skips a beat.

"You wouldn't?" I scowl.

"Try me. I'll say you stole my money too," Patrick replies, his voice dripping with confidence.

I fumble, trying to push the money back, but Patrick's pushes back harder. The scuffle draws attention, and with a woman and kids approaching, panic rises in my throat. I can't afford to make a scene, not with everything that's at stake.

Desperate, I slip the money into my messenger bag, trying to hide it from view just as Patrick's wife and kids walk up.

"Hi honey, this is Christina, the ship's shopping guide. She was just telling me all about the *beauty* she's going to get me next cruise," Patrick says, his tone sickeningly sweet as he hands his wife the shopping map.

"He deserves something nice," Patrick's wife says to me, playing with what hair was left on his head, her smile warm and genuine. "I'm off to spend your hard-earned money again. Come on, kids," she adds, turning to walk off with their children.

As we watch his wife and kids walk off, Patrick leans in close as they leave, his voice a whisper of venom in my ear. "Get me a beautiful girl or I'll tell US Customs all about *this* and have you arrested back in Miami."

I don't respond. I can't. The words are stuck in my throat, choked by the overwhelming sense of dread that's settled in the pit of my stomach. Without looking back, I walk away, the weight of the money and the threat hanging over me like a dark cloud.

I know I'm fucked. And that sting? Yeah, it hurts like hell.

I collect myself as best I can and continue visiting the rest of the stores on the map, trying my best to safeguard the 50k tucked in my bag. How did all of this go south so quickly, I ask myself. The afternoon shadows from the majestic palm trees start to grow as I make it back to the ship, albeit in a mental fog.

Returning to the safety of the ship was like stepping into another world, leaving behind the scorching Bahamian sun and the chaos of Nassau. The air was cooler, but not enough to chase away the sweat beading on my forehead. I wiped my brow with the back of my hand, trying to gather myself as I walk up the metal gangway, behind some tipsy tourist, through the shell-door and approached the security checkpoint. The buzzing of the metal detector filled the otherwise quiet space, a stark contrast to the noise and crowds outside.

As I neared the security checkpoint, I spotted him–Enzo, the friendly and all-too-handsome Filipino security guard who'd made it his mission to flirt with me every time I stepped on board. I've seen him on the other ships I've worked on, a welcomed face on this new assignment.

He was standing casually scanning the guests as they came by, his uniform crisp and perfect, like he'd stepped straight out of a magazine. He caught sight of me and broke into a wide, boyish grin, one that could melt even the iciest of hearts. Not that mine was exactly icy, but you know what I mean.

"Hey, Christina!" Enzo called out, waving me over as if I wasn't already heading his way.

I put on my best smile, the kind that was supposed to say "just another day at the office" but probably came off more like "please don't ask me about the suspiciously full bag I'm carrying." The messenger bag felt like it weighed a ton, even though it was mostly just paper–very valuable paper, mind you, but still just paper.

"Enzo, my favorite security guy," I teased, adding a little extra sway to my walk as I approached him. The filipino security team picking up the slack while Enzo speaks to me.

"How's it going? You keeping all the riffraff out?" I added. He chuckled, a deep, warm sound that made me momentarily forget the anxiety gnawing at my insides. "You know it, ma'am. Just doing my job. How was Nassau? Find anything good?"

"Oh, you know, the usual. Sun, sand, overpriced souvenirs." I shrugged, trying to play it cool as I stepped closer to the metal detector. My heart was pounding in my chest, but I kept my tone light, hoping he wouldn't notice the slight tremble in my hands.

His eyes flickered to my bag, and I could see the gears turning in his head. Enzo wasn't stupid. He'd seen enough to know when something was up. I had to distract him, fast.

"So, tell me, when are you going to show me the best spot on this ship to catch the sunset? You've been holding out on me," I said, leaning a little closer, flashing him a playful grin.

He chuckled again, his eyes crinkling at the corners. "Maybe next time, Christina. I've got a reputation to uphold, you know. Can't have everyone thinking I'm giving you special treatment."

I laughed, hoping it sounded natural. "Come on, you know I'm your favorite. Who else keeps you entertained on these long shifts?"

He shook his head, still smiling, but his gaze drifted back to the bag hanging off my shoulder. "You know the drill, Christina. Bag on the conveyor, please."

Crap. I knew it was coming, but I'd hoped maybe, just maybe, I could charm my way out of it. No such luck. I nodded, trying to look casual as I slid the bag off my shoulder and onto the conveyor belt. The shoe box inside felt like it was glowing neon, screaming for attention. I held my breath as the bag slowly disappeared into the X-ray machine, Enzo's eyes never leaving the screen.

"Anything interesting in there today?" he asked, his tone still light but with a hint of curiosity.

"Just some paperwork," I said, waving a hand dismissively. "You know how it is. Gotta keep everything organized."

He nodded, his eyes narrowing slightly as he watched the screen. I could see the moment he spotted it, the stacks, and huge roll, of cash tucked neatly inside the old Adidas shoe box. His expression didn't change, but I knew he'd seen it. My heart was pounding so hard I was sure he could hear it.

"Paperwork, huh?" he said, raising an eyebrow.

"Yeah, lots of paperwork. You wouldn't believe the amount of forms we have to fill out for these shopping trips," I lied, forcing a laugh. "It's enough to make your head spin."

Enzo leaned back slightly, crossing his arms over his chest, one hand tapping the corner of his cheek, as he regarded me. For a moment, I thought he was going to press the issue, ask me what was really in the bag. But then, he did something I didn't expect. He smiled–just a small, knowing smile, like he was letting me off the hook.

"Well, I hope you get it all sorted out," he said, his tone easy and relaxed, like we were just two friends chatting about nothing important. "Wouldn't want you to get into trouble with all that... paperwork."

I let out a breath I didn't realize I'd been holding, nodding quickly. "Yeah, thanks, Enzo. I'll be sure to keep everything in order."

He gave me a wink as he handed me back my bag. "Stay out of trouble, Christina. And don't forget, you owe me that sunset."

I smiled, the relief flooding through me like a tidal wave. "You got it, Enzo. Next time, I promise."

I slung the bag over my shoulder, the cash still safely tucked inside, and made my way down the corridor, my heart slowly returning to a normal rhythm. As I walked away, I couldn't help but glance back over my shoulder. Enzo was still watching me, his expression unreadable, but there was something in his eyes that told me he knew more than he was letting on.

But for now, he was letting it slide. And I wasn't about to question my luck.

Okay, so here's the thing—everyone who's been around the block on a cruise ship knows the filipino mafia is as real as the ocean beneath the hull.

Now, when I say "mafia," I don't mean a bunch of guys in suits with cigars, but there's definitely a tight-knit group of filipinos that run the show behind the scenes. It's like an unspoken rule. You don't mess with them, and they won't mess with you.

This little shadow organization is all about control, especially in the deck and engine departments. These guys run everything from the cleaning schedules to who gets the cushy jobs, and trust me, they know how to make things happen. And let's not forget security—they've got that locked down tighter than a drum. Every move, every shift, every little thing that happens on board is under their watchful eyes. They can make things disappear or appear out of thin air, depending on what suits their needs.

And here's the kicker—this isn't just one ship or one company. Nope, this is a global thing. Every cruise line, every ship, from the massive floating cities to the smaller, more intimate vessels, has its own version of this Filipino mafia. It's like they're the silent rulers of the seas, keeping everything running smoothly—or not—depending on how you treat them.

Most people think the higher-ups, the captains, and officers are the ones in charge. But the reality? The real power lies with these guys. They're the ones who know where all the bodies are buried, metaphorically speaking, of course. Or at least I hope it's just metaphorical. They've got connections that stretch from one end of the globe to the other, and if you're smart, you'll stay on their good side. They've got a network so tight that if something goes down, they'll know before you do.

You don't really see them much—well, not in the sense that they're flaunting their power. Filipinos are quiet, respectful, but they have this aura that says they could break you without breaking a sweat. Everyone knows not to mess with them because, let's face it, when you're out in the middle of the ocean, you don't want to piss off the people who control the engines or the people who could decide how thorough the security checks are—or aren't.

And what's even more impressive is how they protect their own. You'd think with so many nationalities on board, there'd be friction, but the Filipino crew members stick together like glue. They've got this brotherhood going on—one that's built on years of trust and loyalty. They look out for each other, and they've got a system in place to make sure no one steps out of line or crosses them. It's like they've taken the whole concept of family and cranked it up to eleven.

So, yeah, the Filipino mafia is real, and it's as much a part of cruise ship culture as the midnight buffets and the towel animals on your bed. And as long as you know the rules and play by them, you'll be just fine. Just don't ever think for a second that you can outsmart them. They've been doing this a lot longer than you've been taking cruises, and they've got the upper hand in more ways than you can imagine.

Now, I know what you're thinking–why am I telling you this? Well, let's just say that understanding who really runs the show is crucial when you're carrying around a messenger bag full of cash. You never know who might be watching or what they might do if they see something they don't like.

The walk back to my cabin felt longer than usual, the weight of what I was carrying making each step heavier. I could still feel the adrenaline coursing through my veins, a mix of fear and excitement that left me on edge. I ask myself what have I gotten myself into?

When I finally reached my cabin, I shut the door behind me and leaned against it, letting out a long breath. My hand was trembling as I reached for the zipper of my bag, pulling it open to reveal the shoe box and stacks of cash once more. I stared at it, the reality of what I was doing sinking in.

This wasn't just some small-time hustle. This was serious. And I was in deep.

I thought back to that moment with Enzo, the way he'd looked at me, the way he'd let it slide. I was playing with fire, and I knew it. But I also knew I didn't have a choice. Not if I wanted to keep my job. Not if I wanted to help my mom.

With a sigh, I shoved the cash back into the shoe box and tucked it into the bottom of my closet, hiding it under a pile of clothes. Out of sight, out of mind–or at least, that's what I was telling myself. I pulled an ice-cold beer from the tiny fridge and muttered "Hello, beautiful." I twist off the top, the sound of the bottle opening cutting through the silence like a lifeline. I took a long, deep swig, letting the cold liquid slide down my throat. It was bitter, but familiar. A reminder of simpler times. That first sip was delicious. The next, longer sip was exquisite.

I flopped down onto the bed, staring up at the ceiling as the day's events replayed in my mind. I couldn't shake the feeling that I was teetering on the edge of something dangerous, something that could all come crashing down if I wasn't careful.

But for now, I was safe. For now, I could breathe.

I reached for my beer, the bottle still cold in my hand. As I took another long drink, I thought back to that memory of my dad, the way he'd handed me my first beer with a grin on his face. He always knew how to make the toughest situations feel a little less daunting, a little less terrifying. I could almost hear his voice now, telling me to keep my head up, to keep pushing forward no matter what.

"Cheers, Dad," I whispered", raising the bottle in another mock toast to the old photo on the cork board and obituary program lying on the shelf. Raising the bottle unlocked a memory, one I hadn't thought about in years.

I was seventeen, sitting on the porch with Dad, the North Carolina sun setting in the distance. We were sharing a beer– my first one. It was one of those rare moments when he wasn't the stern, unyielding admiral. He was just Dad. We didn't talk much that evening; we didn't need to. The silence between us was enough, filled with unspoken understanding. He handed me the beer with a small smirk, like he was letting me in on some secret, some rite of passage.

I remember the way the amber liquid tasted, a mix of bitterness and warmth that made me feel both grown-up and still very much like a kid. The memory brought a small smile to my face, a brief respite from the storm brewing inside me. But it wasn't enough to shake off the dread gnawing at my insides. I took another swig of beer, hoping it would drown out the doubts clawing at the back of my mind.

My father, the ever-strict Navy admiral who always seemed larger than life, even after he was gone. "Wish you were here to tell me what the hell to do next."

But I already knew the answer. I had to keep going. Keep playing the game. Keep smiling, keep charming, keep getting by however I could.

And maybe, just maybe, I'd find a way out of this mess before it all came crashing down.

My heart was still racing from the whirlwind of emotions swirling in my chest. I could feel the weight of every single bill inside that shoe box, like a lead anchor pulling me down.

I started pacing back and forth in my tiny cabin, the walls closing in around me. The air felt thick, heavy with the scent of stale air conditioning. I reached for my phone, needing something–anything–to distract me from the mess I was in. My inbox was full of junk, the usual flood of promotional emails and work updates. One email, though, caught my eye. I sit on my single bed and read the email

"CDG Sales are disappointing!"

I could almost hear Artem's voice barking at me through the screen, dripping with disdain. The asshole. As if I didn't have enough on my plate already. I closed out the email app, my heart pounding in my chest. This wasn't helping.

When the app closed it revealed my recently dialed list. Emily's name stared back at me, her number just a tap away. I hesitated, my thumb hovering over the screen. The thought of calling her, of hearing her voice, made my chest tighten with a mix of longing and fear.

I sat up straighter, the beer bottle still in my hand, the weight of the day pressing down on me. Calling Emily would mean facing everything I was trying to avoid, everything I was scared to admit even to myself. But not calling her... that didn't feel right either.

I took another sip of beer, letting the alcohol cloud my thoughts, if only for a moment. I needed to make a decision, but I couldn't. Not yet. The stakes were too high, and I felt like I was standing on the edge of a cliff, unsure if I should jump or step back. One wrong move, and everything could come crashing down–my job, my reputation, everything I'd built on this unstable foundation.

The bitter taste of regret mingled with the beer, but I pushed it down, as I do with all my emotions lately, letting the cool liquid numb my senses. My brain buzzed with all the conflicting voices in my head. Should I stay on this ship, keep playing the game, or finally walk away? Maybe it was the exhaustion talking, or maybe it was the alcohol, but I couldn't shake the feeling that I was drowning in my own indecision.

I glanced at the half-empty bottle in my hand, wondering if I'd ever be able to get out of this cycle, or if I'd keep floating aimlessly, stuck in a never-ending sea of "what ifs."

Chapter 11

SOUTH BEACH DREAMS

The neon lights of South Beach Dreams flickered against the evening sky, casting a glow that seemed both alluring and a bit sleazy on the busy Miami street. Inside, the air was thick with the scent of heavy perfume, faint desperation and bad life choices. Emily sat at her desk surrounded by the soft hum of whispered conversations and the clack of high heels on marble. The office, with its plush velvet chairs and gaudy gold accents, felt like a caricature of luxury–a stark contrast to Emily's own stark, utilitarian workspace.

Emily's desk was cluttered with sticky notes, coffee cups, and schedules scattered about, each column filled with names and times in meticulous detail. She was the master of orchestration behind South Beach Dreams' seamless facade, yet each reservation was a reminder of the life she was desperate to escape. Every call, every appointment scheduled, felt like a chain wrapping tighter around her future.

As she sorted through the evening's bookings, her desk phone lit up. "It's a wonderful evening at South Beach Dreams, how can we make your dreams come true?" she answered with practiced cheerfulness, despite the weariness dragging at her bones.

"Ola, Emily. I see you're finally here, you were late again," came the voice of Bas, her boss. His Cuban accent was thick, his tone dripping with irritation and an underlying threat that wasn't entirely professional.

"Sorry, Bas, I was submitting my mid-term for my online classes," Emily replied, her voice steady despite the flutter of anxiety in her chest.

"You know, Emily, if you put the same amount of effort into this job, as you do with your online classes, you just might do well," Bas's voice was harsh, a reminder of his ever-looming presence in her life.

"When I'm here, I work hard," Emily countered, trying to keep the frustration from her voice.

"Yes, but lately you've been lazy. Our clients demand a level of service I don't think you're capable of providing anymore. I can get someone to fill your position in a minute. Your job is not hard. Don't think you're irreplaceable." Bas takes a long drag of his cigarette and continues.

"Can I count on you to do some fucking work today?" Bas's words were like a slap, sharp and demeaning.

"Yes, Bas, absolutely!" Emily responded, clenching her teeth. The call ended, leaving her to stare at the blinking lights of her phone, each one a reminder of the precariousness of her position.

SeBastian "Bas" Baeza was a ruthless psychopath, a micromanaging tyrant who ruled South Beach Dreams like a dictator. His management style was fear, his motivation greed. Emily knew she needed to escape, to finish her law degree and leave this world behind. But every day, every client she booked, seemed to pull her further away from her dreams of courtrooms and justice.

The weight of her failure was heavy–leaving her law studies at the University of Cincinnati had been a decision born of desperation, not desire. She missed her family, her loving parents, and her younger brother, all of whom she had left behind in a bid to escape the pressure and disappointment. She felt like a failure, not only to her family but to herself.

Later, as the clock nudged past midnight, the gaudy opulence of South Beach Dreams' interior–a kitsch blend of plush velvet chairs and relentless gold accents–seemed to intensify under the dim office lighting. Emily packed her things slowly, her movements deliberate and tired. The nightly ritual of shutting down her computer and stacking papers felt like the closing of a chapter she was too weary to read again. The echoes of phone conversations, scheduling clients and managing escorts, lingered in the air, a reminder of the day's drudgery and her growing disillusionment.

Outside her office door, the hallway was quiet, the buzz of the daytime now a distant memory. As she approached the staff exit, the usual chirpiness that filled her afternoons felt smothered by the night's embrace. Dougy, the security guard, was stationed by the door, his presence both a comfort and a reminder of the world she inhabited.

"Evening, Emily, you heading out for the night? Let me walk you to your car," Dougy offered, his tone friendly but lined with a flirtatious undertone that Emily found more tedious than charming.

"No thanks, Dougy. I can manage," Emily responded with a polite smile that didn't reach her eyes. She was tired, not just from the day but from the accumulated weight of pretending– pretending to be okay, pretending this job was just a job.

As she stepped out into the humid Miami night, the air felt thick against her skin. Her 2007 Camry was parked in the corner of the lot, surrounded by vehicles that screamed of wealth and success–Mercedes, Ferraris, Bentleys. She eyed her car, the paint slightly faded, the driver's side mirror held together with duct tape–a stark contrast to the luxury cars that belonged to the escorts she scheduled daily. The Camry coughed to life, its engine complaining as loudly as Emily's thoughts. "I can do better than this," she murmured to herself, a mix of resolve and resignation washing over her.

Just then, Tina, one of the escorts, pulled up in a sleek new BMW M8 Coupé. The car's engine purred in the quiet night, a sound of smooth assurance. Tina stepped out onto her red-soled heels, her evening still cloaked in the success of a lucrative appointment.

"Hey, Em, car trouble again?" Tina leaned into the window, her voice laced with concern and a hint of amusement.

"Just the usual," Emily replied, forcing a smile.

"You know, with what I made tonight, you could almost get yourself one of these," Tina gestured to her M8, half-joking, half-serious. "Ever think about switching careers? You're pretty enough for it."

Emily laughed, a short, bittersweet sound. "Thanks, but I think I'll pass. It's kind of you to offer, though."

Tina winked. "Offer stands. I *could* teach you a couple tricks to get started. You know, to keep the guys coming back. Give me a call if you change your mind." With a playful salute, she walked to the secure back entrance of South Beach Dreams, leaving Emily alone with her thoughts.

Emily watched Tina's perfect body walk away, the neon signs of South Beach Dreams flickering in the reflection of her car window. Tina's words echoed in her mind, a tempting call to a life filled with more money than she could currently fathom. But deep down, Emily knew that wasn't what she wanted. She never dreamt of being a fuck-toy, her dreams lay elsewhere, in courtrooms and legal briefs, not in the fleeting glances, and man-handling of men who saw everything as a transaction.

With a heavy sigh, she pulled out of the parking lot, her car's headlights cutting through the humid Miami night. The drive home was a blur, and when she finally crawled into bed, staring up in the dark, the silence of her room punctuated by the distant sounds of the city. The decision loomed over her, a crossroads between the life she led and the life she longed for. It wasn't just about a new car or more money; it was about her identity, her future, her sense of self.

As sleep finally claimed her, her last thoughts were of law books and justice and doing the right thing, a world away from the shadowed corners of South Beach Dreams and the life she currently leads.

Chapter 12

CHAIN SMOKE AND COLD SHOULDERS

So, I walk out onto the promenade deck, after my desk hours, to get some fresh air. Very few guests came by to say hi, or complain, or whatever. It's late and I love this time of night when the promenade deck is empty.

As I look out over the railing and feel the salty breeze blow my hair back, my brain begins it's quest to start over-thinking things.

Working on a cruise ship might sound like a dream job to many–a floating palace touring exotic destinations, endless parties, and a never-ending parade of new faces. But let me tell you, it's not all sunsets and margaritas. The reality can be a lot less glamorous, especially when you find yourself feeling more isolated than you'd ever imagined possible.

Picture this: You're surrounded by thousands of guests and hundreds of crew members on a vessel that's Basically a small city at sea. Despite the bustling crowds and constant activities, there's a peculiar form of loneliness that can sneak up on you. It's weird, right? I'm never really alone, but sometimes the sea of unfamiliar faces just makes the isolation feel even more intense.

For one thing, the connections I make are often fleeting. Guests come and go every few days, and while I might remember a face or a name, they usually won't remember mine amid the blur of their vacation experiences. I'm part of their holiday snapshots, a smiling face offering recommendations on the best shopping spots or the tastiest cocktails. But when they disembark, I'm just a part of the ephemeral tapestry of their travel memories. And as for the crew, well, they're in the same boat–literally and figuratively.

Everyone's far from home, missing family, friends, and familiar comforts. Relationships among crew members can be supportive and intense, but also transient. People transfer ships, contracts end, and life moves on.

The irony of it all is that I'm in these incredible locations, the kind of places people save for years to visit.

I'm there, but often it's just a backdrop to the daily grind. I see the Caribbean through portholes and walking to the stores listed on my shopping map. Shopping guides are strictly forbidden to go on tours or enjoy the islands. It's like being at a gourmet buffet but only ever sampling the bread rolls.

And let's not forget the living conditions. Privacy is a concept as foreign as the ports we dock at. Most crew cabins are shared, which means personal space is limited to a few cubic feet. They learn to change clothes with minimal movement and sleep through lights, sounds, and the occasional scent of someone else's midnight snack or shag session. I'm fortunate to have my own cabin in passenger areas, since I'm a concessionaire; in the grey area of being an employee and contractor working on board.

Moreover, the work itself is relentless. Seas might be rough, but schedules are rougher. It's a 24/7 operation where the waves stop for no one. The pressure to be "on" all the time, always smiling, always accommodating, can be exhausting. I'm performing, in a way, part of a well-oiled machine that keeps the dream alive for vacationers seeking escape from their own realities.

Then there's the disconnect from the world. Sure, ships have Wi-Fi now, but it's often slow and expensive. Keeping up with news, sports, or just binge-watching my favorite show can be a challenge. I feel disconnected, adrift from the currents of everyday life that keep you anchored to a sense of normalcy.

But it's not all doom and gloom. This unique lifestyle builds resilience and flexibility. I meet people from all corners of the earth, learn about cultures firsthand, and collect stories that I couldn't get anywhere else. I develop a family with my fellow crew members, bonded by shared experiences and the unique challenges of life at sea.

So, while it might get lonely out on the open ocean, those moments of solitude also give me space to grow. I find strength in the quiet times gazing out at the endless water, learn about myself in ways that might never have been possible on land. And every once in a while, I realize that this floating life, with all its quirks and solitude, is exactly where I need to be–at least for now.

I call my mom, Martina, from the promenade deck, the reception always great on these itineraries; being so close to the Florida coast. Navigating my relationship with my mom, Martina, is like trying to steer a kayak through a hurricane– stressful, chaotic, and frankly, a bit of a disaster. When I tell you it's complicated, believe me, it's an understatement.

Martina, at 60, could easily be the poster woman for life's harsher lessons, a chain smoker whose every exhale seems laced with regret and bitterness. We've always been like oil and water, but ever since the debacle that ended her marriage to dad, the gap between us has only widened. Let me set the scene a bit: Martina got caught cheating on my dad, a decorated Navy admiral who deserved way better. Their divorce wasn't just messy–it was like something out of a telenovela, minus the glamorous outfits and dramatic music.

It crushed my dad, both emotionally and mentally, and I honestly believe it was a contributing factor to his passing. My brother and sister haven't spoken to mom in years and didn't even attend the funeral. We recently laid Dad to rest in Charleston, and that was a day heavier than a double espresso on a Monday morning. To top it off, mom was conspicuously left out of dad's will, a final statement from beyond the grave that spoke volumes of his shattered trust and broken heart.

My brother and sister washed their hands clean of Mom after the divorce. I can't say I blame them–mom isn't exactly the warm, cookie-baking type. More like the smoke-in-your-face-and-complain-about-life type. So now, guess who's left managing this bundle of joy? Yep, that'd be me. Christina, the reluctant glue trying to hold together the remnants of a family that's seen better days.

You might wonder why I even bother. Well, there are days I ask myself the same question. Between managing my hectic life onboard to and dealing with mom's never-ending drama, it's like juggling flaming torches. And let's just say, I never excelled at circus skills.

Staring out over the endless blue expanse from the deck of the Ocean Seduction, I braced myself for the weekly dose of drama–my call to Martina, my ever-cynical mother ensconced in her elder-care castle, Evergreen Manor. Our phone conversations are always a treat. Please note the sarcasm in that statement. Taking a deep breath, I dialed her number, the sea breeze playing with my hair as if trying to whisper calm into the impending storm.

"I was beginning to think you'd never call," she answered, her voice scratchy from years of cigarettes.

"You know I'm the only one of your kids that call," I reminded her, trying to keep the conversation light. "Did you get into any trouble this week?"

"Don't be silly. I stopped going to Fight Club years ago. At my age, a soft shit is the highlight of my day." Her dry humor, as always, was intact despite the circumstances.

"Remember the first rule of Fight Club…" I joked, trying to steer the conversation towards something resembling normalcy between us.

Martina sighed audibly, "That shithead Arthur James died last week, So a better room on the third floor became available. I asked if I could move in there. You know my room is shit. The head bitch here, Lidia, told me there was something up I should speak with you about it. What is she talking about?"

Here we go. "Listen, mom, I don't want you to stress out but I'm a little behind on payments."

"What?" The word came out sharp and loaded, like a gunshot in the quiet of the night.

"Now, before you get upset, just know I have the money and I'm sending a payment to Lidia as soon as I'm back in Miami. I need to visit the bank to deposit the cash I borrowed," I explained as calmly as I could, knowing full well I shouldn't have ended the sentence with the word 'borrowed'.

"Borrowed? Christina, tell me you didn't *borrow* cash to pay your bills?" The concern in her voice was palpable, laced with the sharp tang of fear.

"No, no, it's an advance on future sales and they're *your* bills," I reassured her, stressed I'm doing her a favor.

"You're beginning to sound as stupid as your father. The interest from that loan shark Carlos sucked him dry for years," she snapped, her voice rising with each word.

"Be nice, I'm nothing like dad, so stop saying that," I retorted, feeling the old wound prick at her casual dismissal of his memory.

"You're exactly like your father! Stop denying it," she argued, stubborn as ever. " You work at sea, you never ask for help, you drink like a fish and you despise my existence. I'd say you're exactly alike." Mom wasn't wrong. We both pause for a moment but we start back at it again.

"This loan is from a friend," I tried to explain, hoping to soothe her mounting anger.

"Friends don't loan friends money. You're stupid to think otherwise," she scoffed, her cynicism peaking.

"Go tell Lidia you'll take the better suite," I sighed, tired of the circular argument, feeling the weight of the day pressing down on me.

"I'm not OK with this, and I'm certainly not happy with you. This is bullshit. I need a drink," Martina declared, then abruptly ended the call, leaving me staring at my phone, in my hand, over the railing, the dial tone like a cold dismissal. I felt like throwing the iPhone overboard, but what would that help? There would still be this abrasive tension between us and I'd be phone-less.

I pocketed my phone and leaned against the railing, the ocean's vastness suddenly mirroring my own feelings of isolation. Despite the gentle rocking of the ship, I felt adrift, caught in the undercurrent of familial obligation and my own life choices. Martina, with all her flaws and sharp edges, was still my mom, and no matter how much she infuriated me, I couldn't help but want to make things right for her, even if it meant navigating the murky waters of financial instability myself.

As the ship plowed forward through the waves, I realized that no matter how far I sailed, I could never really escape the ties that bound me to home, to mom, and to the shadows of my father that seemed to stretch as long and as far as the sea itself.

Chapter 13
COLLECTING ON A FAVOR

So, there I was, strolling down Front Street Pier in Key West, the salty breeze gently messing with my hair, making it dance in sync with the laid-back island vibe. Key West is one of those places where the air smells like freedom, mingled with the faint scent of rum and sunblock.

The kind of place where you can lose yourself in a lazy daydream or, in my case, plot the next move in a complicated, slightly illegal chess game of life.

Palm trees swayed above like gossiping old ladies, and the sound of flip-flops smacking against the souls of tourists feet was like a rhythmic island heartbeat. People walked by, all suntanned skin and relaxed smiles, holding hands or cold drinks, or both. It was the kind of place that dared you to be anything but chill. But chill wasn't on my agenda.

Key West stretched out around me, all vibrant colors and easygoing charm. The pier was dotted with little stalls selling everything from seashell necklaces to handmade leather sandals. I could hear a street performer nearby, his guitar strumming out a Jimmy Buffet tune that matched the pace of the day. A couple walked by, laughing and holding hands, their carefree energy making me jealous.

As I walked, my phone buzzed in my pocket. I pulled it out and glanced at the screen, seeing a string of disappointing emails I had no intention of dealing with. But there was one thing I did need to handle. I found Emily's number in my contacts, took a deep breath, and hit call. The phone rang a few times before she picked up.

"This is Emily," she answered, her voice clipped and professional.

"Hey, Emily, it's Christina," I replied, trying to keep my tone casual. You know, like I wasn't about to ask her for a huge favor that dipped its toes into some murky waters.

There was a pause on the other end, then a little laugh. "I know a lot of Christinas, so you gotta be more specific," she teased.

I felt slightly hurt she didn't remember me immediately. "You stole my phone," I shot back, a smirk tugging at the corner of my mouth.

"Ah, hey, cherry chapstick," she said, her tone shifting to something a bit more familiar, maybe even a little flirty. "You calling to collect on your favor?"

Emily's voice had that same undercurrent of sass I noticed at the bar when we met. It's one of the reasons I liked her, even if she was more trouble than I should be getting involved with.

"Actually, yeah," I admitted, feeling a little knot of anxiety twist in my gut. I wasn't one to ask for help often, but desperate times call for this measures.

"I didn't catch you at a bad time, did I?" I ask sincerely, as I turn my face towards the sun. Gosh, I love the heat.

"No, I'm cramming for exams for my online law course. What's up?" Emily asks.

"It's tough for me to say this, but I need your help. I don't know if you remember, but I work on a cruise ship and, funny enough, I ran into a guest looking for *company* on my ship." I slip out trying my best to stress the word company so she understands without having me *say* the words.

There was a beat of silence, and I could almost see Emily's eyebrow arching in that sarcastic way of hers. "Oh, so you're a pimp now?" she asked, voice dripping with amusement.

"Well... no," I said quickly, then sighed. "I didn't mean it like that. Since you have the connections, I was wondering if you can help find a girl to come sail next cruise. You can come as her chaperone, I'll pay for everything. I know it's short notice, but what do you say?"

Another pause, longer this time. I could practically hear the wheels turning in Emily's head. "No," she finally said, blunt and to the point. "I can't just drop everything and take a cruise. I'm broke, and my boss would be pissed. Also, I don't run the agency, so I can't just *get* girls."

"Yeah, I get that," I said, trying not to sound too disappointed, though I was. "You barely know me, and I admire you for staying loyal to your job. Your boss must be a great guy. I should do the same."

"I do remember you saying you '*owe me one*' and that you'd do anything for me not to mention the theft to the police," I said, letting a little edge slip into my voice. "This would be the perfect opportunity to pay back that debt."

There was a long stretch of silence on the other end of the line, and I could almost see Emily biting her lip, weighing her options. She was a smart girl, and she knew when someone had the upper hand. But damn if she wasn't stubborn too.

"I did mention that I would pay for everything for you and your guest," I continued, trying to sweeten the deal. But again, nothing. Just the sound of her breathing, thinking, calculating.

"Alright," I finally said, throwing up my hands even though she couldn't see it. "You can't say I didn't try the easy way. If you receive a call from the police, don't say I didn't warn you."

And with that, I ended the call, my frustration simmering just beneath the surface. I knew I'd hit a nerve with her, but I wasn't sure if it would be enough. Emily was tough, maybe even tougher than I was, but I wasn't about to back down. Not now. Not when everything was on the line. Who am I to think she'd call my bluff.

I shoved my phone back in my pocket and kept walking, trying to shake off the tension. The street performer's song faded into the background as I wandered further down the pier, past more tourists and locals mingling in that effortless way they always seem to do in places like this. The sun was high, casting sharp shadows across the wooden planks beneath my feet. It was one of those picture-perfect days you see in travel brochures, the kind that makes you think the world isn't such a bad place after all. But for me, it felt like the calm before the storm.

My mind kept drifting back to Emily, imagining her sitting there surrounded by textbooks, her hair a mess, eyes tired but determined. But it made sense now, why she was so hesitant to help. She was trying to claw her way out of one life and into another, and here I was, pulling her back in.

And as much as I hated to admit it, I could relate. I'd been there too, more times than I cared to count. Trying to escape, to reinvent myself, only to be dragged back down by the very things I was running from. It's a vicious cycle, one that's hard to break free from, no matter how strong you think you are.

Key West was supposed to be a paradise, a little slice of heaven where you could forget your troubles and just be. But for me, it was just another stop on a journey that seemed to be leading me deeper into the darkness. I looked around at the tourists, all smiles and sunburns, and wondered how many of them were hiding their own secrets, their own struggles. How many of them were just as trapped as I was, but too good at pretending to let it show?

I knew Emily was trying to change, to build something better for herself. And as much as I wanted to respect that, I couldn't. Not when my own back was against the wall. Not when I was running out of options.

The pier ended, spilling out onto a sandy beach lined with palm trees and dotted with colorful umbrellas. I could see a group of kids playing in the waves, their laughter echoing across the water, and for a moment, I envied their innocence, their freedom. But that moment passed, and I was left with nothing but the weight of my own decisions, the choices I'd made that had led me to this point.

I took a deep breath, letting the salty air fill my lungs, and made a decision. Emily might be trying to change, but I wasn't about to let her off the hook. Not when I needed her, my last hope. Not when everything was on the line. I'd give her some time to think, to stew over my words, but I wasn't giving up. Not yet.

And with that, I turned off Duval Street at Sloppy Joes, from the tourists and the carefree laughter, and started down Greene Street. There was still work to be done, plans to be made, and I wasn't about to let a little thing like a guilty conscience get in the way.

Key West has always been one of those places where the sun feels like it's trying to burn off a hangover, and the vibe is so laid-back it's almost horizontal. The air's thick with the smell of saltwater, sunscreen, and a hint of stale beer, but it's a comfort in its own right–kind of like a warm hug from a friend you haven't seen in a while. I made my way down Greene Street, the heart of Key West, where the colors are just a bit too bright, and the characters a bit too quirky to be anywhere but here.

I ducked into a souvenir shop on the corner, the kind of place where the walls are plastered with t-shirts screaming "I Got Wasted in Key West!" in neon colors, and shelves are stacked high with keychains, shot glasses, and questionable alligator-shaped trinkets. The air conditioning hit me like a blessing, and I let out a sigh of relief. If the outside was a sun-drenched fever dream, inside this shop was a kitschy cave of wonders–overly tanned tourists mingling with dusty, sun-bleached curios.

The shop's owner was a sight to behold. Raggedy would be a polite way to describe him. He was the human equivalent of an overused leather belt, or more like an old cigarette butt, all cracked skin and sun-worn edges, with a permanent scowl etched into his face like he'd seen one too many stupid tourists in his lifetime. His tank top was probably white in a past life, and his shorts looked like they'd been cut from a pair of jeans sometime in the Reagan era. He gave off the vibe of someone who had found paradise and then promptly got sick of it.

"Welcome, I guess," he grumbled as I walked in, his voice a raspy drawl, like gravel being kicked around. He barely looked up from the counter, where he was half-heartedly rearranging a display of seashell magnets.

"Thanks," I replied, flashing him a smile that was met with the enthusiasm of a damp sponge.

"My name is Christina Delgado and I'm the shopping guide on the Ocean Seduction." raising my chin as I politely introduce myself.

"What happened to the last guy?" He quipped angrily, wiping the sweat from his over-grown, fluffy eyebrows. "They're changing you all faster than I change sock, if I wore them." Questioning what was happening in the real world. I begin to explore the trinkets this gaudy souvenir shop has to offer. He follows along on the other side of the long glass display case, not sure to trust me with his seemingly worthless wares.

"They move us around a lot. It all depends on our sales and how we perform for the stores" I admitted.

My phone started ringing just as I spotted a particularly gaudy flamingo figurine that was too hideous not to love. I grabbed it, balancing it in one hand while I dug my phone out of my bag with the other.

"Hello?" I answered, waving at a few cruise guests who were meandering around the shop, picking up random items as if they were ancient relics instead of mass-produced junk.

"Yes, this is she," I said, moving toward the back of the un-air-conditioned store where the noise from outside was just a distant hum. The conversation was about to get personal, and I didn't need a bunch of strangers hearing it.

"I made a payment, like, yesterday, so it shouldn't be so high. When was the last payment?" I asked, trying to keep my voice low. My stomach did a little flip-flop as I waited for the response, which didn't sound promising.

"Oh, well, I'm doing my best to make payments," I said, feeling the weight of the flamingo in my hand like it was suddenly made of lead. I was doing my best, but sometimes your best isn't good enough when you're juggling bills, a job that's more hustle than pay-check, and the kind of life that doesn't leave much room for error.

"I should have some money in my account by the end of the week, so I can make a payment after that," I continued, my eyes darting around the shop as if the kitschy souvenirs could somehow offer me some financial advice. Instead, my gaze landed on the shop owner, who had perked up ever so slightly at my conversation.

"No, I don't need help filing for bankruptcy. Fuck you, don't call me again," I snapped, hanging up the phone and shoving it back into my bag with more force than necessary.

The shop owner's eyes twinkled with a sort of creepy curiosity, and before I could make a break for it, he piped up.

"Sounds like you've got some money troubles, sweetheart," he said, leaning on the counter with a look that could be mistaken for concern if I squinted hard enough.

"Who doesn't?" I replied, trying to keep my tone light, even though I was itching to get out of there.

"Ever thought about moving somewhere a bit more... off the grid?" he suggested, his voice taking on an almost conspiratorial tone. "Someplace where no one's gonna find you if you don't want them to."

I raised an eyebrow, trying to keep my cool even though the way he said it sent a shiver down my spine. "I think I'll pass, but thanks for the tip," I said, plastering on a smile that didn't reach my eyes.

"Suit yourself," he shrugged, turning his attention back to the tourists wanting to purchase seashell magnets, like we hadn't just had a borderline creepy conversation.

"I'll do my best to keep Ocean Seduction guests flocking in here for the best selection of Key West souvenirs." I blare so the entire store can hear me.

I made a beeline for the door, tossing the flamingo figurine back onto the shelf as I went. As I stepped out into the blazing sunshine, I let out a breath I didn't realize I'd been holding. Key West was weird, but that guy was on a whole other level. I needed to clear my head, and fast. I had other stores to hit on the map, and I wasn't about to let some sun-baked curmudgeon's advice mess with my game.

After a day spent trudging through the vibrant streets, dodging wayward spring breakers and avoiding aggressive vendors, I was ready to return to the ship, my temporary floating home. Shopping in Key West was a challenge, not just because the whole place isn't duty-free but because every store seemed to cater to the least sophisticated of tourist tastes. It was all about neon shirts, cheap flip-flops, and those horribly tacky souvenirs that scream, "I went to Key West and all I got was this lousy T-shirt."

The sun was starting to dip low in the sky, painting everything with that golden hour glow that could make even a dive bar look magical. I made my way back to the ship, weaving through groups of tourists who seemed more interested in finding the next bar than appreciating the beauty of the sunset. As I walked, I spotted a family–the one with the young daughter, Hana, I had met on the first day of the cruise. They looked slightly lost, map in hand, clearly trying to decide their next move.

"Hey there!" I called out as I approached them. The little girl looked up and beamed, recognizing me instantly.

"Christina!" Hana exclaimed, tugging at her parents' hands. "She's the nice lady from the ship!"

Her parents, relieved to see a familiar face, smiled warmly at me. "Hello again," the mother said. "We're just trying to figure out how to get back to the ship."

"Absolutely," I replied, pulling out a map from my bag and grabbing a pen. "If you want the quickest way, just stay on Duval. It runs straight into the pier." I circled the pier on the map and handed it to them.

"Thank you so much, Christina," the father said, his relief palpable. "We really appreciate it."

"No problem at all. Enjoy your evening!" I waved goodbye to Hana and her parents as they headed off, map in hand, a clear plan now guiding their steps.

Feeling slightly better after helping Hana's family, I continued my walk back to the ship, darting in and out of the stores on my map. To me, trying to sell people jewelry in Key West is a lesson in futility, like trying to convince a fish to buy a bicycle. But hey, at least you're in Key West, where even the most nonsensical endeavor can be wrapped in a warm sea breeze with a side of key lime pie.

I get back to the ship, the gangway looming ahead, and I could see Camila, the new Cruise Director, my ex, standing at the top, greeting the returning guests. Despite the heat of the day and the chaos that always accompanied a port stop, she managed to look impeccably sharp in her uniform, though the strain around her eyes betrayed her stress.

As I trudged up the gangway, I caught Camila's eye and she gave me a nod of acknowledgment. "Are you staying out of trouble?" she asked as I reached her, a slight smirk playing on her lips.

"Yes, ma'am, just focusing on work," I replied, trying to keep the conversation light despite the fatigue pulling at my limbs.

We moved together towards the security checkpoint, where I placed my messenger bag on the conveyor belt and stepped through the full-body scanner. The hum of the machine was a familiar discomfort by now, a reminder of the never-ending scrutiny we all endured on board.

As I collect my messenger bag I turn to Camila. "Camila, just so you know, my dad..." Camila cuts me off. She leans in and whispers so no-one else hears our conversation.

"Listen, I'm sorry for slapping you. I'm still hurt and doing my best to keep it together. This new Cruise Director position is so stressful. So many moving parts, responsibility, it's paralyzing. I need a stress reliever. What I wouldn't give for a mind-numbing orgasm right now? You down? No strings."

The question hung in the air between us, stark and unexpected. Working on ships has a funny way of making every sexual encounter casual. Like...really causal. One could easily have sex with multiple partners a day, if you want...or need to. Just sayin'.

I paused, taking in her serious expression and the tired slump of her shoulders. Camila wasn't just making a pass; she was reaching out in her own, unique way for a connection, for something to ease the stress that was clearly eating away at her.

Without a word, I followed her lead, and we made our way to her cabin, a silent agreement forming with each step. As we entered, the door shut behind us, sealing away the responsibilities, the titles, and the stress of our roles.

In Camila's cabin, the world narrowed down to just the two of us. That first kiss was soft and inviting, just as I remembered. Camila and I were a perfect match physically and we both knew exactly what made us tick. It was a little different this time, though. Clothes were shed not with passion but with a mutual understanding of need, a shared escape from the pressures that weighed us down. We found what we were seeking in each other, a temporary solace that was as intense as it was fleeting.

The emotional and physical release left us both quieter, more reflective. We lay there, not touching, wrapped in our own thoughts. The encounter hadn't solved anything, really; it was a mere respite, a pause in the relentless cycle of our lives aboard the cruise ship. But sometimes, a pause was all you needed to gather the strength to face another day.

After the whirlwind of what just happened between us, the cabin felt unusually still, like the pause after a storm. I was still processing the intense emotions, the rush of our encounter, as I sat on the edge of Camila's bed, trying to gather my thoughts and my clothes.

Camila's cabin was a stark contrast to the vibrant, chaotic energy of Key West where I had spent my day. It was meticulously organized, with every item in its place, which now seemed like a reflection of her attempts to keep her life just as orderly, despite the evident cracks. Her walls were decorated with framed photos of her cruise ship adventures and tranquil sea vistas, probably meant to instill a sense of calm but now feeling more like a facade.

I picked up my polo shirt from where it had landed on a sleek, modern chair–a stark reminder of the line we'd just crossed. As I buttoned it up, I could feel Camila's eyes on me, her gaze heavy with questions that neither of us were ready to address.

"Camila," I started, breaking the silence as I slipped on my sneakers, "I need to head out. My desk hours start soon, and I gotta get changed. You know how it goes."

She gave a small, wry smile at that, the tension easing slightly. "Yeah, I get it. Duty calls. I gotta get back to the gangway. I need to get a lot of positive comments if I want to stay in this position." Her voice was lighter, but I could see the confusion still clouding her eyes, mixing with something else– relief, maybe, or just the remnants of stress fading away.

I stood, adjusting my skort and smoothing down my hair, an attempt to bring some normalcy back. I looked around for my bag, finding it under a throw pillow that looked too expensive to touch. Camila watched me, her expression unreadable.

"Thanks, Camila," I said sincerely, clutching my bag. "For... you know, everything."

She nodded, crossing her arms behind her and leaning back against the door. "Yeah. Thanks, Christina. I..." She trailed off, shaking her head as if to clear it. "I guess I'm more relaxed now but somehow more confused after what just happened."

I couldn't help but let out a short laugh. "Welcome to the club. If this job has taught me anything, it's that nothing is ever simple." I gave her a hug at the door. "Just, you know, take it easy. Chill. And maybe don't slap anyone else anymore."

A genuine smile broke through her previously stoic facade, lighting up her features. "No promises," she quipped, and it was almost as if nothing had happened. Almost.

I left her cabin, the door closing softly behind me with a click that sounded too final. I get out of crew areas and up on my deck the hallways of the ship were bustling with guests heading to dinner, chatting and laughing, a stark contrast to the complexity of what I was leaving behind in Camila's cabin.

Walking through the ship, I could feel the weight of the day settling over me. Key West had been a mix of sun, stress, and shopping mishaps, none of which could really compare to the emotional cocktail of the past hour. I needed a moment to reset, to shift back into the role of Christina the shopping guide, not Christina the... whatever I had just been with Camila.

As I approached my shopping guide desk, the familiar sights and sounds of the cruise ship's main concourse wrapped around me like a comforting blanket. The clink of glasses at the bar, the murmur of excited conversations about dinner plans, and the occasional burst of laughter from a group of tourists– all of it helped me to refocus.

I arranged the brochures on my desk, each one promising the best deals and the most exclusive shopping experiences. I smiled and greeted the guests, slipping seamlessly back into my role. Every interaction felt like a step back toward normalcy, each smiling face a reminder of why I did this job.

But as the evening wore on, the energy of the day began to fade, and the memories of my impromptu visit to Camila's cabin lingered in the back of my mind. I was left with a sense of unease, wondering if I had just complicated things further, or if perhaps, in some convoluted way, I had found a new ally on this floating city.

Whatever the case, I knew one thing for sure: on a cruise ship, just like in life, you never really know what the next wave might bring.

Chapter 14

TICKET TO RIDE

Under the relentless Miami sun, I perch at an outdoor table at Bayside, in downtown Miami, the bustling shopping haven that served as a playground for tourists and a pitstop for crew members craving a slice of shore life. The mall, a vibrant collection of shops and eateries, sprawled across the shoreline like a colorful, chaotic canvas, pulsating with the rhythm of commerce and casual chatter. Situated just a bridge away from the Port of Miami, it offered not just retail therapy but a panoramic view of the marina, where boats danced lazily on the glittering waters under the expansive blue sky.

My spot at the cafe provided an unobstructed view of this maritime ballet, but my focus was elsewhere. I fiddled with my phone, anticipation mingling with the faint thread of desperation that had crept into my plan. It was a last-ditch effort, calling Emily to join me on today's cruise, not just as a guest but as part of a hastily concocted scheme that reeked of necessity rather than opportunity.

I dial Emily's number.

"Emily? Hey, it's Christina," I say as soon as the call connected, my voice carrying that unmistakable hint of mischief mixed with urgency.

On the other end, Emily's response came through, tinted with surprise and amusement, "Ah, cherry chapstick, what a surprise."

We both spoke over each other excitedly, a cacophony of urgent whispers and breathless updates.

I rushed her words, "I'm asking one last time, I really need your help."

"I want to take you up on your offer," Emily interjected, her voice a mix of resolve and excitement.

I pause, confusion making my eyebrows arch in surprise, "Wait, what?"

"For me and a friend to come for a cruise today. My roommate has agreed to come," Emily clarified, her words rushing out as if to cement the decision before she could reconsider.

"Hang on, that is great news, but why the sudden change of heart?" I probed, my mind racing to align this new development with the day's demands.

Emily's voice softened, conveying a depth of sincerity that was rarely necessitated by their usual exchanges. "I realized last night that my integrity needs work. That has to start today. I gotta do right by you. And, I need a break from work, so I told my boss, and he let me take some vacation time."

"Well, that's profound. Let me check some last-minute cruise tickets websites, hang on."

My response was immediate and instinctual, my earlier stress dissolving into a mix of relief and renewed purpose. I whipped out my laptop from my sleek messenger bag, fingers dancing across the keyboard with practiced ease.

The marina's backdrop faded to a blur as my focus narrowed to the glowing screen, my search punctuated by the rapid clicking of keys. Within moments, my search bore fruit, "We're in luck, I found some cruise tickets. Text me you, and your roommates, details like full name, address, passport numbers, and I'll buy the tickets."

"I'm on it. I'll get all our details to you within the hour," Emily responded, the relief in her voice mirroring Christina's.

I couldn't help but smile, a genuine expression of gratitude spreading across my face. "Hey Emily, thanks. I'm really happy you reconsidered. I'll head back to dock and wait for y'all there."

As the phone conversation ended, I sat back, allowing myself a moment to take in the scene before me. The sun cast long shadows across the outdoor seating area, the air filled with the salty tang of the sea and the sweet melody of distant laughter. The weight of the morning's anxieties seemed to lift, replaced by an adventurous anticipation for what lay ahead.

I pack up my things, my movements brisk and purposeful. I cast one last glance over the marina, the boats bobbing gently in the water as if nodding in approval of my plans. With a renewed sense of direction, I stride away from the table, my steps light, almost buoyant, ready to embark on this unexpected journey that promised not just a reprieve from the daily grind but a chance to redefine boundaries and test the waters of this newfound camaraderie.

As the afternoon sun shone brightly into her kitchen, Emily's fingers hovered over her phone, her mind racing as she crafted the lie that would grant her a brief reprieve from her life at South Beach Dreams. The locked black screen of her iPhone stared back at her face, reflecting the furrow of her brow as she grappled with the deceit necessary to secure her escape.

Emily knew the power of words; as a scheduler, she wielded them daily to weave the seamless fabric of appointments and engagements that kept the agency running. Now, those same skills were repurposed to construct a plausible sickness–a contagious illness that would ostensibly keep her and her escort roommate, Rebecca, quarantined and out of work for the next few days.

She typed out a message to Dina, her coworker, who also juggled the complex schedules of their demanding clients. Dina, reliable and unsuspecting, would be the perfect ally in their unwitting deception.

"Hey Dina, bad news 😕," Emily began, infusing her text with a casual tone to mask her underlying anxiety. "Rebecca and I caught a nasty bug. We're super contagious and the last thing we'd want is to bring it into, or spread it around, the office. Doctor's orders are strict: stay home and rest for the next three days. Can you cover for us? Really sorry for the hassle. 😔"

Sending the message felt like dropping a stone into a still pond, the ripples of her lie spreading out to alter the surface of their carefully maintained reality. She held her breath, waiting for Dina's response, knowing that her compliance was the linchpin in her hastily constructed plan.

Dina's reply came quickly, a testament to her ever-ready helpfulness. "Oh no! Get better soon! Don't worry about work; I'll handle everything. Just focus on getting well soon 🙏."

Relief washed over Emily in an almost physical wave. She knew the cost of her deception went beyond mere words; it was a crack in the ethical foundation she strived to maintain. Yet, the urgency of her need–to escape, to breathe, to find a moment's peace away from the relentless demands of her job– justified the moral compromise, at least in her tumultuous heart.

As Emily set down her phone, the silence of the room seemed to press in on her, heavy with the weight of her decision. She was now semi-committed to the secret journey, shielded by a veil of falsehoods that Emily hoped would be enough to protect her from the consequences of discovery.

In the quiet of her kitchen, Emily contemplated the delicate balance of truth and fiction, her resolve hardening with each passing moment. This brief escape was not just a respite; it was a necessary act of self-preservation, a chance to reclaim a piece of herself that South Beach Dreams threatened to consume. As the night deepened, Emily steeled herself for the days ahead, her resolve tinged with the silent hope that her return might bring a new beginning, or at least a temporary reprieve from the chaos of her life.

Emily, having just concluded a phone call and work text that would chart a new course for both her and her roommate, walked the sunlit hall with a sense of urgency, her steps echoing softly against the sleek marble floor. At her roommate's door, she paused for a moment, collecting her thoughts before knocking gently.

"Hey Becca, you up?" Emily called softly, pushing the door open.

Inside, the room was a stark contrast to the minimalist aesthetic of the rest of the apartment. It was vibrant and colorful, adorned with posters of K-pop idols and Disney princess memorabilia. At the center of this kaleidoscope was Rebecca Nguyen–*Becca* to her friends–a 23-year-old whose appearance was as dazzling as the pop culture icons she idolized.

Becca was 'Drop-dead gorgeous', but once you had the opportunity to speak with her, you'd determine she was as sharp as a marble. Emily couldn't figure out if it was all an act or if she was born lucky. Men sure love her, though. She was booked solid months in advance.

At the moment of Emily's entry, Becca was performing a perfect Salamba Sirsasana, her body inverted in a graceful yoga headstand, showcasing the disciplined agility that made her one of the most sought-after GFE escorts at South Beach Dreams.

"What's up, buttercup?" Becca's voice was cheerful, her demeanor unfazed by the challenging yoga pose.

"You got a gig, and it sounds awesome. It's super secret and on a cruise ship that leaves in a couple of hours." Emily joyfully states, sounded as exciting as the cruise itself.

The news seemed to disrupt Becca's physical harmony, and she tumbled out of her headstand, landing on the plush carpet with a surprised giggle.

"What? OMG! I always wanted to go on a cruise. I have to thank Bas for this. What the hell am I going to wear?" Her excitement was palpable as she sprang from the floor, pirouetted and Grand Jeté'ed into her walk-in closet, a treasure trove of glittery dresses and high-end accessories, her dance background clearly evident.

Becca's was as colorful as her wardrobe. Born to Korean parents who prized education and traditional values, Becca was supposed to be studying at the University of Florida. They believed she was pursuing a degree in marketing, unaware of the double life she led in Miami. To maintain her secret, Becca had become adept at juggling her two worlds, her charisma and charm serving as perfect veils for her activities.

In her bedroom walk-in closet, Becca sifted through her outfits with the excitement of a child in a candy store, each garment sparking ideas for her upcoming adventure. Meanwhile, Emily watched, her expression a mixture of amusement and conflict. She knew the truth–the cruise was not a job from Bas but a necessary escape she had orchestrated for both of them. Her deceit weighed heavily on her, a necessary evil to ensure Becca's cooperation and safety.

"I just got off the phone with Bas. He's busy now, I'll tell him you said thanks later. This assignment pays double and you keep the commission going to the house. You can't tell anyone we're going," Emily fabricated, maintaining her ruse.

"We're going? You and I are going?" Becca paused, a puzzled look crossing her face as she held up a sequinned gown.

"Yes, I was as surprised as you. I'll be there as a chaperone to throw off US customs. They get suspicious when a pretty girl travels alone," Emily explained, her voice steady despite the inner turmoil. The lie was elaborate, a tapestry woven from necessity and desperation, crafted to protect not just her roommate but herself from the consequences of their realities.

"If anyone asks, we'll say it's a vacation. We'll be gone a couple of days. Dina will cover my shifts," Emily continued, watching as Becca resumed her enthusiastic search for the perfect outfit.

"I can't believe Bas has me working on a cruise. I'm so excited. Bas has been good to me. I need to thank him for this assignment," Becca mused aloud, her innocence regarding the true nature of their trip making Emily's heart sink even further.

"No. Again, I can't stress this enough. This job is secret. Focus on packing. Bikini's, smart casual, a sexy LBD. I'll be in contact with Bas the entire time. We have to get to the port of Miami, like, before 2 pm. I'll need your passport number for the tickets. I gotta go pack." Emily urged, her voice firm yet gentle, steering her friend away from contacting their supposed benefactor.

"Thanks, Emily. It's so great I can trust you to have my back. You're such a great roomie," Becca beamed, her trust in Emily complete and unshakeable.

As Emily exited the huge closet to exit the room, her fingers brushed against a pair of earrings on Becca's dresser. Being an uncontrollable kleptomaniac when stressed, she pocketed them quietly, a small act of theft that went unnoticed. It was a momentary lapse in her struggle to beat her condition, a minor sin in a sea of larger deceptions, a reminder of the blurred lines she navigated daily.

Leaving Becca's room, Emily felt the weight of her decisions settling around her. The path they were about to embark on was fraught with risks and uncertainties, but it was a path paved with good intentions. Emily knew lying to Becca was forgivable, but lying to Bas was dangerous...if he found out, and she promised herself not to let that happen.

Chapter 15

BON VOYAGE

The Florida sun blazed overhead, the kind of day where you could fry an egg on the sidewalk, or so they say. It felt like a scene straight out of a movie, complete with a glossy black UberSUV Escalade pulling up at the bustling Port of Miami.

Emily and Becca, cradling designer handbags, emerged from the air-conditioned cocoon of the Uber, stepping into the sultry tropical heat.

The driver, a young guy with a too-bright smile and a flirtatious twinkle in his eye, awkwardly juggled their suitcases, trying to maintain an air of professionalism while clearly enchanted by the duo.

He's trying hard, maybe too hard, especially when his eyes linger just a little longer than necessary. Emily, ever the fateful envoy, handles it with a polite nod, probably used to brushing off much worse at South Beach Dreams.

"You made it," I call out as they approach, ready to help with the luggage.

That's when Becca, in true dramatic fashion, spins around and plants a kiss on me. It's slow, deliberate, and way too sensual for a public greeting. Heat rises to my cheeks–not from displeasure, but from the shock of it. This isn't exactly the discreet arrival I was hoping for.

"Um, Becca, that's Christina." Emily blurts, a note of embarrassment in her voice. Becca's eyes widen with a mischievous sparkle.

"Oops, so sorry. I thought you were my client." A little disappointment trails from her voice.

Brushing off the kiss with a laugh, I retort, "What the fucks' with you girls and the kissing?"

Standing there, I'm hit with a mix of amusement and admiration. Becca thinks a moment, then adds "You're right, Emily, her kisses are fire. Call me Becca. And careful, Emily has an incredible memory. It's unbelievably good."

"It's a blessing and a curse," Emily adds, playing along with the light mood despite the awkward start.

"Good to know. We gotta hurry!" I add, helping them with their bags. I hustle them towards the escalators, eager to get away from any more potential scenes and onboard the ship.

The cruise ship terminal is buzzing as we arrive. The process of signing in is smooth—my crew ID helps bypass the longer lines, and soon, we're stepping into the ship and make it to the ship's grand atrium area. The elegance of the grand staircase and the buzz of excited new passengers hit us all at once. Becca's already pulling out her phone to snap pictures, and Emily looks around, wide-eyed.

"I can't believe we're doing this," Emily whispers, and I nod, feeling a mix of relief and excitement.

Unbeknownst to me, and out of the corner of her eye, Camila, my ex whom I recently got naked with, sees me walking with Becca and Emily in the atrium. Camila catches a glimpse of Becca affectionately grabbing my arm, pulling me in and fixing my smudged lipstick with her thumb. This sends her into a jealous rage and she does her best to hide it from the guests coming on board.

The polished brass glass elevator whisks us up to deck 8 and we exit and weave around a group of older ladies.

As I lead them to their cabin, Becca's still bubbling with energy, chattering nonstop about all the things she wants to do first. The cabin door is conveniently open and I roll their cases in and up to the tiny desk. The cabin itself is cozy, with a view that promises endless ocean and skies from the balcony.

"This view is amazing!" Emily exclaims, stepping out to lean on the railing.

Becca, not one to stay still, spins around the room. "This is nice, I've done it in worse places," she jokes, pressing down on the mattress testing it's strength. Emily returns from the balcony and pushes Becca onto the bed playfully, making us all laugh.

I feel a tug of responsibility and a flicker of pride. This might actually work, I think to myself.

"I gotta run and get ready for my show," I say, pulling out a pen to scribble down my number on the daily events flyer. "Here's my deck phone number. You can call it from any phone located all around the ship. I'll come by the cabin and get you two at 6:45 pm. I have a shopping presentation to host now, so go explore the ship and have fun."

Just as I'm about to leave, Becca playfully shoves Emily, who in turn bumps into me. We lock eyes and I smile confidently.

"I know this was a big ask. Thanks!" I say sincerely, feeling genuinely grateful for their willingness to jump into this crazy plan with me.

"Consider us square," Emily replies with a cheeky grin, giving me finger guns as exit the cabin and start my journey to my cabin to get ready for my presentation.

The ship feels like it's pulsing with life, ready to set sail. As I head back to my quarters, I can't help but feel like this might just be the start of something doable.

As I hustled towards the backstage area of the main entertainment venue. My deck phone buzzed in my pocket–a jarring intrusion into my already frazzled state. Flipping it out, I saw 'Cruise Director' flash across the screen, and my stomach knotted up slightly. I answer.

"Hey Camila. I was just thinking of you, How you doin'?" I tried to keep my voice light, upbeat, despite the gnawing apprehension.

"How am I doing? I'm pissed! You should've been backstage twenty minutes ago?" Camila's voice was sharp, a finely honed blade of accusation and barely contained anger.

"Hey, hey, hang on." I paused, taking a breath to temper my rising irritation. "I'm running a bit behind, but not late. I have some friends cruising and just now helped them to their cabin. I'm heading backstage now to set my show. What gives?"

As I navigated through the throngs of guests, her next words stopped me dead.

"I saw you getting cosy with some girl in the atrium. It's sad to see you lose focus so quickly. We were just with each other yesterday." The hurt in her voice was palpable, laced with a venomous jealousy that seemed to seep through the phone.

Camila was clearly hurt and jealous, assuming I had cheated or moved on. The complexity of our relationship, a tapestry of intense passion and professional entanglements, often felt as volatile as the ocean surrounding us. We had been together, then apart, and then somewhere in a limbo that neither of us could navigate cleanly. Her next words were a cold reminder of the power dynamics at play.

"Didn't I tell you I'd be watching you and if you screwed up just once I'd have you removed? Mark my words, this will not go unnoticed." Her tone was icy, each word a deliberate thrust meant to wound.

The phone line went dead with a click that echoed slightly in my ear. I stood for a moment, the tiny Nokia phone still pressed against my cheek, the sounds of the ship around me muffled by the rush of blood in my ears. Camila, as the cruise director, had a certain authority over many aspects of onboard life, including my role as the shopping guide. Her threat wasn't just emotional blackmail; it was a professional guillotine that could sever me from this gig I loved.

Taking a deep breath, I pocketed my phone and quickened my pace. The familiar smell of the back stage area– a mix of old wood, metal, and the faint linger of fog machines used in the last show–greeted me as I pushed through the backstage door. The area was bustling with activity; dancers stretched in their vibrant costumes, techs buzzed around adjusting lights and sound, and the air vibrated with the pre-show energy I had come to love.

I approached my setup, where brochures and props for my shopping presentation were arranged meticulously from earlier preparation by my trusted steed, Victor. As I straightened a stack of maps, my mind replayed Camila's words. The threat of being removed from the ship for merely socializing was absurd, yet I knew Camila's capacity for dramatics–both on and off the stage–could turn this threat into a stark reality.

The inner conflict was gnawing at me. On one hand, I cared deeply for Camila; we had shared moments that stretched beyond the confines of casual romance into something profound. On the other, her possessiveness was suffocating, and the professional overlap added layers of complexity that I was increasingly finding hard to navigate.

As I continued my preparations, I couldn't shake the feeling of being watched. I glanced around subtly, half-expecting to see Camila lurking in the shadows with that intense, scrutinizing gaze of hers. Nothing. Just the usual pre-show chaos.

"Christina, five minutes till curtain," one of the stage managers called out, snapping me back to reality.

"Thanks, got it!" I called back, forcing a smile. As I adjusted my presentation materials one last time, I resolved to handle the Camila situation with as much grace as I could muster. Maybe after the cruise, a serious conversation was due–one that would either mend fences or burn bridges.

For now, though, the show must go on. I stepped into the wings, the lights of the stage beckoning me forward, the murmur of the expectant crowd fueling my resolve. Tonight, I would be the best version of Christina the shopping guide, the entertainer. Whatever personal dramas awaited offstage would just have to wait. My guests, my audience, deserved that much.

Chapter 16

THE SPARKLE AND THE SPITE

Sebastian "Bas" Baeza, at 43, is the epitome of a man who has mastered the art of living multiple lives, each as complex and intricately woven as the next. Born into the turbulent streets of Havana, Cuba, his early life was a cocktail of vibrant culture and stark violence, a dichotomy that would shape his worldview irreversibly.

As a boy, he witnessed the harsh realities of survival, where the lines between right and wrong were blurred by necessity and ambition.

Bas's father, a charismatic but ultimately doomed figure, operated on the fringes of Havana's underground economy. It was from him that Bas learned the harsh lessons of power and its costs. The elder Baeza's life ended abruptly, a casualty of the very shadows he had navigated so adeptly. This loss propelled Bas into a life of determined self-reliance, his father's demise serving as a stark reminder that in their world, vulnerability could be fatal.

By the time he was a teenager, Bas had developed a keen instinct for survival and an even keener ambition to escape the life that had claimed his father. His journey from Cuba to Miami was nothing short of cinematic—a harrowing midnight escape aboard a drug runner's speedboat, crashing through the tempestuous waves of the Florida Straits.

It was a baptism by fire, one that marked the end of his life in Cuba and the beginning of his American dream—or so it seemed.

Miami offered a fresh canvas, but the colors of his past painted his new life in hues of grey. Bas quickly learned that the underworld of his new home mirrored that of his old. He adapted, his inherent charm and ruthless pragmatism propelling him up the ranks of Miami's shadow economies. Eventually, he established South Beach Dreams, the city's most notorious escort agency, a business that catered to the wealthy, the powerful, and the depraved.

As he sipped Cuban coffee in the sprawling kitchen of his Palm Island mansion, Bas reflected on the paradox of his existence. The kitchen, a masterpiece of modern design with sleek lines and high-end appliances, contrasted sharply with the dark operations he coordinated from his marble-topped island. On speakerphone, he listened to Dina, one of his most loyal schedulers, list off the availability of girls for the evening.

"...Ava, Paige, Madison, Samantha, Jenna and Brooke are on tonight." Dina answered her inquisitive boss.

"That's it? Where are the other girls?" Bas's voice was calm but carried an edge, a hint of the impatience that lay just beneath his polished surface.

"Cindy, Akiko, and Becca are either off or sick and are not available this weekend," Dina responded, her voice tinged with hesitation.

"No no no, call them all and get them ready. The governor is hosting political clients tonight," Bas commanded, his voice now sharp, the facade of calmness fading. The stakes were always high, and tonight was no exception.

"I can call Cindy and Akiko, but Emily let us know Becca is really sick, so she's unavailable," Dina added quickly, trying to manage the situation.

Bas paused, his mind racing. "Becca makes me a lot of money. When did Emily tell us this? And where is Emily? Is she gone again? Let me know when the other girls are ready. I'll send you the governor's location details now. Chau."

Ending the call, Bas scrolled through his phone to reread any messages from Emily, his brow furrowed in concern and irritation. Nothing. Becca's absence was a complication, and Emily's unexplained unavailability added to his suspicions.

As he stood in his kitchen, the afternoon sun casting long shadows across the sleek surfaces, Bas felt the weight of his existence. Outside these walls, he was a devoted father to two daughters, their innocent laughter a balm to the chaos of his professional life.

His wife, a gorgeous woman who knew her husband was a successful businessman with murky but legal ventures, continued the facade of the '*perfect family*', hiding the true nature of his work.

This dichotomy was Bas's greatest challenge. The love he felt for his family was genuine, as was the joy he derived from his role as a provider and protector. Yet, he was also a man who orchestrated the darkest of deeds, a puppet master whose strings controlled more than just the operational aspects of an escort service.

The conflict within him was a constant battle between the warmth of his paternal affections and the cold pragmatism of his business decisions. His life was a precarious balance, a daily dance on the tightrope of morality, each step calculated to maintain the facade that kept his family safe–his daughters the dark.

Bas's story was one of survival, ambition, and the ceaseless quest for power in a world where the stakes were life itself. As the sun dipped lower, casting golden hues through the windows, Bas prepared for the night ahead, a night that would require all his cunning and control. In the quiet moments between calls, he wondered about the path he'd chosen, the lives he'd touched, and the legacy he would leave.

The mansion, as beautiful as it was, often felt like a gilded cage. But for Bas, freedom had never been the goal; power was. And power, he knew, came at a price–one he had been paying since that fateful night on a speedboat speeding away from Cuba.

Bas snaps back from replaying his childhood in his minds eye and scrolls through his phone in search of Emily's phone number. With Emily's contact details open on his screen, he pauses for a moment before hitting the call button. He know's he has a tendency to jump to the worst conclusion in any situation and the reprieve always gives Emily the benefit of the doubt for not being at work. Then Bas remembers what his father told him about trusting people.

"Never trust anyone, mi hijo. Everyone is going to fuck you over in the end." Then Bas's father just died in his arms, the blood loss from multiple stab wounds too great a challenge to survive. Noticing his father slip to the other side he stopped applying pressure to the open wounds, wiped the blood from his hands on the tall grass they lay in and slowly walks away. The moment still as painful and accurate today as it was those many years ago.

Bas presses the call button and takes a sip from his potent cuban beverage.

The promenade deck of the cruise ship was a vibrant tableau of holiday revelry, buzzing with the energy of guests who were clearly making the most of their sea day.

The sun cast a brilliant sheen over the ocean, reflecting off the water in dazzling bursts of light that seemed to dance along with the laughter and music filling the air. Amid this festive atmosphere, Emily and Becca, the former burdened with secrets far heavier than her suitcase, were taking selfies, their faces alight with the carefree joy that only such an escape could provide.

Mid selfie, Emily's phone rings and Becca sees it's a call from Bas.

"Is that Bas? Should I thank him now for this amazing assignment?" Becca's voice was playful, her eyes sparkling with mischief as she glanced at Emily's phone, which had started vibrating.

"He's probably calling to confirm some details. Let me check." Emily responded, her voice a notch too high, betraying her nervousness. "Oh and don't post any images to social media," she added, as she stepped away from Becca, distancing herself from the noise and the deceptive mirth that now felt like a mask she couldn't afford to drop.

Emily's hand trembled slightly as she answered the phone, her voice unnaturally bright. "Hey Bas," she greeted, injecting a fake cough for good measure. The act felt hollow, her stomach churning with guilt.

"Amiga, how are you? I just heard you were off tonight," Bas's voice came through, casual yet carrying an undertone of suspicion that Emily knew all too well.

Echoes of the lively atmosphere inadvertently filled the background of her call, a detail she hadn't considered in her hurried decision to step aside. "Where are you?" Bas pressed, his tone sharpening.

"I'm just out getting cold medicine, at the drug store, for Becca and me. She's really sick and in bed," Emily lied smoothly, the words tasting bitter on her tongue. She glanced around nervously, her gaze catching Becca's carefree antics by a ship life ring, snapping yet another selfie.

"You should stay home and rest," Bas advised, his voice a mix of concern and command.

The sudden blast of the ship's horn cut through the air, a sound so distinctive and loud that Emily's heart skipped a beat. In a panic, she fake coughed again, louder this time, hoping to mask the incriminating noise as she quickly moved inside the ship, seeking the sanctuary of quieter surroundings.

Finding herself in the ship's gift shop, a haven of trinkets and souvenirs, Emily continued the charade. "Nothing to worry about here Bas, just two roommates sick and resting for the weekend," she reassured him, her eyes scanning the shelves lined with colorful magnets, postcards, and assorted baubles. As she spoke, her fingers brushed against a fridge magnet, a quaint little piece that seemed to whisper temptations.

Under the mounting stress, her old, compulsive habit kicked in–the urge to steal, a misguided attempt to exert control over something, anything, in a moment where everything felt dangerously out of control.

"OK. Get well soon," Bas concluded, his voice softening, the suspicion seemingly allayed for the moment.

With that, the call ended, and Emily pocketed the stolen magnet, a small act of defiance that brought no real relief, only a deeper sense of sinking.

Stepping back onto the promenade deck, Emily's eyes found Becca, who was gleefully reviewing her social media feed, oblivious to the tightrope Emily was walking. She puts her phone away and steps over to Becca.

”Did you tell Bas thanks from me?" Becca asked, her tone light.

"Yes, he was super grateful," Emily replied, her voice hollow as she navigated through her tangled web of lies.

"Cool. Let's get a drink so you can tell me all about my client.” Becca hugs Emily. “

Are those my earrings? They look just like a pair I used to have," Becca remarked, her sharp eyes catching the familiar sparkle of her own jewelry on Emily's ears.

Caught off guard, Emily quickly changed the subject, steering Becca towards the bustling bar area. The weight of her decisions, the lies, the thefts–each felt like a chain around her neck, pulling her deeper into waters too turbulent to tread alone.

As they mingled once again with the carefree cruisers, Emily's smile was a mask, painted on for the world to see, hiding the turmoil that churned like a stormy sea within her. The cruise ship, a vessel of escape for so many, had become her prison, sailing further away from the shore of truth she had left behind.

Chapter 17

KEVIN, CHAOS, AND A QUIET BOND

The smell of sea salt and stage sweat mingled backstage at the Starlight Theatre, creating a cocktail of scents that should've been bottled and sold as "Eau de Overworked." It was another Embarkation Day, another show done, and here I was juggling more props and guest giveaways than a street vendor at Carnival.

Victor stood at the end of the stage handing out flyers and instructing guests to go meet me at my desk on Deck 7.

I was busy bundling up the last of the promotional flyers when the clatter of confident footsteps announced his arrival. Kevin Ronanfeld, the poster child for Midwestern charm turned corporate shark, strode onto the stage. As my direct supervisor at Shipboard Media, he wore his authority like a crown, albeit one that seemed to pinch his head a bit too tightly at times. This was an unannounced, and unexpected, visit, to say the least.

"Holy fuck, Christina, no wonder you were demoted to this ship," Kevin blurted out, his voice echoing off the walls like a misplaced thunderclap. "Where did your passion for this amazing job go? You've done, what, like over 500 shows all with such fire and intensity. You used to make people *want* to shop during their cruise. This show was terrible. Looks like you lost what made you, YOU. I'm speechless."

His critique stung, slicing through the already thin veil of my professional composure. I turned to face him, my hands instinctively clenching around a stack of luxury watch brochures.

"Wow. Thanks for the constructive criti..." I began, but Kevin was already steamrolling over my words.

"The Christina I knew years ago would crush the Christina I see here today. Didn't you learn anything in my sales seminars? I pray these guests buy something this cruise. If not, I'm here to take over till a replacement arrives." His words were a slap, his presence a looming shadow that threatened to swallow what little light was left in the room.

I swallowed the lump of frustration in my throat and grabbed my laptop and the remnants of my dignity. We exited the stage, heading toward the darkened backstage area. The tension between us was a observable, living thing, snaking its cold fingers around my neck.

As we exited backstage to the crew area elevator, my arms were laden with the burdens of the night—props, personal grievances, and unmet expectations. I nudged the elevator call button with my elbow, lacking any free hands, while Kevin made no move to assist. Typical.

"If you weren't such a cocky fuckhead, people might actually like you," I snapped, the words leaping from my tongue like caged birds set free.

Kevin's smirk was a thin slice of moonlight, sharp and cutting. "I'm not here to be liked, I'm here to make sure shopping guides, like you, do what they're supposed to do— motivate guests to shop."

The elevator dinged open, a merciful escape from the verbal sparring. As I stepped inside, Kevin's voice followed me, a relentless echo of past mistakes and present tensions.

"By the way, this ex-girlfriend shit-talk has to end. We ended years ago. You're the one that got confused, remember?"

Fumbling through my messenger bag, I searched for something, anything, to hurl back in defence. But all I found was the empty space where my patience used to be. I turned, a sharp retort perched on my lips.

"Ex-girlfriend? You wish. We didn't *end*, Kevin, we never ever got started." Trying to stab him with my words.

I add, "Hey Kevin, I almost forgot, I have something for you." My hand emerged from the bag, fingers curling into a gesture as old as time–the middle finger. The elevator doors slid shut on his stunned face, cutting off whatever retort he'd been gearing up to deliver.

Safely ensconced in the moving elevator, I leaned against the wall, letting out a long, slow breath. The drama with Kevin was exhausting, a rerun of a show I'd seen too many times. The memory of that one drunken night years ago, when lines had blurred and mistakes had been made, was a ghost that haunted both of us. Kevin's continued interest, or whatever it was–resentment, lust, or a cocktail of both–made working with him, albeit sporadically, a tedious experince.

By the time I reached my desk on the Promenade Deck, a crowd had gathered, buzzing with anticipation for whatever deals I might conjure from the remnants of my disastrous show. Patrick, the slightly-too-enthusiastic black-mailer from the last cruise, was at the front of the line, his eyes lit with the kind of hope usually reserved for lottery drawings.

"Great show, Christina. Got anything 'special' for me this cruise?" he asked, leaning in with a conspiratorial grin.

"Hi Patrick, yes, I have something so amazing you'll want to come back and cruise every week," I replied, my sales smile snapping back into place as I pulled out a VIP card. I scribble the words 'Ocean Seduction' on the back before handing it over. "Tomorrow, in Nassau, you're going to walk into the Jewelry Box and ask for a man named Sunny. Show him this card and say you're here for the '*Ocean Seduction Collection*'. You will not be disappointed."

So here's the deal with the Ocean Seduction VIP cards. Guests come to me, all wide-eyed and excited, asking where to go shopping on the islands, like I'm their personal luxury GPS. Depending on what they're looking for–diamonds, watches, or some overpriced tchotchke–I whip out one of my trusty, postcard-sized VIP cards. It's got the ship's name branded all over it, so it looks *fancy*, like they're getting something extra special. Spoiler alert: they're not.

I scribble down the best store for whatever they're hunting for–whether it's a diamond the size of their ego or a watch they can show off at their next backyard BBQ–and hand it over like I'm giving them the golden ticket to shopping heaven. Our office like us to push CDG only, because Artem paid millions to advertise with Shipboard Media, but I like to spread it out so it's fair for all stores on the map.

Guest take that *VIP* card to the store, make their big purchase, and guess what? I get credit for it. It's a clever little system. The store tracks the sale back to me, I rack up some points, and everyone leaves thinking they've scored some exclusive deal.

Yeah, I play the game, but I play it well. And those cards? They're like my secret weapon–foolproof, and let's be honest, who doesn't love being called a VIP, even if it's all part of the hustle?

Patrick's excitement was perceptible, his departure quick as he made way for the next eager guest. A woman behind him piped up, her curiosity piqued.

"What is this '*Ocean Seduction Collection*'? I want in on this."

"The Ocean Seduction Collection is the finest collection of secret, hard to resist, luxury items exclusive to this cruise line. They can only be acquired with a signed VIP Card," I explained, the words flowing easily now.

As I dealt out VIP cards like a seasoned card shark, my gaze drifted across to the casino area, where I caught Kevin watching me. His expression was unreadable, a mix of annoyance and something else–something like admiration, maybe? No, that couldn't be right. Whatever it was, Kevin Ronanfeld remained an enigma, wrapped in a riddle, and cloaked in a designer suit. And as the night drew on, the sparkle of diamonds wasn't the only thing catching the light.

Later, after my chaotic but potentially lucrative desk hours, I met up with Emily and Becca in the main dining room.

If there's anything more chaotic than the backstage of a theater, it's the dining room of a cruise ship during peak dinner hours. Trust me. And tonight, with the incessant clinking of cutlery and the soft murmur of a hundred conversations, I found myself craving the comparative peace of the backstage. But here I was, at a corner table in this grand dining hall, caught between the allure of the sea and the complications of my life back on land.

The table was set with a precision that would make a drill sergeant weep with pride—each fork and knife perfectly aligned, every wine glass gleaming. And the lighting, soft and dim, made everything feel a little more glamorous, a little more like we were living a life we didn't quite deserve.

Emily and Becca sat across from me, deep in conversation, probably trying to figure out which European waiter was themes attractive. I should've been doing the same, but instead, my mind was elsewhere, floating somewhere between guilt and confusion. It hit me then, right as I stared at the delicate fold of the napkin on my lap—I hadn't thought of my father in days.

How could that be? Just a week ago, I was burying him, heart heavy and swollen with grief. And now, what? I'm here, sipping wine and pretending like everything's fine. Is that okay? Should I be feeling guilty? Part of me thinks I should—after all, wasn't I Daddy's little girl? The one who was supposed to be devastated? Yet, here I was, at sea, lost in menus and trying to keep up with this weird charade of luxury.

I took a deep breath, forcing myself to stay present, but the thought lingered like a shadow I couldn't quite shake. Maybe it was the ocean, or maybe it was the constant buzz of ship life, but somehow I'd pushed the grief aside, packed it away like one of my suitcases, only to be opened when I was ready. Was it wrong to want to forget, even just for a moment?

I glanced at Emily, who was deep in conversation with Becca about some cocktail with an absurd name. They seemed so carefree, so detached from any real-world problems. Meanwhile, my world was crumbling on land, and I wasn't sure if I was relieved or ashamed that I could escape it, even for a little while.

An attentive busboy whisked away our empty plates, a silent ballet of efficiency, as my iPhone buzzed with the persistence of a neglected lover. It was a text from Mom: "When are you back in Miami? We need to talk."

Becca, ever the curious cat, glanced over with raised eyebrows. "You get cell service in the middle of the ocean?"

"We're not in the middle of the ocean, we're always close enough to land to get US cell service." I replied, thumbing a quick message back to Mom. I told her I'd be in Miami in a couple of days and promised to text then. Privacy on a cruise was a myth, like low-calorie buffet options.

"Wicked. I'm going to go check my emails. I'll find you later, Emily," Becca said, pushing back her chair with a flourish that caught the attention of every waiter in a ten-foot radius. She strutted off, her confidence a tangible trail in her wake.

Left alone with Emily, the air seemed to shift, charged with an electricity that had everything to do with her and nothing to do with the storm brewing on the horizon. Emily's presence stirred something in me—a mixture of intrigue and a deeper, more dangerous kind of desire that I was loath to acknowledge. Her green eyes sparkled with mischief, hiding the chaos just beneath the surface.

"Are you going to let me in on the plan for Becca and her client?" Emily's voice broke through my reverie, pulling me back to the present with the effectiveness of a cold shower.

"Yes, sorry, my mind is elsewhere. My mom's sending cryptic texts and my boss Kevin is up my ass. I need to get organized for tomorrow, send emails, you know, work stuff.

You should catch up with Becca. I'll have everything for tomorrow ready to go in my cabin."

Emily's expression softened, her gaze holding mine with an intensity that made my heart do a traitorous little skip. "You shouldn't stress about life so much. Nothing is in our control, so let it go," she murmured, her voice a soothing balm to the frenzy of my thoughts.

Then, with a grace that seemed at odds with the chaotic backdrop of our conversation, she reached out and scooped my dark brown hair behind my right ear. Her touch lingered just a second too long, sparking a trail of heat down my neck. I looked up at her, from my phone, and smile warmly. She stood, her movement fluid, her intent clear. She bent over and whispered.

"You'll know where to find me when you come to your senses," she continued, her words tinged with a challenge and a promise. Her wink was the punctuation mark at the end of a particularly compelling sentence, leaving me more unsettled than ever.

I watched her walk away, spinning around to tease me, playing with the cross on her long sliver necklace, her figure a focus of admiration not just for me but for every waiter in the room.

The sway of her hips was poetry, the kind that was better suited to the pages of a risqué novel than the dining room of a cruise ship.

Alone now, I mulled over her words, turning them over in my mind like smooth pebbles in a stream. Emily had this way of seeing through the façade of chaos I wore like armor. She knew, somehow, the turmoil that churned beneath my sassy, controlled exterior–a maelstrom of duties, desires, and doubts.

I toyed with the edge of the linen napkin, considering. Emily was a temptation, one that I wasn't sure I should indulge. Yet the way she moved, the way she looked at me, spoke of possibilities that were as thrilling as they were terrifying. My heart was a traitor, my body a rebel, and my mind? Well, my mind was a battleground where sense and sensibility waged a war that had no winners.

I knew I should follow Emily's advice, to let go of the stress and embrace the moment. But it wasn't just stress that needed releasing–it was a host of emotions I wasn't sure I was ready to confront.

Yet as I sat there, the echo of her touch still warm on my skin, I couldn't help but wonder if coming to my senses meant succumbing to the pull of something–or someone–I had tried so hard to deny. The thought, of Emily, was as intoxicating as it was daunting. Would I find her, as she suggested, when I finally decided to come to my senses? Or would I find myself, lost in a sea of what-ifs and might-have-beens?

As the night deepened and the dining room began to thin out, I realized that the real journey wasn't to Miami or any port on the map. It was a voyage into the uncharted waters of my own heart, with Emily as the North Star guiding me into tempests and towards treasures alike.

Chapter 18

WINDS OF CHANGE

You know that feeling when the universe aligns just right, like all the stars hitched a ride on the same cosmic bus? That was me, today, right there on the pier in Nassau, heart hammering in sync with the thumping of my footsteps.

My phone had just lit up with the kind of news that could make a girl scream–and scream I did, right there with the blue Bahamian waters lapping at the cruise ship's massive hull, echoing between the towering ships docked like behemoths at rest.

I had just tripled my sales target. Tripled! I haven't done that in, like, never. The numbers danced on my screen, teasing and bold, igniting a firework of elation in my chest. This wasn't just a good day at the office–it was record-breaking, history-making, shout-it-from-the-rooftop kind of good.

With a whoop that could have startled the seagulls into a new migration pattern, I sprinted back towards the ship. The gangway under my feet felt like the yellow brick road, and honey, I was clicking my imaginary heels all the way home.

The air was thick with the scent of the sea, a tangy blend that mingled with the intoxicating aroma of freedom and success. But amid all the physical and metaphorical sunshine, a storm brewed on the horizon of my heart–a storm named Emily.

After my victorious howl on the pier and a sprint worthy of an Olympic medal, I bounded back onto the ship with the kind of buzz that could only come from smashing records. The buzz of my Nassau sales win still thrums through my veins. I practically float toward the ship's security checkpoint scanner, my feet barely touching the ground.

And who's there to greet me? None other than Enzo, the Filipino security guard who somehow manages to look both bored and amused at the same time. He's seen it all, but today, apparently, I'm giving off some kind of radiant glow even he can't ignore.

"Ma'am Christina," he says with that signature smirk of his. "You look like you just won the lottery."

"More like I made the lottery, Enzo," I shoot back, dropping my bag on the conveyor belt and stepping through the scanner like I own the place. The machine beeps, as if in agreement with my swagger.

Enzo chuckles, the kind of laugh that says he's used to my antics. "Big sales day, huh?"

"Big? Please. Massive." I grin, feeling my energy light up the whole damn security area. "Nassau never knew what hit 'em."

He shakes his head, grinning as he checks my bag on the x-ray screen. "Well, whatever you did today, you're beaming like a lighthouse. It looks great on you."

"Aw, thanks," I reply, grabbing my bag off the belt. I wink as I head toward the crew area, feeling every bit the conqueror I am. "Don't worry, Enzo. I'll make sure you get something shiny for Christmas. Maybe a VIP discount."

Dashing through the corridors of the ship, I couldn't help but notice how the carpet–once a garish pattern of maritime blues and golds–seemed to blur into a royal runway under my feet. The scent of polished wood and a faint, lingering odor of antiseptic from the cleaning crew filled the air, wrapping around me like a promise as I made my through this tired, but welcoming, ship.

Before heading to Emily and Becca's cabin, I decided a quick pit stop at my own quarters was necessary. The corridors of the ship seemed to cheer me on with each of my steps. I reached my cabin, slipping inside to drop off my trusty messenger bag, complete with a luxury timepiece gift for

Becca, and switch gears from business powerhouse to whatever this evening had in store.

My cabin, a compact but cozy slice of solitude, was just as I left it, except for the garment bag hanging on the bathroom door. It had a note pinned to it in Victor's unmistakable scrawl, *'Here's outfits you requested. Victor'* my loyal assistant, had a way of handling all my requests. His reliability, although paid handsomely for, was as comforting as the warm Caribbean breezes we sailed through.

Grateful for his efficiency, I grabbed the garment bag containing Becca's costume for tonight's festivities, mentally thanking him for his part in my convoluted day.

With the garment bag in hand, I took a quick glance in the mirror to assess the damage a day of running around had inflicted. Surprisingly, the reflection staring back showed no signs of the day's chaos—just a woman with a spark in her eyes and a smile tugging at the corners of her mouth.

To add the final touch, I reached for my bottle of 'Good Girl' perfume, a scent that was as bold and complex as the persona I put on each day. A couple of sprays in the air, and I walked through the mist, letting the rich, floral notes cling to my skin, a fragrant armor for whatever lay ahead.

Before departing my tiny cabin, I turn toward the small corkboard on the wall, where the picture of Dad—Eric Delgado, Navy admiral, larger-than-life—still hangs, pinned there like a permanent reminder of who I'm trying to live up to.

"Hey, Dad," I say softly, taking a deep breath, my fingers grazing the edges of the worn picture. "I had a great day today. You'd be proud of me."

The words come out shaky, but I don't let them linger. He'd hate that—me getting all emotional. I can almost hear him now: "No tears, kid. Focus on the win."

"Well, I did it," I continue, straightening up and forcing a smile. "Crushed sales in Nassau. I mean, I owned that town.

You should've seen it, Dad." I laugh softly, my voice echoing in the small cabin.

For a moment, it feels like he's here, just over my shoulder, nodding his approval. But reality creeps back in, the emptiness settling like a familiar ache. I kiss my fingertips and touch the picture. "I miss you," I whisper, before quickly brushing the feeling aside.

I grab the garment bag and head for the door. No time for emotions right now. I've got a life to hustle, and somewhere, I know Dad's watching–probably telling me to keep pushing.

Feeling refreshed and ready, I leave my cabin, garment bag with an extra small "cabin steward" outfit inside, in tow, the perfume leaving a subtle trail behind me as I make my way to Emily and Becca's cabin. The ship's interior was a familiar maze, but tonight it felt different, as if each turn and each deck were leading me not just through spaces but through the chapters of my own unfolding story.

The anticipation of seeing Emily again, combined with the high of my professional triumph, created a cocktail of emotions that was intoxicating. As I approached their cabin, my heart, usually so sure and steady, thumped a nervous rhythm. This was more than just delivering a garment bag; it was stepping into a new possibility, one that could change the course of my journey in ways I was only just beginning to understand.

Knocking on their metal door, I felt the ship sway gently, as if it too was holding its breath, waiting to see what winds of change would blow my way next. The swaying meant that we were casting off onto our next port of call, the cruise lines private island named "Ambergris Cay". A tiny strip of land you could barely call an island, full of plenty of places to unwind in the hot Bahamian sunshine.

I knocked on the metal door and Emily swung it open, and there she stood–like a vision in white, a bikini-clad siren with skin kissed by the sun into a shade that could best be described as 'temptation bronze'. The smell of coconut oil wafted from her, mingling with the salty residue of a day well-spent by the sea.

"Hello scrumptious, here's Becca's outfit and my room key," I said, stepping into the room and hanging the garment bag on the hook of the open bathroom door. Becca was sprawled out on her bed, the very picture of innocent repose in the hot and humid afternoon.

"I'll let her know once she gets up from her nap," Emily whispered, her voice a soft caress that seemed to stroke the humid air between us.

I nodded, my eyes taking in her form with an appreciation that was both aesthetic and achingly personal.

"I'll be around just in case something goes sideways. We can meet up at 7:50 pm, by my cabin, to go and get a drink while Becca works her magic. It's formal night tonight, so try and wear something nice." I say teasingly.

"I'll see what I can throw together," she replied, her voice light, teasing, a counterpoint to the heavy drumbeat of my pulse.

The space between us was charged, a magnetic field of tension and unspoken words. It was the kind of energy that makes your pulse quicken, even if you're not sure why. Every glance felt heavier, every breath more deliberate, like we were teetering on the edge of something we weren't ready to admit yet.

Without thinking, aw, who am I kidding, I was thinking about this all day, I reached out, drawn by some unseen force, and pulled her by the hips towards me. Her skin was warm, her body a beacon, and as my lips met hers, the taste of salt and adventure lingered deliciously between us.

This kiss wasn't just a momentary sneaky treat in a quiet room, it was a declaration, a silent confession of the feelings I'd kept hidden away like precious cargo on this vast ocean liner.

It was the kind of kiss that said more than words ever could–about hope, about fear, about the endless possibilities that lay ahead. As our lips met, it felt like we were the only two people in the world who understood the language we were speaking, a dialect of longing, desire, and danger communicated through the gentle pressure of salty lips and the hesitant exploration of touch.

As we continued to passionately kiss, in that brief, beautiful moment, time seemed to stretch and bend around us, the sounds of the ship leaving port–the distant laughter softly drifting in through the open balcony door, the soft hum of the engines, the gentle sway of the sea–all fading into a hazy backdrop to the clarity we found in each other's embrace. It was a kiss that acknowledged past hesitations and future uncertainties, yet boldly declared a willingness to leap into whatever came next, together.

I slid my hands down from her hips to her perfectly eatable ass. I pull her closer, grinding myself into her while playfully slipping my tongue into her eagerly inviting mouth. Emily is as eager as I as her left hand caresses my b-cup, revealing her pent up sexual energy. Her right hand enjoys a handful of my Latina booty. YAS! This is what I'm talking about, finally.

It gets hot real fast only ending with Emily friskily nibbling on my bottom lip. I pull away, looking over Emily's shoulder making certain we didn't disturb the sleeping beauty on the bed.

The room, usually just a simple, functional space, transformed under the weight of our newfound intimacy into a sanctuary, a secret place carved out of the routine and the mundane where we could explore the depths of what we might become. It was as if, with that kiss, we were setting sail on a new journey, one not charted by navigational stars but by the beating of our entwined hearts, and sexual tension between us ignitable, making us really horny.

"You should go before I rip your clothes off." Emily whispers which makes me wetter than a submarine with screen doors.

In a super-smooth move, I reach behind Emily's back, pull the ties on her string bikini top and impetuously undress Emily. The whiteness of her perky breasts almost glowing on the cabin. She doesn't intervene, beginning to kiss me passionately again, her hands slowly caressing the curves my latina body showcases.

I slowly bring my hands up to her chest and gently play with her nipples. Emily softly moans as she kisses me, a little too loud, and digs her hips into me again, which makes Becca inhale and drift back from her dreamland, waking and shifting on the cabin bed.

We stop and giggle to each other like school girls getting caught doing something naughty.

"I should go." I whisper. "Yes, you should!" Emily states and covers her breasts with her left arm, pushing me to the door with her right. I slide out the door into a group of middle aged men who literally eye-fuck me as begin walking down the hall. Do they know what just happened? Do I look all flushed and rosy-cheeked? Dripping wet? Don't care. I haven't been this turned on since Camila beat me like a dog in the crew hallway.

As I made my way back to my cabin, ready to trade my daytime hustle for evening flair, I couldn't help but feel a flutter of excitement–or was it nerves?–at the prospect of the night ahead. The ship was a labyrinth of sparkling lights and soft music, setting the stage for an evening that promised more drama than a telenovela marathon.

Turning the corner, I almost bumped into Preston, my cabin steward, his smile bright enough to rival the polished brass fixtures lining the hallway. "Hey, Preston! Thanks for all your help today, and keeping the cabin nice and tidy," I said, genuinely grateful for his knack for keeping my life in order less chaotic.

"No problem at all, Christina! Any 'ting for you. You light up this place." he replied, his Jamaican accent wrapping around his words like a warm hug.

With a quick thanks and a promise to snag him some of the less-disastrous dessert from the staff mess–if such a thing existed tonight–I continued to my cabin. Inside, the real transformation began. My cabin, usually a tight but cozy refuge from the chaos of ship life, transformed into a backstage dressing room.

The tiny bluetooth speakers blasting out some Becky-G as I hop into a hot shower for a quick masturbation session after making out with that Lolli-pop, Emily. What I wouldn't give to have her right here with me.

My body is electric, and fully satisfied, as I exit the shower to get ready. On ships, you get really good at getting completely ready in under 15 minutes. Make-up, outfit, and I finish curling my hair in not time flat. My hair would be hideously flat in the Caribbean humidity without my Dyson Airwrap.

I slipped into the stunning formal gown I had picked out earlier, a creation that hugged every curve of my Latin figure as if it were custom made just for me, which, let's be honest, it might as well have been.

The gown was a deep emerald green, shimmering with every move like the calm seas under moonlight. Checking myself in the mirror, I adjusted the b-cup rocket-tits god blessed me with, making sure everything was in place and tighter than a tiger. A spray of my favorite perfume, a quick fluff of my hair, and voila–Cinderella was ready for the ball, or at least a very complicated evening. Looking at my reflection in the mirror, I suddenly realize making out with a gorgeous blonde, and frantically masturbating, has made me hungry.

Heading towards the staff mess, I prepared myself for the hit-and-miss adventure that was dining onboard. The staff mess was like a high school cafeteria but with more languages and less enthusiasm. The room buzzed with the subdued energy of staff members catching a quick meal in between their shifts. The crazy smells from the crew mess next door to the staff mess, which caters to the deck and engine crew, cabin stewards, waiters and bar servers, wafts in intermittently.

The food in the staff mess is slightly more refined. Fluorescent lights flickered occasionally, adding a strobe effect to the otherwise drab decor. Long tables filled the space, each one a patchwork of department uniforms–officers, entertainment staff, gift shop attendants, and spa managers like Charles, who was currently hunched over a tray as enthusiastic as a completing at a tax return. I take a large dinner plate and add rice, a chicken breast and some undefined white sauce and drizzle it over my choices. I walk over to Charles after grabbing an orange juice.

"Hey, Charles," I greeted, sliding into a seat across from him, my gown making a soft swishing sound. "How's spa life treating you?" I immediately begin devouring my dinner which was surprisingly tasty.

Charles looked up, his expression a mixture of surprise and relief. "Christina, it's been brutal. You wouldn't believe the number of no-shows and last-minute cancellations this cruise. I feel like I'm running a ghost town." He attempted a smile, but it was clear the stress was wearing him down.

"Ouch, that sounds tough," I interject. Charles asks "How was your day in Nassau?"

"I had a stellar sales today. Broke records, and possibly a few hearts, with large diamond deals," I replied as I wash down my chicken with juice, trying to lighten the mood with a dash of my usual sass.

His eyes lit up, a mixture of curiosity and something close to desperation peeking through. "Seriously? Congratulations, that's amazing, Christina. How do you even get into something like being a shopping guide? I'm–I'm honestly at a point where I'd try just about anything to get out of this financial rut."

As I gobbled up my rice, the raw honesty in his voice tugged at me. Charles was a good guy caught in a bad wave, and here I was surfing a diamond tide. "Look, it's not a walk in the park, but it definitely has its perks. If you're really interested, I can show you some sales techniques, give you some advice," I offered, the words out before I could second-guess the commitment.

His relief was audible, and he leaned forward, his voice dropping to a whisper. "I'd owe you big time, Christina. I'm— I'm kind of broke, and this could be my lifeline."

I nodded, understanding more than I let on. "I've got your back, Charles. But keep this under your spa towel for now, and stay in your lane while I figure things out. We can't have you jumping ship just yet, literally or otherwise."

He almost seemed to tear up, his eyes glossy with gratitude. "Thank you, Christina, really. You have no idea..."

"Don't mention it. And now, I have to run to fulfill a client's special request. We'll chat more soon, okay?" Just as I stood, smoothing down my gown, one of the spa attendant girls, a staff member Charles manages, arrives with a full plate of chicken breasts. In her tight mint-green spa tunic outfit, her figure turned all the heads in the staff mess, mine included.

"Hey." I say, looking at her plate first, then up at her. "Those breasts are amazing!" I playfully throw out.

"Thanks, I love it when they're dripping with sauce." She skillfully responds, in a deep-toned Scottish accent, without missing a beat. At sea, there is LOT'S of leeway when it comes to what would be classed as harassment. Comments like this on land, back in the real-world, would have anyone fired.

Charles nodded, his usual reserve melting into a look of deep appreciation. "Thanks again, Christina. This is Claire, the assistant spa manager. Come to think of it, you too would get along swimmingly. Christina is the shopping guide and knows everything about the fire things in life." Charles boasts. Claire scooches into the bench seat where I just stood from, making it look easier than in a full length gown.

"Well, let's make it a plan to meet up in the crew bar one night." I flirtingly state, confidence oozing from my lips.

"Can't wait to learn more about your *finer things*." She answers with a flirty smirk. Clare and I lock eyes and share something exciting.

I turn around, and there she is–Camila, standing just two feet away, balancing a tray of food like it's the last thing holding her together. Her face, once calm and composed, now betrays a storm of emotions. Jealousy, disappointment, maybe even a little hurt, all mixed into one toxic cocktail that's hard to miss.

Her eyes narrow slightly, scanning me like she's trying to figure out what exactly she walked in on.

The food on her tray trembles a little as she grips it tighter, her knuckles turning white. The smile she usually wears is gone, replaced by something cold, something edged with bitterness. It's painfully clear she overheard every word of my naughty conversation, every flirtatious exchange, and now she's wrestling with whatever's going on inside her head.

The way she's looking at me, it's not just anger. It's deeper than that. It's the kind of look that says, I knew this would happen, but I hoped I was wrong. The jealousy burns beneath her skin, making her normally composed face twist ever so slightly with betrayal.

There's disappointment, too–a sadness she's trying to mask with her usual confidence, but it's not working. The whole scene feels like a punch to the gut, like we've hit a moment we can't walk back from.

Her eyes flick to the space between us, then back up to my face, and I can practically hear the thoughts racing through her mind.

I felt the heat rising to my cheeks, the awkwardness of the moment pressing down on me like the weight of the ship itself.

Camila's eyes burned into me, her tray of food suddenly feeling like a weapon in her hands. I wanted to say something–anything–but words were stuck in my throat, trapped behind the guilt bubbling up. The jealousy on her face wasn't just a fleeting emotion; it was the culmination of all the unspoken things between us, things I'd been avoiding for too long.

"Camila, I–" I started, but the look she gave me shut that down faster than I could even attempt to explain.

She didn't need to say a word. The disappointment in her eyes spoke louder than anything she could have said. It wasn't just about what she overheard; it was about everything. The tension between us that had been building for weeks, the unresolved feelings, the awkward middle ground we were both tiptoeing around.

I shifted on my heels, feeling like a kid who got caught sneaking out after curfew. My bravado, my usual sass? Gone. I suddenly felt small under her gaze, like I didn't belong in that moment, like I should've just stayed quiet. But there was no undoing this now. The damage was done.

"I should go," I muttered, the words barely escaping my lips as I took a step back. She didn't move, didn't say a thing. She just stood there, her eyes never leaving mine, the tray of food a sad, silent reminder of the awkwardness between us.

Without another word, I turned and walked away, my feet moving faster than I intended.

Striding out of the staff mess, my gown trailing behind me like a regal banner, I felt a mix of emotions swirling within.

All I could see was Camila's face. Her eyes, dark and sharp, cut through me like shards of glass. The hurt she tried to hide beneath that iron mask of indifference was crystal clear. And I knew why. I was the reason.

Flirting. Why did I even bother? For a moment of ego? A distraction? Whatever it was, it left me with that tight knot in my stomach, like I'd swallowed something I shouldn't have. I knew what I did, and worse, I knew how it must have made her feel.

This must've been how Dad felt when he caught Mom cheating on him. The way he used to look at her–devoted, like she was his whole world, even though she didn't deserve it. And then, the betrayal. I remember that night too well. Dad's face turned stone cold, not because he didn't care, but because if he let any of that hurt slip out, he'd shatter. The silence between them, the weight of it–it was the kind that crushed you without a word spoken.

God, I always hated Mom for that. How could she? How could she do that to him, to us? And now here I was, doing the same thing to Camila. It made me sick just thinking about it. The guilt was crawling up my spine, prickling at me, and I couldn't shake it off. I wanted to scream at myself, 'Get it together, Christina! Stop being like your father!'

But no, I had to go and flirt, toss out those smiles and sweet little nothings like I was some damn charmer. And for what? To prove something? To feel like I still had it? Well, guess what? All I did was make myself feel like a grade-A jackass, and now I had Camila looking at me like I was the biggest disappointment in her life.

And I knew that look too well. That same look Dad had when he found out about Mom's affair. The tightening of the lips, the way his eyes would harden when he thought no one was watching. He never said it out loud, but it was there, simmering under the surface. I'd seen it.

And now, I'd put that same look on Camila's face. I felt like I was becoming the very thing I swore I'd never be. But I couldn't keep running from it forever, could I?

I couldn't let any of that sink in–not completely. Not here, not now. I had a job to do, and there was no time for wallowing. If there was one thing I'd learned working on ships, it's that you can't let feelings drag you down. I had to brush it off, push it deep down where all the other unresolved things go, and get on with it. This wasn't the time for guilt or second-guessing. Not if I wanted to survive.

Helping Charles and flirting with Claire was a reminder of the strange, beautiful web of relationships formed in the unique bubble of cruise ship life.

Tonight was about more than just sales or schemes; it was about connections, the kind that could either weave you into the safest net or tangle you up in knots.

As I approached the theatre, I mentally shake off the drama from the staff mess and think about how cool it is that there is a 'show' most nights on board.

There's something about a theatre on a cruise ship that just feels like magic is about to unfold–or in my case, a little mischief mixed with some heavy-duty wheeling and dealing. The Starlight Theatre was this gaudy gem in the heart of the ship, decked out in velvet and gold, with carpets so plush you'd think they were trying to compete with the clouds. The seats were lined up like little soldiers ready for the onslaught of tourists, and the air was thick with a mix of perfume and anticipation.

Tonight, the theatre was buzzing more than usual. There was a vibe, a sort of electric pulse, as if everyone knew they were about to witness something spectacular. It was, in all accounts, formal night, but someone forgot to mention that to half the passengers. These cheaper cruises, on smaller cruise lines, don't insist passengers wear formal attire. It's a shame. When everyone puts the effort in and all are dressed to the nines, it makes the night just a little more spectacular.

I made my grand entrance, right on cue, just as the crowd was settling down, the murmur of their chatter a backdrop to the twinkling lights that dotted the ceiling like a makeshift sky of stars.

As I sauntered down the aisle, the scent of fresh popcorn mixed with a floral perfume someone must have bathed in, I spotted Patrick, with his wife and kids, a regular gem herself.

She was flaunting a sparkling 3-carat diamond ring that caught the light and threw it back out into the crowd like it was sprinkling glitter. The guests behind her were practically drooling, eyes wide, as if the ring was the real show.

"Patrick, that is absolutely beautiful! And that ring is beautiful, too," I quipped as I approached, giving them my best show-stopping smile. Patrick's wife, caught off guard, blushed a shade of red that rivaled the theatre curtains and playfully slapped my hand. I always enjoyed cheesy little exchanges with random guests; there was something refreshingly genuine about their amusement.

"Patrick, I know this is last minute, but I wanted to speak to you about that amazing piece you purchased from The Jewelry Box," I continued, widening my eyes and lowering my voice a tad to keep our conversation just between us as the theatre lights began to dim. The signal that the show was about to start sent a little thrill through me; timing was everything in this game.

"We shouldn't be long. I just need some signatures for his diamond certification papers," I explained, turning to his wife with a conspiratorial wink. She was all grace and giggles, clearly still on a high from her new bling.

"Take him as long as you need him, I'll watch the kids. He got me this today; I won't be needing anything else," she replied, her voice a melodic whisper that carried a hint of indulgence.

Patrick and I made our way out just as the curtain was rising, our exit as smooth as the slide of silk. His small talk on the way to my cabin was a nervous chatter, a stark contrast to my calm, collected demeanor. Poor guy was blissfully unaware of the whirlwind he was about to step into—a carefully choreographed dance of distraction and deceit.

My passenger cabin was a functional space turned into a stage for tonight's act. As we entered, I ignored Becca, dressed as a cabin steward, puttering away the bathroom. Her disguise was both a ruse; assurance and a reminder of the everyday operations behind the scenes and made this setting look and feel normal. Patrick was none the wiser.

Patrick took a seat at the desk, looking like he was trying to blend into the decor–my mirror reflecting his awkwardness perfectly as I adjusted myself in my formal gown. Creepily, he eye-fucked me in my dress. Gross. I ignored that due to his significant purchase, at The Jewelry Box, today.

"I really appreciate the huge purchase today. The show, your wife and kids are at, is 45 minutes long, so you have about 35 minutes to get back to your family before it ends," I informed him, keeping my tone light but firm.

The groundwork was laid, now it was time for the play within the play.

Just then, my cell phone buzzed–a text from Mom that read: "We REALLY need to talk." I slipped the phone into my clutch with a mental note to brace myself for whatever that was about.

Patrick leaned back in the chair, his eyes narrowing slightly as he studied me.

"You ever think about what you're going to do when this cruise gig is over?" he asked suddenly, catching me off guard.

I raised an eyebrow, leaning against the desk with my arms crossed. "What do you mean?"

"This ship stuff," he waved his hands around, indicating the cabin, the ship, the whole situation. "It's fun for now, but you've got a lot more potential than just selling diamonds and watches to drunk tourists."

I blinked, taken aback by his comment. I'd been called a lot of things in my line of work, but "*having potential*" wasn't usually one of them–especially from a guy like Patrick.

"I'm good at what I do," I said, a bit defensively. "People like me. I make sales."

He chuckled. "No doubt about that, sweetheart. But let me ask you something–don't you want more? I mean, selling jewelry is great, but what happens when you're tired of living out of a suitcase and hustling tourists every day?"

I opened my mouth to snap back with something snarky, but paused. He wasn't entirely wrong. The thought had crossed my mind before, more than once. The glamour of the ship life fades pretty quickly when you're counting down the days until your next contract ends.

We both look toward the bathroom, as Becca, her back to us, flushes the toilet and mills about, waiting for me to leave.

"What are you getting at, Patrick?" I asked, turning back and narrowing my eyes at him.

He leaned forward, lowering his voice like we were sharing some kind of secret.

"I've got a business. Pharmaceuticals. Big clients, big deals. We're expanding, and I could use someone like you on the team. Someone who knows how to close a deal, make people feel good about spending money."

I blinked. This was the last thing I expected. "You're offering me a job? In pharmaceuticals?"

Patrick smiled, that sleazy charm oozing from his every word. "Why not? You've got the sales skills. I've seen you work. Plus, I can tell you're not exactly thrilled with this cruise life. Think about it—stable income, no more living out of a cabin, and way more money than you're pulling in selling necklaces to rich ladies on vacation."

I crossed my arms, my b-cups on full display in my gown, eyeing him suspiciously. "And what would I be selling exactly?"

"Oh, we deal in supplements, enhancers. You know, the stuff that keeps men and women... happy," he said with a wink. "Legal, of course, but highly in demand. You'd fit right in."

I almost laughed. Here was this guy, a walking stereotype of mid-life crisis in motion, offering me a job selling what, sex pills? It sounded insane. But then again, was it any crazier than what I was doing now? The thought lingered for a moment before I shook it off.

"I don't know, Patrick," I said slowly, "That doesn't exactly sound like my kind of gig."

He shrugged. "Think about it. It's a lot more money, a lot less hassle, and I can tell you're smart enough to handle something bigger. Besides, I could use someone like you–someone I trust."

"Trust, huh?" I raised an eyebrow.

"Yeah, trust," he said, taking a pen from my desk and holding it out to me. "Give me your number and I'll send you the text with the details. We'll talk."

This guy was something else, but the crazy part was... I wasn't entirely dismissing the idea. I reluctantly take the pen and write my number on a post-it note. He slips it into his pocket without a word.

Becca clears her throat from the bathroom and I snap back to reality and focus on the task at hand.

"Oops, I forgot the diamond certificate at my desk on Deck 7. Hang tight while I get it," I said with a feigned scatter-brained charm.

"Wait, what? Should I stay here?" Patrick's confusion was almost comical, his voice a mix of uncertainty and misplaced trust.

"Yes, just make yourself comfortable!" I chirped, already halfway out the door. As I closed it behind me, the hallway greeted me with its own drama.

I bump into Camila, a storm dressed in evening wear, her eyes flashing with a mix of curiosity and accusation.

"I'm going to overlook the pathetic flirting you and that spa girl got up to in the staff mess," Camila spat, her voice low but full of venom.

She stepped closer, her eyes locking onto mine with that familiar fire. "But don't think I didn't see it, Christina. You think you can just play me like that? Like I'm some idiot who doesn't know exactly what you're doing?" Guests approach and Camila steps back and smiles at them as they walk by. Once they're far enough not to hear, she starts in on me again.

"So, who are these hoochie 'friends' you brought on board? You're clearly into the *skinny* blonde, but the K-pop princess, I can't figure out why she's here," Camila hissed, her words sharp as the heels she was balancing on.

Back inside my cabin, while I was out navigating the unexpected confrontation from Camila, a different kind of performance was unfolding–one I had orchestrated but wouldn't witness firsthand. As Patrick sat there, a mix of nervousness and naivety playing across his features, the bathroom door creaked open.

Out stepped Becca, complete in a, dare I say, sexy cabin steward uniform and a playful glint in her eye that would have tipped off anyone who knew her well. The rubber gloves she peeled off added a layer of theatrics to her guise, and she tossed them aside with a flourish that was pure Becca–always in character, always on cue.

She sauntered over to Patrick, who looked momentarily confused–his mind likely trying to bridge the gap between this unexpected cabin steward and the surroundings he'd become momentarily accustomed to. Becca, seizing the moment with the confidence of a seasoned actress, opened up her top fully to showcase perfectly shapes D-cups, courtesy of Dr. Mendlecorn in Boca Raton, in a tastefully expensive Honey Birdette lingerie and straddled him as he sat in the chair at the desk.

"So sorry for not having your cabin ready for your return," she cooed, leaning close enough for her words to be a whisper, but loud enough to ensure they carried the weight of her playful deceit. "How can I ever make it up to you, sir?"

Like a coin dropped, the change in Patrick was instantaneous, his earlier apprehension melting into a wide, almost incredulous smile. Any lingering doubts or nerves dissolved under Becca's expert attention, as he played along with the scene unfolding, clearly enjoying the unexpected twist to his evening.

This little charade, while light-hearted on the surface, was another layer in the complex game of cat and mouse we found ourselves in–where every player had a role, every action had a purpose, and every moment could turn the tide in our favor or send us adrift. Back out in the hallway, the storm continued.

"Hoochie? Please. Emily is far from a 'hoochie'. I don't think this is the time or place to discuss this," I retorted, feeling my patience thinning faster than the ice in a tropical drink, and clearly wanting to leave the area. We both nod and smile at the omnipresence of passing guests. Once they clear, Camila continues.

"I agree. Let's go somewhere more private," she snapped, reaching for my cabin door handle, her movements as subtle as a sledgehammer.

Just then, like a scene straight out of a spy movie, Emily stepped in front of Camila, blocking her path with a cool, collected presence that made my heart skip a beat. "Can I help you?" Emily's voice was calm, but her eyes were steel.

Camila, taken aback by her sudden magical appearance, stepped back. "Sorry, I didn't notice you there."

"I guess I'm too '*skinny*' to notice," Emily shot back, her tone icy enough to chill the hallway.

Camila, now clearly realizing she had overstepped, turned back to me, her eyes narrowing. "This conversation is not over," she declared before retreating down the hall, her retreat as dramatic as her entrance.

I let out a breath I didn't realize I was holding and glanced at Emily, her presence a sudden and unexpected comfort in the chaos of the evening. Whatever storms were brewing, it seemed I had an ally, and possibly, something more. But first, there was a show to run, and the night was just getting started.

Chapter 19

DANGEROUS CURRENTS

Under the silvery glow of the moon, the Palm Island mansion's pool area shimmered like a jewel in the night, its waters still and serene, mirroring the calm before the storm. Bas, the master of this opulent domain, lounged on a plush outdoor couch, his presence commanding even in relaxation.

However, peace was fleeting this evening as his phone vibrated with an urgency that sliced through the tranquility.

The text message read: "I thought you said Becca was sick?"

Attached was an image of Becca's Instagram account–a selfie with the cruise ship's life-ring clearly visible in the background, the ships name 'Ocean Seduction' reflecting from the flash. The caption was a taunt wrapped in naivety: "Working the high seas! #cruiseshipGFE."

Rage clouded Bas's features as he scrolled through his phone, his jaw clenching with each swipe. The audacity of the betrayal struck him like a physical blow; Becca, one of his most trusted, had brazenly stepped out of line. With a growl, he dialed a number, his voice a low thunder.

"Get over here in the morning. One of my girls has stepped out without permission."

As he ended the call, his twin daughters, two giggling bundles of joy, came rushing toward him, oblivious to the storm brewing in their father's eyes. They jumped into his arms, their innocent laughter piercing the veil of his anger, reminding him momentarily of the different roles he played–tyrant to some, loving father to others.

"Daddy, we came to say goodnight!" they chimed, their voices a soothing balm.

Bas's features softened as he enveloped his daughters in a gentle embrace, his demeanor shifting from a menacing overlord to a doting parent. His heart lightened momentarily, but the dark cloud of Becca's betrayal lingered, a reminder of the dualities of his life.

"Run along now, darlings. Daddy has to talk to mommy about something important," he said, his tone gentle yet firm.

The girls scampered off, their laughter echoing down the hall and out the open wall of the house. As the sound faded, Bas's wife, Alejandra–Aly for short–approached, her intuition sharp as ever. She sensed the shift in his aura, the undercurrent of fury mingled with betrayal. She walks right up, places both her hands on his cheeks and looks deep into his eyes.

"What's wrong, Bas?" Aly's voice was both a caress and a blade, soft yet slicing to the core. He stares at her a moment, his blood pressure increasing with every breath. He turns, grabs his phone and unlocks it.

He showed her the image on his phone, the evidence of Becca's indiscretion stark against the light of his screen. "Becca decided to play games. On social media, no less."

Aly's eyes hardened, her lips curling into a smile that did not reach her eyes. It was the look of a queen chess piece poised for a deadly move. "¡La puta! We can't allow this, Bas. It sets a dangerous precedent. We need to send a message–a clear, unequivocal one."

The discussion that followed was a dance of darkness, two minds weaving plots with the precision of a spider spinning its web. Aly, ever the strategist, suggested a plan that was both chilling and effective, a demonstration of power that would ripple through their ranks like a cold wind.

Bas listened, his respect for his wife deepening with each word. She was his equal in every sense, her cunning and ruthlessness matching his own. Together, they were unstoppable, a duo forged in the fires of ambition and the shadows of the underworld.

Alejandra bore the unmistakable charisma of a woman who had risen from the smoldering streets of Havana to the opulent corridors of power. Her origins, like many before her, were woven into the colorful and relentless tapestry of Cuban life. Her beauty was arresting, with deep olive skin that shimmered under the sun and eyes dark and piercing as the midnight ocean. Her figure moved with a grace only cultivated by years of dancing–a skill that had both defined her past and carved her path to the present.

Aly had been a dancer at one of the city's less reputable strip clubs, a place where the glitter of sequins barely outshone the desperation and raw ambition of its inhabitants. It was here, amidst the haze of cigarette smoke and the pulsing neon lights, that she first encountered Bas, who was then a burgeoning figure in the underworld. Unlike the other patrons, Bas wasn't there solely for the cheap thrills or the flowing liquor. He was a man on a mission, always scouting for potential, always looking to expand his flourishing empire.

From the moment Bas saw Alejandra sway rhythmically on stage, he saw something beyond her physical allure–an innate toughness and a sharp wit that many of her admirers overlooked. Her movements were hypnotic, not just in their sensuality but in the sheer power they conveyed; each step, each twirl spoke of her fierce determination and unspoken dreams.

For Aly, Bas was initially just another customer, albeit one whose gaze held more than a mere flicker of lust. There was a depth to him, a seriousness that set him apart from the drunken revelers she was used to.

When he approached her after her set, his demeanor was respectful yet assertive, his proposal straightforward but laden with possibilities. He saw potential in her beyond the club's smoky corners–a potential to rise alongside him in a life filled with risk and reward.

Their partnership began as a business arrangement, with Aly providing Bas with information about the city's less savory characters–ones she learned of through overheard conversations and whispered confessions. However, as they spent more time together, their relationship deepened into something more complex. Aly wasn't just a source; she was a confidante, an equal in a game that was typically ruled by men. Her insights were sharp, her intuition unmatched, and her loyalty unshakeable.

As Bas's empire grew, so did their bond. They became a formidable duo, not just in love but in business. Aly transitioned from the nightclub's spotlight to the shadowy realms of Bas's operations, her transformation both literal and metaphorical. She traded her dancer's attire for sleek dresses and sharp suits, her role now that of a strategist and advisor.

Their marriage was a culmination of shared ambitions and mutual respect. It was a union forged not just in affection but in an understanding of power–how to wield it, how to maintain it, and how to expand it. Aly's past life as a dancer in Havana, and then in Miami, seemed like a distant memory, but the skills she honed there–the ability to read a room, to enchant an audience, to negotiate her worth–remained integral to her new identity.

In the world Bas and Aly inhabited, love was often a vulnerability, but for them, it was their greatest strength. Together, they navigated the precarious waters of their life, not just surviving but thriving, their pasts not as chains but as ladders to a future only they could envision.

As they plotted, an electric charge filled the air, the thrill of the hunt, the excitement of the game. It was what had drawn them together, what had fused their lives into one unbreakable bond. Aly leaned in, her breath a whisper against his ear.

"Let's remind them why we're the ones in charge," she murmured, her words sending a shiver down his spine.

Their conversation veered between cold logic and heated whispers, the tension morphing into an intoxicating allure. They were two sides of the same coin, equally obsessed with control and power, their love intertwined with their ambitions.

"Nobody plays us, Aly. Nobody," Bas reiterated, his voice a growl of promise.

"Exactly, darling. We play them. Always," Aly replied, her eyes alight with a fierce joy.

The night grew deeper, their plans more intricate. They were artists painting a canvas of fear and respect, their brushes dipped in shadows and strategy. As they finalized their approach, a sense of satisfaction settled over them, the pleasure of a job well planned fueling their desire for each other.

This dance of darkness wasn't just a part of their marriage; it was the bedrock. Each scheme that brought them closer to their goals also drew them closer to each other, each plot a thread in the tapestry of their twisted romance.

In the quiet of the night, with the stars bearing witness to their machinations, Bas and Aly solidified their resolve. No betrayal would go unpunished, no disloyalty overlooked. They were the masters of their universe, and woe betide anyone who forgot that.

As they retreated from the planning into the sanctuary of their bedroom, their conversation shifted from strategic to intimate, the thrill of power seamlessly blending into the passion of their relationship. Tonight, they had reaffirmed their dominion, not just over their empire but over each other's hearts. They were partners in every sense, their love as deep and dangerous as the sea that surrounded their island fortress.

Over on the ship, stepping into the Martini Lounge felt like walking onto a movie set where the set had seen better days but nobody had the heart to tell it. This place clung to its fame like an actor hanging onto a single memorable role from decades ago, its glitz faded but just enough charm to keep the guests coming back. The dim lighting tried its best to hide the wear and tear, while the crystal glasses still sparkled under the warm glow of strategically placed spotlights.

"Okay, Emily," I chuckled as we dodged a particularly loud group of tourists, "we've got about twenty minutes to collect Patrick from my cabin and his tryst with Becca and get him back to his unsuspecting wife. This should be fun."

Emily, ever the calming presence, gave me a soft smile. "Thanks for sticking up for me back there with Camila. It's been a long time since anyone's done that for me."

Navigating through the sea of guests, I could feel the sticky residue of spilled cocktails beneath my heels, the carpet holding onto each spill like a memory. "I hear you," I confessed, pulling out a bar stool for her before taking my own. "I ran away to work on ships because I saw the disappointment in my father's eyes. Always felt like I didn't measure up to my brother and sister. Tried my best to help but somehow always managed to fuck things up more. Hence, another delightful addition to my growing list of flaws. Why does it always feel like I'm running?"

A Filipino bartender greeted us with a warm, knowing smile, perhaps too accustomed to overhearing confessions across his bar. "Two Lycée martinis, please," I ordered, trying to shake off the heaviness of our conversation with a wink.

As he set to work, Emily leaned in, her voice low, "We're all running to or from something. Your perception of it all depends on your direction." Her eyes flicked towards the other end of the bar, then back to me, a silent question lingering between us. "Now, let's address the elephant in the room. Is the Cruise Director your old girlfriend or something?"

The bartender chose that moment to place two beautifully crafted martinis before us. The glasses caught the light, sending prisms dancing across the polished wood. "Hold that thought," I said, standing abruptly. "Nature calls. Be right back."

Making my way to the restroom, I passed by the starboard side entrance where Enzo, one of the Filipino security guards, stood watch. I smiled at him and he smiled back. His gaze followed me, and I could tell he was putting pieces together he shouldn't even know existed.

Just then, Captain Bjorn Olsen, the ruggedly handsome Norwegian in command of the ship, made his entrance. He had a way of appearing exactly where he was least expected but most needed. The lounge buzzed anew with his presence, guests straightening up as if his gaze could peel back the layers of their vacation personas.

Captain Bjorn Olsen is the epitome of the sea-worn mariner, a figure who might have leaped from the pages of a nautical adventure. At 55, his presence is as commanding as the ocean waves, marked by a rugged handsomeness that speaks of years spent navigating the world's waters. With his steel-gray hair, often tossed back in a windswept style, and a beard that seems perpetually caught between stubble and full-grown, he carries the aura of a man who has seen it all.

Bjorn was born in a small coastal village in Norway, where the sea was both playground and teacher. From a young age, he was drawn to the ocean, spending his days aboard local fishing boats and his evenings poring over maps and maritime books. His heart was set on the horizon, and by the time he was in his late teens, he had enrolled in a maritime academy, eager to turn his passion into a career.

His ascent through the ranks was swift, driven by a mix of raw talent and an unquenchable thirst for knowledge. Bjorn was not content with mere competence; he sought mastery over every aspect of seafaring, from navigation to engineering to meteorology. His dedication paid off when he became one of the youngest captains to helm a major cruise liner. It was a role he stepped into with both pride and a profound sense of responsibility.

As a captain, Bjorn is known for his unshakeable calm in the face of storms–both literal and metaphorical. His leadership style is firm but fair, and he commands with a respect born of confidence rather than fear. Crew members, from the deckhands to the highest officers, speak of him with a mixture of admiration and affection, acknowledging his ability to bring out the best in those under his command.

Despite his decades at sea, Bjorn has never lost his love for the quieter, more introspective moments that life on the ocean can afford. He is often found at the ship's prow at dawn, coffee in hand, gazing at the sunrise with the contentment of a man who knows he is exactly where he belongs. These moments of solitude are precious, a time for Bjorn to reflect on his journey, both physical and personal.

Off the ship, Bjorn's life is less documented, shrouded in the privacy he cherishes. However, it is known that he has a family –a wife and two grown children–who share his love for the sea, though they prefer to enjoy it from the shore. His home in Norway is filled with relics of his travels: shells from Caribbean beaches, woven fabrics from Asian markets, and photographs of sunsets so vivid they hardly seem real.

Captain Olsen's reputation extends beyond his seamanship. He is a staunch advocate for marine conservation, driven by a deep-seated belief that the sea, which has given him so much, deserves protection. Under his leadership, his ships have pioneered several environmental initiatives, earning accolades and setting standards in sustainability within the cruise industry.

For those who travel with him, Captain Bjorn Olsen is more than just a ship's captain; he is a symbol of adventure and the enduring call of the sea–a reminder that the journey, not just the destination, is what truly matters.

Back at the bar, unaware of the Captain's entrance, Emily was a beacon of tranquility amid the growing storm. When Captain Olsen approached her from behind, the surprise didn't quite reach her eyes before her training kicked in.

"Good evening, Emily, are you enjoying your cruise?" his voice boomed, smooth yet piercing.

Turning to face him, her response was measured, "Yes, very much so. Thank you." Emily thinks for a moment and continues. "Have we met? How did you know my name?"

"I'm the Captain. I know everything happening on my ship," he said, a twinkle in his eye that didn't quite reach the rest of his face. "You're a friend of the shopping guide, Christina. I trust she's keeping you entertained."

I returned from the loo to the Martini lounge to see the Captain speaking to Emily at the bar. From out of nowhere, Kevin grabs my arm, his grip tight, his face a mask of frustration and something darker. "I got to hand it to you, you really stepped it up today."

"Uh, thanks," I muttered, trying to pull away, my eyes on Emily and the Captain.

"How is it that your sales were the highest the Jewelry Box has ever seen, EVER?" Kevin's voice was a hiss, his anger barely contained. "Artem at CDG found out and is furious. Those sales should have been funneled to and made at CDG's."

Trying to focus on, and understand, the scene unfolding at the bar, I ignored Kevin, which sent him into a tizzy.

"Since those sales didn't happen at CDG, we're going to hold back your commission as a penalty," Kevin declares with attitude.

My eyes narrow as I snap back to Kevin, my voice sharp. "What the hell did you just say? Why are you men so fucking hard on me? I tripled my sales target, and you're not going to pay me the commission I rightfully deserve? With no help from you, or anyone at the office, I tried a different strategy and you know what...it worked." I snarl, nose to nose with this arrogant fuckwad.

"Well, you should have focused on smashing sales for CDG instead of smashing your girlfriend," Kevin retorted, venom in his voice.

"It's not my fault you couldn't ring my bell," I snapped back, tugging my arm free from his grasp.

Fuming, Kevin spat out, "Whatever. Keep telling yourself that. The office wants me to communicate to you the importance of pushing Artem's store, CDG, over everyone else. And, just so you're consistently pushing CDG *above* everyone else, we're assigning you an assistant."

I blink, stunned for a second, then snap back. "What? No. I don't need help. I have Victor."

Kyle smirks, like he knows something I don't. "Not an assistant to stock brochures. An assistant to help with sales. The office will make their decision on who that will be in the next couple days."

I scoff, annoyed and frustrated, and leave Kevin simmering in his own rage and slide back onto the stool next to Emily just as the Captain was issuing a veiled warning.

"Don't do anything that could get you removed from the ship. That goes for you too, Christina."

He walks off, leaving a chilling silence in his wake. Emily downs her drink and grimaces.

"What was that about?" I whispered, glancing at her.

She shook her head, her eyes wide. "I think someone is catching on to why we're here."

"Ah, fuck. Let's get out of here and get Becca and Patrick back to safety," I said, standing up, adrenaline pumping. My heart races–not just from the danger, but from the thrill of the unknown and the magnetic pull of the woman standing next to me.

Chapter 20

SWEATING BULLETS

Just after dawn, Bas's mansion basked in a serene glow, the morning light reflecting off the opulent pool and casting elongated shadows across the immaculate grounds at this Palm Island estate. Seated by the pool was Bas, his mind as turbulent as the sea in an autumn hurricane.

Beside him stood two men, Luis and Angel, his most loyal enforcers–thugs by job description but not necessarily by aptitude.

Luis, the Venezuelan, was the more boisterous of the duo. He stood gripping a large cup of Dunkin' Donuts coffee, the steam mingling with the morning mist. His love for the American coffee chain was a running joke in their circle, as was his insistence that it somehow tasted better than anything back home. Angel, the Colombian counterpart, was leaner, his features perpetually scrunched in a mix of suspicion and annoyance–mostly directed towards Luis's caffeine habits.

"Luis, if you keep chugging that coffee like it's water, you'll float before we even board the plane," Angel scolded, his voice a mix of jest and genuine concern.

"Ah, Angel, you worry too much. This," Luis said, raising his cup as if toasting the sun, "fuels my superpowers. How else do you think I keep up with all of Bas's orders?"

Both men had stumbled into Bas's service under less than ordinary circumstances. Luis had been a small-time crook in Caracas, running scams and petty thefts, when he crossed paths with Bas during a botched deal, in Miami, that almost cost him his life. Bas, seeing potential in the rough-edged man, offered him a choice: work for him or face the consequences of his failed scam. Luis chose the former, bringing along his childhood friend Angel, who had been looking for a way out of Colombia and the violent street wars that had claimed his family.

Over the years, Luis and Angel had become Bas's go-to guys for operations requiring a mix of muscle and intimidation, though their lack of sharpness often led to comedic, if not entirely efficient, outcomes. Their loyalty, however, was unmatched, and Bas valued that above all.

This morning, as the sun crept higher, casting a golden sheen on the water, Bas's mood was anything but light. He scrolled through Becca's Instagram feed, his expression darkening with each swipe. When he came across a photo that clearly showed all three girls, and Christina's name badge, he zoomed in and took a screenshot.

"Becca and Emily are on a cruise ship named the Ocean Seduction," Bas stated, his voice cold and calculated. He sent the screenshot to their devices, the familiar ping of the airdrop echoing slightly in the open air.

As the information settled in, Bas's orders were clear: "Alvaro, our go-to pilot, is waiting at the airport to fly you to Nassau. The Ocean Seduction is in port today, in Nassau. Find Becca and Emily and bring the girls back to me. And find out who this Christina girl is. Don't be shy to twist her for information."

Luis pocketed his phone, his other hand still clutching the coffee. "Bueno, you got it, boss. We'll bring them back and squeeze that Christian for everything she know."

Angel nodded, his usual stern demeanor tightening even further. "We won't let you down, Bas."

As they turned to leave, Luis's thoughts were already shifting to the logistics of the trip–and his caffeine supply. "Hey, Angel, you think we have time to swing by Dunkin' before the airport? I could use a refill."

Angel sighed, the corners of his mouth twitching in reluctant amusement. "We're about to handle serious business, and you're planning a coffee run. You're unbelievable, Luis."

"Hey, a man needs his fuel. And who knows? Maybe we can stop by the Dunkin' in Nassau. We could use a local taste test," Luis joked, his attempt at humor easing the tension as they headed to their sleek black Escalade.

The bickering continued, a familiar soundtrack to their preparations. "Just make sure your passport is up to date, and for heaven's sake, don't lose it this time," Angel reminded, throwing a pointed look at Luis who was notoriously forgetful.

"Relax, I've got it all under control. And after we grab the girls, it's straight to Dunkin'," Luis declared with a grin, his priorities amusingly skewed but his determination clear.

As they drove out of the long, paved brick driveway, the morning's tranquility was restored, but the undercurrents of their mission promised anything but a peaceful outcome.

Later, in Nassau, The Cove at Atlantis isn't just any hotel—it's like stepping into one of those glossy travel magazines that promise paradise and actually deliver.

As I usher Emily and Becca towards a cabana draped in elegance by the pool, Emily's eyes light up like she's just won the lottery.

The pool itself is an oasis. It stretches languidly across the expansive deck, its waters crystal clear and inviting, mirroring the cloudless azure sky above. Around it, an assortment of lounge chairs and plush cabanas are sprawled invitingly, offering sanctuary to sun-seekers and shade-lovers alike. Each cabana, draped in sheer, flowing fabrics that flutter gently in the breeze, offers a private slice of this paradise, creating little pockets of tranquility amidst the buzz of activity.

As we settle into one of these elegant havens, the visual splendor of The Cove isn't the only thing drawing appreciative glances. Becca, with her effortless charisma, tiny bikini, flawlessly toned yoga body and radiant smile, seems to magnetically attract the admiring stares of many around the pool. It's not just her beauty but the vibrant energy she exudes, laughing heartily at a joke one moment and playfully splashing water the next, that makes her the unwitting center of attention. Men lounging nearby nudge each other, their eyes following her every move, a mix of awe and something a bit more palpable hanging in their gazes.

Emily, on the other hand, exudes a carefree aura that's almost palpable. There's a noticeable shift in her demeanor from the usual stress-lines of worry that mar her features.

Today, her laughter is more frequent and genuine, her movements more fluid, as if the serene setting of The Cove has smoothed out the usual tension she carries like a second skin.

She lounges in a deck chair, her legs stretched out elegantly, a cocktail in hand, her eyes closed in contentment as she soaks in the warm sun. Every so often, her lips curl into a smile at a private joke or a passing thought, suggesting a mind unburdened, at least for the moment.

The atmosphere around us is thick with the scent of sunscreen and tropical florals, mingling seamlessly with the salty kiss of the ocean breeze. Servers move gracefully through the crowds, balancing trays of colorful drinks and gourmet snacks, their polite smiles never faltering even in the face of demanding guests. The entire scene is a well-orchestrated symphony of luxury and relaxation, designed to make every guest feel like royalty.

Despite the occasional overzealous admirer, our little trio maintains a bubble of jovial camaraderie. We share stories that make us laugh until our sides ache, we dive into the cooling embrace of the pool to escape the heat, and we indulge in the kind of light-hearted banter that can only come from true comfort and familiarity with each other's company. In this slice of paradise, it's easy to forget the world beyond the deck– a world of schedules, responsibilities, and lurking threats.

For now, at least, The Cove offers more than just a physical escape; it provides a mental respite, a temporary reprieve from life's relentless pace. And for Emily, it seems to unfurl her tightly wound springs, allowing her a freedom that is rare and, by all appearances, deeply cherished.

"Wow, this place is beautiful. I could get used to this," she marvels, sinking into the plush cushions of our cabana.

"I know, right?" I chuckle, scanning the horizon where the water meets the sky in a perfect postcard moment. "I can only stay for an hour, though. I should be in stores hustling." Winking at them, I add, "BRB," before I trot off to swap my uniform for something less...official.

Strolling down the pathway towards the change room, the balmy breeze plays with the edges of my uniform, reminding me that duty calls—but so does a quick change. I think to myself that the sun over The Cove at Atlantis Hotel is relentless, beating down on me like it had a personal vendetta. It was one of those days when the heat made the air shimmer, and the palm trees looked almost too relaxed, swaying lazily like they didn't have a care in the world. I love this kind of heat.

Just as I'm lost in thoughts of potential sales and the lingering excitement of being in such a stunning locale, I spot two overdressed men approaching. They're comparing something on their phone to... well, to me. Angel, apparently the head thug of this dynamic duo, flags me down with a grin that's too sharp to be friendly.

"Hey, Christina, what luck, we were just looking for you." Angel's tone is casual, but his body language screams trouble.

"Looking for me? Why? You looking for some deals on diamonds or watches?" I quip, eyeing them both skeptically. My heart's pounding—not just from the heat or Emily's form in her bikini.

Their smiles don't reach their eyes. As one thug—Angel—slides his phone back into his pocket, I catch a glimpse of a gun in a holster. Oh, this is not good.

"You could say that," Angel replies smoothly. "My name is Angel and my boss, Bas, is looking for Becca and Emily." His words hang between us, heavy and ominous.

Things escalate quicker than a sale on Black Friday. One minute, I'm minding my own business, and the next, this guy named Angel is in my face, demanding answers like I'm the Jeopardy champion of the day. And because I didn't respond fast enough, this dude decides to give me a lesson in "hands-on communication" with the hardest open-hand slap I've ever received. Holy fuck that hurt.

Seriously, I saw stars–like, I could practically hear 'Bohemian Rhapsody' kicked in, and I could practically hear Freddie Mercury belting '*Mamaaaa, just killed a man!*' in the background. Now I'm rethinking every life choice that led me to this moment, courtesy of Angel's slap-happy hand.

The sand beneath me was scorching, sticking to my skin, clothes and just about everywhere at this point as I tried to shake it out of my hair. My ears were still ringing from the hit Angel unleash on me, and everything around me felt muffled, like I was underwater. Laying in the sand behind the dwarf sugar palms, I could hear the angry muttering of the thugs above me, their shadows darkening the already hot sand.

"How'd you like that one?" Angel sneered, his voice oozing with arrogance. The leader, probably. I didn't even bother to look up.

I spat out a mouthful of sandy blood, tasting grit and metal. My mouth hurt like hell, but I wasn't about to give them the satisfaction of knowing that.

"The song playing in the grocery store hits harder than you," I shot back, forcing a smirk even though it hurt to move my lips.

I didn't give them time to react. I sprang to my feet, adrenaline coursing through me, and took a swing at the nearest goon. But I wasn't quick enough. His hand caught me mid-swing, and before I knew it, he slapped me down so hard I saw stars. The impact knocked the breath out of me, and I hit the sand again, hard. Brings back memories of being raised by a no-nonsense, military dad and my roughhousing brother.

Before I could even catch my breath, he had me by the hair, yanking me up like I weighed nothing. I struggled, but he tightened his grip.

"You want another?" he snarled, then growled "Where are the girls?" shaking me so hard I thought my head might pop off.

Through the dizziness, I locked eyes with him.

"Harder," I whispered, barely audible, but I knew he heard me. I saw it in the way his eyes narrowed. Just like dad did.

He pushed me to my knees, and I felt the cold metal of a silenced Glock G30 pistol press against my thigh. He pulls the hammer back and I close my eyes. My heart was pounding so loud I was sure they could all hear it. This is going to be loud.

Chapter 21

ENTER, THE TOURIST

Out of nowhere, a voice cut through the tension. "Christina, what are you doing way back here? I'm heading back to the ship but, silly me, I just can't find my cruise card." I glanced over, my heart skipping a beat. A tourist, probably in her late 40s, early 50s, walks towards us, completely oblivious.

She was wearing this huge floppy beach hat that made her look like a lost 'extra' from a bad tropical movie. She was rummaging through a beach bag, not even paying attention to what was happening.

"You need to go back that way," I said, trying to keep my voice calm, but there was an edge to it. I didn't have time to deal with this. But she kept coming closer, still looking down, digging through that damn bag.

"Looks like this party is getting a little rough. Can I join in?" she asked, finally looking up from her bag. Her eyes met mine first, then she noticed the gun, and I could see the gears turning in her head.

Angel, clearly losing patience, barked at her. "Bitch, you stupid or something?"

Her face changed in an instant. "Who you calling bitch?" she snapped, her voice like a whip.

Before I could even process what was happening, she dropped the bag and moved like lightning. She landed a roundhouse kick right to Angel's face. Teeth scatter. The other thug went for the gun that had fallen to the sand, but she was faster. She knocked him out with a punch that made me wince, then quickly disassembled the gun and tossed the pieces into the sand seemingly like she'd done a thousand times.

"Let's go," she said, grabbing my hand and yanking me to my feet. She didn't wait for me to respond, just started dragging me down the path towards the hotel entrance, her grip firm and unyielding, like she was my mom and I'd just gotten caught doing something really stupid.

As we hurried down the path, the loose, floral-patterned sundress billowed around her in the breeze, giving her the appearance of a carefree tourist just soaking in the scenery. But her appearance was deceiving.

To anyone who noticed her, she was just another tourist enjoying a day in paradise, but for those who could see beyond the surface, she was a lioness in sheep's clothing, a woman who could disarm and disable an attacker in seconds without breaking a sweat.

The floppy hat and the carefree outfit were just a disguise, masking the instincts of a seasoned warrior who was always prepared for the unexpected.

As we reached the main entrance of The Cove, I could feel the heat radiating off the pavement by the valet. Tourists were milling around, completely unaware of what had just gone down a few yards away. Then, out of nowhere, a flat black Range Rover screeched to a halt in front of us. My heart was still pounding, and I was trying to catch my breath as two Hasidic Jewish men, armed to the teeth with assault weapons and looking like they meant business, stepped out and flanked her.

She finally let go of my hand and turned to face me. "Christina, why is it that you fuck up every good thing going for you?" she asked, her voice calm but sharp.

"Count yourself lucky I was watching your dumb ass and my investment."

I blinked at her, trying to process everything that had just happened. The heat, the pain, the confusion—it was all swirling around in my head, making it hard to think straight. She noticed the state I was in and pulled a water bottle and an

Hermes scarf from her bag, starting to clean the sand and blood from my face with surprising gentleness. Meanwhile, the guards silently kept a watchful eye on everything around us.

"I suggest you head back to the ship, have a drink, and get your shit together," she said, her voice softening slightly. "Heaven knows you want one. You're a bit of a yard sale right now. I'll connect with you later with instructions on your next move. Keep this to yourself, got it?"

"Who are you?" I managed to ask, my voice barely a whisper.

Sliding into the backseat of the Range Rover, she paused before closing the door closed, a faint smile on her lips.

"Who am I? I'm the only one in your corner by the looks of it."

The guards climbed into the vehicle, and the Range Rover sped off, leaving me standing there, still trying to catch my breath, the world spinning around me.

Everything hit me at once, and before I knew it, I was screaming–screaming out all the anger, frustration, and fear. I stood there, fists clenched, until the scream died in my throat and all that was left was exhaustion.

The skinny Bahamian valet stood there silently, staring at me for a moment longer than comfortable. His dark eyes traced my disheveled appearance, his lips pressed into a neutral line. I could feel the weight of his gaze, though he did his best to mask it. His fingers twitched at his sides, fidgeting nervously as if unsure whether to offer assistance or pretend he hadn't seen anything at all.

Slowly, as if by some internal cue, he diverted his eyes, shifting them toward the bright blue sky and the swaying palm trees, as if nothing was amiss.

I felt a surge of frustration rising in my chest, the kind that came from knowing you looked a mess and people were trying their best not to notice. The valet's attempt to maintain a facade of casual disinterest only made me more self-conscious.

I could practically hear his thoughts: What the hell just happened? But he kept it all buttoned up behind a veneer of polite detachment. Don't ask. Don't tell.

I wiped my hand across her face, trying to clear the damp strands of hair clinging to my forehead. The remnants of sweat and sand still stuck to my skin, making everything feel sticky and uncomfortable.

"*Everyting* okay, miss?" the valet finally asked, his voice soft, almost hesitant, as if he were walking on eggshells with the question. His Bahamian accent added a melodic lilt to his words, but it didn't mask the awkwardness in his tone.

"Yeah, just peachy," I said, with as much sarcasm as I could muster. I forced a tight-lipped smile, hoping it would communicate the message: Please, just drop it.

The valet gave a small nod, his expression unchanging, and went back to staring at the horizon as if the scene in front of him was the most ordinary thing in the world. It was clear he wasn't about to involve himself in whatever mess I had been through–self-preservation instincts, I supposed. The less he knew, the safer he was.

I wiped the last of the blood from my face, blew the sand off and out of my sunglasses and slipped them on to hide the damage, and walked into the hotel's main entrance like nothing had happened. The blast of air conditioning hit me like a wall, and I shivered despite the heat outside. But I kept walking, head held high, trying to figure out what the hell just happened and what I was going to do next.

I staggered through the dimly lit corridor of The Cove, my vision still hazy from the scuffle that had just gone down. My heart was pounding, and I could feel the sting of sand still clinging to my skin, irritating the cuts and bruises that had started to form. I adjusted my crooked sunglasses, feeling the grit between my fingers as I tried to regain some semblance of composure.

The hotel's interior, with its sleek design and luxurious finishings, felt at odds with my current state. My once pristine outfit—a casual yet stylish Shipboard Media polo shirt that I wear so guest know we work for the cruise line—was now a rumpled mess, stained with patches of sand and blood. My comfy Nike runners full of sand, scratch against the marble floor with each step, echoing the disarray that clung to me like a second skin. My hair a mess and full of sand.

As I weaved through the hallways, dodging clusters of guests who were blissfully unaware of the chaos that had just unfolded, I couldn't help but notice the contrast between their carefree expressions and my current disheveled state.

A couple passed by, their laughter ringing in my ears as they chatted about dinner plans, completely oblivious to the war zone I had just escaped from. Another group of tourists, clad in colorful beachwear, were huddled around a map, discussing which poolside bar to hit next. They barely gave me a second glance as I sidestepped them, trying not to draw any more attention than necessary.

The opulence of the resort, with its grand archways and cascading indoor waterfalls, suddenly felt suffocating. Each step felt like a mile as I made my way through, what felt like, a labyrinthine hallways, my mind racing with a mix of panic and determination. I could feel the stares of a few curious onlookers, their eyes lingering a moment too long on the wild-haired woman who clearly didn't fit the picture-perfect image of a resort guest.

I could almost hear their thoughts: Who let this mess in here? Then my nose started to bleed again. Great.

Pushing through the grand doors that led out to the pool deck, the bright sunlight hit me like a slap to the face. I quickly grab a napkin from a dirty tray of drinks and hold it to my bloody nose. The sudden transition from the cool interior to the blazing heat of the afternoon made me squint, the intensity of the sun only adding to the headache that was building behind my eyes. The sound of splashing water and distant laughter filled the air, a stark contrast to the quiet tension that had filled the corridors.

The sight of glistening bodies Basking in the sun made me acutely aware of just how out of place I was, now.

I'm a mess–bruised, beaten, and barely holding it together. I find Emily and Becca exactly where I left them, Becca blissfully unaware, headphones on, world tuned out. I arrive, pull the bloody napkin down my nose, and toss it aside.

"We gotta get out of here!" I gasp, pulling Emily up so fast she stumbles.

"What the fuck happened? Are you OK?" Emily's face is a mixture of concern and confusion as she takes in my battered appearance.

"No. Some fucking guys kicked the shit out of me around the corner," I spit out the words, and some blood, as anger and adrenaline courses through me. "They were looking for you and Becca. They said some guy Bas is pissed and sent them to bring you back."

Emily's drink crashes to the deck, splattering ice and liquid like her suddenly shattered peace. It suddenly clicks, like a lightbulb going off in my head–Emily isn't just scared; she knows these thugs. She knows exactly who they are, and I can feel the weight of that realization settle in my gut. What fuck have I gotten myself into?

"The guys are still around. We *need* to go. This will not end well if they find us," I urge, my voice a harsh whisper of urgency.

As Emily processed my breathless revelation, a chill that had nothing to do with the pool water trickled down her spine. The bright Bahamian sun, moments ago a comforting embrace, now seemed glaring and intrusive, casting harsh shadows that mirrored the dark turn in her thoughts. The carefree bubble that had enveloped her since arriving at The Cove burst abruptly, replaced by a sharp, clawing anxiety.

The name Bas, tied to a threat so visceral, reverberated in her mind like a sinister echo. The fact that he had dispatched thugs to retrieve her and Becca, in another country, transformed her perception of their situation from a distant danger to an immediate threat. Emily's heart pounded with a ferocity that drowned out the mundane sounds of poolside laughter and splashing water. My hands felt clammy, my throat dry, as the implications of my words fully registered.

Gone was the lighthearted tourist, sipping cocktails by the pool without a care in the world. In her place stood a woman suddenly aware of her vulnerability, of the precariousness of her seemingly idyllic surroundings. The realization that their actions on the cruise could draw such a targeted response from Bas was both frightening and infuriating. Emily felt a surge of protectiveness over Becca, coupled with a fierce determination not to be intimidated or controlled by anyone, least of all a man like Bas.

Emily's mind raced with potential escape routes and plans. The weight of responsibility to ensure their safety pressed heavily on her, but beneath that weight was a budding resolve. Emily knew they needed to act swiftly and smartly, not just to evade Bas's immediate reach but to dismantle the hold he seemed to have on their lives.

Snapping into action, Emily yanks the headphones off Becca's head. "Becca, we have to return to the ship. It's leaving soon. Grab your stuff, let's go."

The three of us bolt from The Cove pool area without a glance back, our footsteps echoing like a warning behind us. Hearts racing, we weave through the chaos, dodging sunbathers and servers like it's some twisted obstacle course. Just another day in paradise–if paradise came with a side of panic.

Chapter 22

SUN, SAND, AND A SUCKER PUNCH

After the unexpected thrashing they received at the hands of the enigmatic Tourist, Luis and Angel found themselves staggering back to the taxi stand at The Cove, each step punctuated by groans of pain and the muffled sounds of the bustling hotel grounds.

The sharp, tropical sunlight seemed to mock their defeat as they tried to navigate through the crowd, blending their battered forms with the casual elegance around them. Angel, clutching his jaw, spat blood with every other step, mumbling curses under his breath.

Seven of his teeth had been dislodged in a manner so brutal, it seemed the Tourist had been extracting years of pent-up vengeance rather than merely incapacitating him. Luis, on the other hand, held his broken nose, the blood staining his hand and dripping onto his shirt, creating a stark contrast against the crisp white fabric.

They made a pathetic sight–two tough men reduced to stumbling wrecks. The pain was excruciating, but the humiliation of being bested so thoroughly stung even more. As they reached the taxi stand, the attendant gave them a wide berth, eyeing their disheveled appearance with evident alarm.

"Take us to the nearest hospital," Luis managed to say through clenched teeth, his voice muffled by his swollen nose.

The taxi driver hesitated, his gaze flicking to the rearview mirror where the reflection of their bloody and bruised faces gave him pause.

"Move it!" Angel snapped, the pain igniting a fierce impatience. Reluctantly, the driver complied, pulling away from the curb with a speed that suggested he couldn't wait to be rid of them.

Inside the cab, the air was thick with the iron scent of blood and the harsh breathing of two men in agony. Angel used his phone's front-facing camera to inspect the damage perpetrated to his face and to count the missing teeth.

Luis fumbled with his phone, his fingers slick with blood as he dialed Bas's number. The call went through, and soon, Bas's voice, icy and expectant, filled the tiny space.

"We got... ambushed," Luis started, pausing to suck in a breath as a jolt of pain shot through his nose. "The target had... backup. A woman. She took us down before we could complete the extraction."

On the other end of the line, Bas's response was a cold silence that seemed to stretch over miles of ocean. When he finally spoke, his voice was a calm that belied the fury brewing beneath the surface. "What? You were taken down by a woman? Both of you? Was it the shopping guide, Christina?"

The humiliation was complete. Angel snatched the phone from Luis, his tone defensive. "No. She was a tourist walking by. She wasn't ordinary, Bas! She knew exactly how to hit. Seven teeth, Bas! She kicked seven damn teeth out of my mouth!"

Luis grabbed the phone back, a mix of pain and anger flashing in his eyes. "And she broke my nose. We didn't see her coming. It's not like we—"

Bas cut him off, his voice sharp as a knife. "I don't pay you to get beaten by tourists, I pay you to handle things smoothly. This incompetence will have consequences."

As the call ended, the silence that followed was filled with the harsh reality of their failure. Angel and Luis glanced at each other, each nursing not only physical wounds but also the sting of Bas's words.

"Who the hell was she?" Angel muttered, wiping the blood from his mouth with the back of his hand.

"No idea, but she's trouble," Luis replied, his usual composure drowned out by the throbbing in his face.

The rest of the ride was spent in a bitter exchange of blame and the recounting of their respective beatings. "You should have seen it coming," Angel grumbled, wincing as he prodded at the empty spaces in his gums.

"You think I let her break my nose on purpose?" Luis retorted, his frustration boiling over. "Maybe if you had taken the left side like we planned–"

"Enough," Angel cut him off, the pain making him irritable. "We messed up. Bas isn't going to let this slide."

The taxi pulled up to the hospital, and they shuffled out, each step reminding them of their defeat. As they entered the emergency room, the clinical brightness felt harsh, unwelcoming, yet it was a sanctuary from the judgment waiting for them back at their Base.

Back at the mansion, Bas paced, his mind racing through the implications of this failure.

A job that should have been straightforward had unraveled spectacularly, leaving him to reconsider the reliability of his men. This setback was not just a physical defeat for Luis and Angel; it was a strategic blow for him, forcing a recalibration of plans that couldn't afford disruption.

This was more than a physical brawl lost–it was a stark reminder that in the shadows of the underworld, the unexpected could be lurking around any corner, ready to upset the precarious balance of power. For Bas, it was back to the drawing board, with the added burden of reinforcing his ranks and perhaps, reevaluating the loyalty and effectiveness of his closest enforcers.

In the seclusion of his study, Bas sat enveloped in the shadows that seemed almost palpable, mirroring the turbulent thoughts swirling in his mind. The room, usually a sanctuary of strategic planning and control, felt stiflingly close as he mulled over the phone call from Angel. His fingers drummed a slow, steady rhythm on the mahogany desk, each tap a punctuation mark in his internal monologue of frustration and recalibration.

His thoughts were abruptly interrupted by the soft click of the door. Alejandra entered, her presence as commanding as ever. She moved with a fluid grace that belied the seriousness of her intent. The subtle swish of her silk dress seemed incongruously gentle in the charged atmosphere.

"How did the recovery go?" Her voice was calm, almost casual, but her eyes, sharp and discerning, searched his for the unspoken truths that lingered beneath the surface.

Bas's expression hardened as he met her gaze, the weight of disappointment and irritation clear in his features. "It didn't. Luis and Angel were incapacitated. Beaten by a tourist, of all things," he confessed, the words tasting bitter as they left his mouth.

Aly's eyebrows arched slightly, her initial surprise morphing quickly into a cool, measured disdain. "A tourist?" she echoed, the word dripping with disbelief and a thinly veiled scorn. "And our two most reliable men were laid low by some guy on vacation?"

"The tourist was a woman." Bas reveals.

Aly paused, her expression unreadable as she absorbed Bas's words. The revelation that a woman had single-handedly bested their most capable enforcers was unexpected, and her eyes flickered with a mix of surprise and a recalibrated respect for the unseen adversary.

"A woman," she repeated slowly, the corners of her mouth twitching into a wry smile that didn't quite reach her eyes. Her gaze sharpened, focusing intently on Bas as if seeing the scenario play out before her. "That's... interesting."

She leaned back against the desk, her mind racing through the implications. "It appears we underestimated our opponents—not just in strength but in capability. Luis and

Angel are no amateurs; for a woman to take them down... she must be exceptionally skilled. Trained, perhaps."

The thought seemed to intrigue as much as it irked her. Aly's stance on power was rooted in respect, earned through strength and intelligence. "This woman," she continued thoughtfully, "she's not just a random tourist caught up in the moment. She could be a significant variable we failed to account for."

Aly's expression then hardened, the initial flicker of amusement at the gender surprise shifting to a strategic contemplation. "We need to find out who she is," she stated decisively, her voice carrying the weight of command. "Her involvement isn't coincidental. She could be connected to Emily and Becca more deeply than we anticipated, or she might be an operative protecting them."

The room was charged with a new energy, a mix of challenge and opportunity. "Let's not make the mistake of underestimating her again Based on gender. We should prepare for a formidable adversary," Aly concluded, her eyes alight with the thrill of the hunt. "This woman could change the playing field, Bas. We need to adapt our strategy accordingly."

Her words hung in the air, a testament to her adaptability and foresight. Aly wasn't just contemplating a setback; she was already moving chess pieces in a game that had suddenly become much more complex.

Bas knew her critique was as much about their failure as it was about the implications of that failure. "They underestimated the threat. It won't happen again," Bas assured her, his voice a low growl of promise.

Aly moved closer, perching on the edge of the desk, her posture relaxed but her mind anything but. "We can't afford such... amateur mistakes, Bas. This isn't just about failing to retrieve Emily and Becca–it's about how we're perceived by everyone watching. Strength is currency in our world, and right now, we're paying out more than we're earning."

Bas nodded, the truth of her words sinking in deep. "I know. We'll handle it when they return to the U.S. It's better we deal with this at home, avoid creating any international incidents. We have enough leverage and resources stateside to manage this quietly and efficiently."

Aly considered this, her mind already turning over the possible scenarios, calculating risks and plotting courses of action. "Make sure Luis and Angel understand the gravity of their failure. We rely on fear and respect, Bas. Without them, we're vulnerable."

"They understand," Bas assured her, though the assurance was more for himself. He planned to make an example of the situation–one that would ensure such a failure was never repeated.

"We'll tighten our network, keep a closer watch on Emily and Becca's movements. When they step back onto U.S. soil, we'll be ready," Aly strategized out loud, her brain working through logistics with a cold efficiency that had always been her strength.

Bas's features softened slightly, admiration mixing with affection. "What would I do without you?" he murmured, reaching out to touch her hand lightly.

Aly's smile was slight but genuine. "Let's hope you never have to find out." Her tone was light, but the underlying message was clear: they were in this together, for better or worse.

"Once we have the girls back, we'll need to reassess our operations. Perhaps it's time to expand our oversight, tighten security measures around our more vulnerable assets," Aly suggested, her mind always one step ahead.

Bas nodded, his respect for her acumen a cornerstone of their partnership. "Agreed. I'll have our team on standby, ready to move as soon as they arrive. And this time, there will be no mistakes."

Aly stood, her silhouette framed by the dim light filtering through the blinds. "Ensure that everyone understands the stakes, Bas. We cannot show weakness, not now." Her voice was as much a command as it was advice, a reminder of the empire they had built together–one forged in the fires of ambition and the shadows of ruthlessness.

As she left the room, Bas felt the weight of the empire on his shoulders, heavier in that moment than it had been in a long time. But alongside the weight was a fierce, unyielding determination. They would recover from this setback. They would deal with Emily and Becca. And they would remind everyone why their names were spoken with a mix of respect and fear. In the world they navigated, every failure was merely the setup for a greater comeback–and Bas was ready to prove that once again.

Chapter 23

CLEAN UP OR CLEAR OUT

Stumbling into The Jewelry Box felt like crashing into another world—a sanctuary glittering with gems and precious metals that contrasted sharply with my battered appearance. I was a mess; my face was a map of bruises and dried blood.

Sunny, the store's flamboyant manager, was a whirlwind of color and motion, his attire as loud as his personality, as always. As soon as he saw me, his usual exuberance flipped into high gear.

"Christina! What on earth happened to you?" Sunny's thick Pakistani accent was thick with concern as he rushed over, his vibrant silk shirt a blur of electric blues and pinks.

"You should see the other guy, Sunny," I managed to joke through the pain, trying to lighten the mood even though every inch of me screamed in protest.

Sunny was instantly all business, snapping orders at Surjeet, his assistant who seemed perpetually on the brink of a nervous breakdown thanks to Sunny's explosive energy. "Surjeet, first aid kit, now!"

While Surjeet scuttled away, I sank into one of the plush velvet stools, by the diamond counter, that made The Jewelry Box feel more like a lavish boudoir than a shop. As I tried to collect my thoughts, Sunny hovered, his concern etched across his normally cheerful face.

"Who did this to you, Christina? Tell me everything," Sunny insisted, his tone a mix of anger and worry.

"It was a couple of thugs," I began, wincing as I adjusted my sitting position, Sunny adjusting the mirror on the counter as Surjeet arrived with a first aid kit that had seen better days. Sunny tried his best to clean me up.

"They were asking me questions that I didn't have answers to. You wouldn't believe it, Sunny, but I was saved by this... this superhero tourist or something. She was incredible– beautiful, exotic, and looked like she could kill a man with her pinky."

Sunny's eyes widened. "A superhero, here in Nassau?" His skepticism was palpable, but then again, Sunny lived for drama and intrigue.

"Yes, and not just any superhero. She was like something out of a movie, you know? Came out of nowhere, knocked those goons down like they were nothing. She was... I don't know, she was something else," I explained, still in disbelief over the encounter myself.

As I recounted the details, Sunny seemed to absorb every word, his usual flamboyance dimming slightly as he processed the gravity of the situation. "And you have no idea who she was?"

"No clue. But she was like a guardian angel or something. Just appeared when I needed her most." My voice trailed off as I glanced around The Jewelry Box, feeling suddenly out of place amidst the luxury, my beaten state contrasting sharply with the polished surfaces and sparkling jewelry.

I fretted aloud about my next steps, "Sunny, I look like hell. How am I supposed to visit all the stores looking like this? I'll scare off the customers!"

Before Sunny could respond, and deep in my recount of the terrifying events, he slowly moved away, his expression unreadable. I was too wrapped up in my own discomfort to notice at first, until I felt someone in the space where Sunny once sat. Turning, I found myself staring not into Sunny's colorful visage but at the enigmatic figure of the woman who had saved me.

She was indeed beautiful, with a regal bearing that made her seem both untouchable and intensely present. Her eyes were a striking shade of green, and her hair, a cascade of dark brown curls, framed her face with an air of mystery.

"I'm Yael," she introduced herself simply, her voice a smooth contralto that hinted at a thousand secrets. "I'm the owner of The Jewelry Box. And the one who provided your loan."

My mouth went dry. "You–You're the one who saved me."

Yael nodded, a small smile playing on her lips. "I have a vested interest in keeping my top salespeople alive and well, Christina." Yael continued where Sunny left off, applying ointment to my cut lip and fixing my hair as we spoke. "And you, my dear, have been breaking records, here at The Jewelry Box, left and right."

I sat there, dumbfounded, my earlier confusion morphing into a mix of awe and a strange sense of relief. As I looked for the right words, a man standing behind the counter by the back office caught my eye–a man in Hasidic attire, complete with peyot and a black hat, cradling what looked unmistakably like an AR-15 assault rifle. He was one of the men guarding the Tourist back at The Cove by the Atlantis Hotel.

Here was this powerful, mysterious woman who not only owned the store but had stepped into the fray to pull me out of it.

"Thank you," I finally managed to stammer out, my usual sass deflated by the gravity of her presence.

Yael's smile widened, but it didn't quite reach her eyes. "You're welcome."

Yael was a striking figure, poised and composed, with an aura that commanded attention without a word. "It's not every day you get saved by a vigilante jewelry store owner." I say looking up to Yael like a fan meeting their idol. "Where did you learn how to do all that...ass kicking?"

"I'm not a vigilante, but I don't like to see men overstepping their bound with women. I'm from Israel and was in an elite special forces unit. Enough about me." catching herself revealing too much.

Yael offered a small, knowing smile as she sat opposite me. Her eyes, sharp and assessing, seemed to take in every detail. "I'm glad I was there, Christina. It's not often I get to make such a dramatic entrance. But let's talk about why you were targeted. This isn't just about being in the wrong place at the wrong time, is it?"

I sighed, the weight of the world settling on my shoulders. "It's complicated. I've been... bending some rules to make ends meet. It's caught up with me now."

Yael's demeanor remained unflinchingly calm. "In this line of work, the lines often blur. I understand more than you might expect. But bending rules can become breaking them if you're not careful. What's your plan with Emily, and the escort Becca, now?"

I couldn't believe she knew about what was going on. How? That just happened, like, yesterday. Terrified, I shook my head, a bitter laugh escaping my lips. "Plan? I was mostly trying to stay afloat. Now, I think I'm just trying not to drown."

"Surviving isn't living, Christina," Yael remarked softly, her tone serious yet sympathetic. "You're playing a dangerous game. And from what I've seen today, it's one you're not fully prepared for."

"Guess I never really was," I admitted, meeting her gaze. "I'm good at the sales part, at the charm and the spiel. But when it comes to the cutthroat side of things, I'm out of my depth."

"That's where I come in," Yael said, leaning forward, her hands clasped together. "Consider me a... strategic ally. But, remember, Christina, keep driving sales here. And pay off your loan before you either get yourself killed or fired. You're no good to anyone after that." She stressed.

"And let me know if you need more funds. You know, for any other unexpected expenses," she added with a sly grin, like we both knew '*unexpected expenses*' was code for something way more sketchy than cab fare. Her eyes lingered on mine for a second longer than they should, making it clear there was more to her offer than just money.

"If Artem gets too aggressive, you let me know. I have ways of dealing with men like him."

I raised an eyebrow, a mix of skepticism and curiosity lighting up my bruised face. "And why would you help me? What's in it for you?"

Yael's smile was enigmatic. "Let's just say, I invest wisely. Keeping you safe ensures my interests are protected as well. Plus, I despise bullies."

"And Artem is definitely that," I muttered. "Walking into CDG is like entering a lion's den. He's always there, watching, waiting for me to slip up."

"Then we'll make sure you're prepared," Yael assured me, her confidence infectious. "Artem relies on intimidation. If you show him you're not afraid, that you have powerful friends, he'll think twice before crossing you."

"Sounds good in theory," I mused, still trying to wrap my head around the turn my life had taken in just one day, and how the hell she knew about Emily and Becca.

The conversation was surreal. Here I was, bruised and battered, receiving business advice from a woman who could probably afford to buy the entire island but chose instead to run a jewelry store and occasionally play the hero. This was no ordinary jewelry store owner, and I was no ordinary shopping guide.

"Life isn't lived in theories, Christina. It's lived in actions. Be bold, be smart, and let me worry about the rest."

She took my hand, feeling the firm grip of an ally, I couldn't help but feel a spark of hope. Maybe, just maybe, I wasn't as alone as I had thought. With Yael's backing, I could navigate the treacherous waters I'd found myself in. It was a small comfort, but in my world, small comforts could make all the difference.

As Yael walked away toward the back office of The Jewelry Box, the reality of my situation settled in. I was in deep–maybe deeper than I'd ever been. But for the first time, I felt like maybe, just maybe, I wasn't in it alone.

As Yael disappeared into the labyrinth of glittering displays, Sunny hurried back to my side, first aid kit in hand. His usual flamboyant demeanor was replaced by a more subdued urgency, his eyes darting around to ensure no one was close enough to overhear us.

"Christina, you must take this seriously," Sunny whispered, his voice laden with an intensity I'd rarely seen in him. He began to carefully tend to the cuts on my face, his hands surprisingly steady despite the vibrant tremor of his personality.

"You've been given a second chance here, a lifeline. Yael isn't just any store owner; she's your savior in more ways than one. You can't afford to mess this up," he continued, dabbing gently at a cut above my eyebrow. The sting was sharp, but his words stung deeper, echoing the gravity of my situation.

I nodded, absorbing his concern. "I know, Sunny. I didn't even realize who she was until she sat down next to me. This changes everything."

Sunny glanced around once more before leaning in closer, his voice dropping to a near murmur. "Yael is more than she appears. She's connected, powerful. And she has resources that we can't even begin to comprehend. If she's taken an interest in you, it's because she sees potential–or utility. Either way, you need to leverage this. Be smart, Christina."

His fingers were deft as he applied a small bandage, his care a stark contrast to his usually boisterous self. "I've seen many come and go, burn out or get run out because they couldn't handle the pressure or navigate the complexities of these relationships. Don't be one of them."

"Thanks, Sunny. I'll tread carefully. I promise." I say.

Sunny finished and stood back, examining his handiwork with a critical eye. "There, you look... well, less like someone used your face as a punching bag."

I managed a weak smile. "Thanks for patching me up, Sunny. And for the advice."

He nodded, his expression serious. "Just remember, Christina, people like Yael don't do things out of the goodness of their hearts. There's always an angle, always a strategy. You need to be one step ahead, or you'll find yourself two steps behind."

With that, he busied himself with cleaning up the first aid supplies, but his words lingered in the air between us. Sunny had seen his fair share of the dark underbelly of the luxury retail world, and his advice was not to be taken lightly.

As I stood up, steadying myself on the plush chair, I felt the weight of the path before me. Aligning with Yael could either be the best decision I had ever made or a dangerous game that could end disastrously. The bruising on my face was a stark reminder of the risks involved, but now, with potential new allies like Yael and always reliable confidants like Sunny, I felt a renewed sense of purpose.

I needed to navigate this new relationship with precision and care, mindful of the potential benefits and wary of the inherent risks. It was a tightrope walk, but I was no stranger to balancing acts. With Sunny's cautionary words echoing in my mind, I was ready to step back into the fray, a little wiser and a lot more wary.

I limped my way through the string of small boutiques and kiosks dotted downtown Nassau's Bay Street, the port's main drag. Each shop was a blur of vibrant colors, eager tourists, and the overpowering scent of fresh leather and ocean spray. Despite my efforts to make a 'quick appearance' at each, my mind was reeling from the day's earlier events, and my body wasn't faring much better.

As I stumbled toward the next store on the map, I ran into Victor making his rounds picking up fresh brochures from all of the store. Victor's sharp intake of breath was almost comical if it hadn't been for the worry that immediately clouded his eyes. "Christina, who did this to you?" he growled, his Russian accent thickening with every word, like vodka poured over ice –chilling and stark.

"I tripped earlier, it's nothing, Victor," I tried to brush off, but he wasn't having any of it.

"This is not right. I will help you get the person who 'tripped' you," he vowed, each word a hammer of cold resolve. Victor might look like he was straight out of a spy thriller, but his loyalty was the kind that you couldn't buy, only earn.

I shook my head, a smile tugging at the corners of my bruised face. "Thanks, Victor, but it's more complicated than that. I've... I've gotten into something bad." I trailed off, the weight of my confession hanging between us.

Victor leaned in, his expression serious. "Christina, you must ask for help. This is what friends do, yes?"

For a moment, I smiled. His use of the word 'friend' was surprising. But the smile didn't last long. I sighed, my stubbornness flaring up. "I know, I just..." I couldn't finish the sentence. Asking for help felt like admitting defeat, and that wasn't something I was ready to do, not yet.

"I'll meet you back on the ship" I exclaimed giving Victor a weak pat on the shoulder and making my exit, heading towards my next stop: Caribbean Diamonds and Gems (CDG), Artem's flagship store.

The cool air of CDG hit me like a wall as I entered, a stark contrast to the humid heat outside. I tried to do my best to slip in without being noticed, but who was I kidding. There were more security cameras in this place than a Vegas Casino.

The store was bustling, with a young couple examining engagement rings at the counter, their faces lit with the soft glow of new love and bright display lights.

I approached them with a practiced smile. The young woman spotted me and beamed "Hey, it's the *Shopping Girl*, from the ship. Babe, ask her for help." She cooed to her man. He notices the bandages but quickly averts his eyes.

"How can I help you celebrate your love today?" I began, slipping into my professional persona despite the throbbing pain in my head.

As I started guiding them through the selections, the Bahamian sales woman who was helping vanished and Artem appeared across the counter. His presence was always imposing, but today it felt particularly oppressive. His eyes narrowed as he took in my disheveled appearance.

"Missing most of the day, and then showing up looking like a street brawl participant, Christina? This is not the image we want to project," he hissed under his breath, keeping his smile intact for the couple.

I met his gaze without flinching, the image of Yael, my unexpected guardian angel, bolstering my courage.

"You know, Artem, diamonds are a lot like life. They appear tough, but they require careful handling and polish if you want them to shine bright," I replied, my voice steady.

Artem's smile twitched. "Indeed, and like life, they can also shatter under extreme pressure," he retorted smoothly, turning his attention back to the diamonds. "For instance, this exquisite piece," he gestured to a diamond ring in front of the couple, "needs the right setting to truly shine, much like how people need the right... environment to perform their best."

The couple glanced at us, a flicker of confusion passing between them. They could sense the tension, the undercurrent of something darker beneath our polished exteriors.

I leaned in, lowering my voice so only Artem and the couple could hear.

"And yet, despite the pressure, diamonds can cut through just about anything. The right stone will find a way to emerge stronger, more brilliant."

Artem pulls out a beautiful two and half carat solitaire diamond and hands it to the young woman. While the couple drool over the exquisite brilliance of the diamond, he and I get into it.

Artem's jaw clenched. "Be careful, Christina. Diamonds cut, yes, but they can also be cut imperfectly. And when they do, they become... less valuable, more trouble than they're worth."

The young man of the couple shifted uncomfortably. "We just... uh, we want a ring that shows our commitment... not one that's going to cause drama." He hands the ring back to Artem.

I gave them an apologetic smile. "Of course, let's find you something with a bit less... history."

As they moved down the counter, Artem leaned closer. "Watch yourself, Christina. You're not as untouchable as you think."

I straightened, feeling the sting of his words but not letting it show. "Neither are you, Artem. Remember, even the most beautiful diamond can still end up in the wrong hands."

He scowled, then turned his attention back to the couple, his salesman smile snapping back into place.

As I helped the young couple, my mind was racing. The game I was playing was dangerous, maybe more dangerous than I'd realized. But with Yael's cryptic protection and Victor's unwavering support, I felt a strange concoction of dread and exhilaration.

I knew one thing for sure: Artem Hadad, with all his power and threats, was not going to scare me off. The stakes were high, but I wasn't ready to fold—not yet.

Chapter 24

THAT'S WHAT FRIENDS ARE FOR

As the dessert plates were cleared from our corner table, the cacophony of scraping chairs and excited chatter filled the air. Guests, eager to secure the best seats for the farewell show, scurried towards the theater like ants to a picnic.

I couldn't help but smile at the spectacle, despite the weight of the day's events still pressing heavily on my mind. The day had indeed gone sideways, starting with the harrowing encounter with the thugs.

Walking from shop to shop in Nassau today, I was constantly looking over my shoulder, the fear of another attack making my heart race with every shadow that twitched. The vibrant streets I once loved now felt like a maze of potential threats. How did they know I knew Emily and Becca? What did they want with me? Why would they use violence on *me*? These questions, along with about a million others, filled my every thought.

When I finally returned to my cabin after my day in Nassau, the relief was palpable. I stripped off the dust of the day and stepped into the shower, letting the hot water cascade over me, attempting to wash away the negativity, the fear, the grime of vulnerability. Yet, the water couldn't rinse away the deep-seated anxiety that had taken root. Only the remnants of sand in my hair.

Under the shower, my thoughts turned to Emily. Her carefree nature today contrasted sharply with my own frayed nerves. Could I really get involved with her deeper in her chaotic world? Was it smart to fall further into a situation fraught with danger, all because of what? Feelings that might not even be fully reciprocated?

These questions haunted me as I dressed for dinner with the girls, the fabric of my gown brushing against skin still tingling from the heat of the shower. I have to hand it to myself –I did a damn good job hiding the bruises with makeup. You'd never know there's a dark purple mark under this perfectly blended concealer.

As I prepared to leave my cabin, the weight of responsibility for Emily and Becca's safety pressed heavily on me. I needed to keep them safe, not just from Bas and his goons but perhaps, from my own reckless heart.

At the dinner table, I kept it light and friendly since this was our last evening together.

"Before you two join the stampede to find seats for the show," I said, reaching for the small package I'd carefully hidden under the table upon my arrival. "I have something for you, Becca."

I pushed the beautifully wrapped gift across to her, the twinkling lights of the dining room reflecting off the metallic paper. Becca's eyes widened with surprise and curiosity, a delightful contrast to the usual savvy composure she carried.

"Today went a little sideways for all of us," I confessed as she peeled back the layers, "but, Becca, I couldn't have done any of this without you and Emily. This week, and the sales recorded in the stores, is going to help me out tremendously."

The final layer fell away to reveal a luxurious Omega watch box. Emily leaned in, her interest piqued. "What is this? Come on, open it already, Becca."

Becca's fingers trembled slightly as she lifted the lid, her gasp audible when the contents came into view.

She carefully removed the Omega Seamaster Aqua Terra from its leather-wrapped home, her eyes sparkling as much as the watch. Stuffed in the box along with the watch was an envelope of cash. Payment for services, to Patrick, rendered.

Becca picks up and opens the envelop, quickly flips through the stack of Benjamin's sleeping inside, looks at me then Emily and says "Make sure you thank Bas for this, Emily. I'll come on a cruise anytime he needs me to. This was fun!" Emily and I exchange glances knowing Becca is still in the dark of this operation. Becca stuffed the envelop of cash into her clutch then returns her focus to the watch.

"It's beautiful," she murmured as she picks up the watch, almost in awe.

Emily helped fasten the new watch onto Becca's wrist, her movements gentle and precise.

"This is the Omega Seamaster Aqua Terra and it is an impeccably handcrafted timepiece," I explained, watching their interactions with a mix of satisfaction and a twinge of envy. "My boss owns this exact model. It sports a self-winding movement with Co-Axial escapement, free sprung-balance, 2 barrels mounted in series, automatic winding in both directions, and the power reserve is 60 hours."

"I don't know what you said, but, I love it!" Becca laughed, her gaze fixed on the shimmering dial.

"Em, your memory is scary good," she added, giving Emily a playful nudge.

"Yeah, she's the brains; I'm just the brawn," I joked, trying to lighten the mood as the shadow of the day's earlier violence lingered at the edges of my mind, and clearly on my face.

After a pause, I stood up, feeling the need to move, to do something. "I have to get backstage for the farewell show. You girls should go get a good seat; I make an appearance onstage. I'll find you after the show. We'll get drinks. Thanks again."

As I squeezed Emily's hand, a jolt of something undefinable shot through me—appreciation, fear, maybe even a hint of desire. It was complicated, and as I walked away, the complexity of my feelings for Emily swirled chaotically within me.

As I slipped through the side door of the Starlight Theatre's backstage, the pulsing energy of the cruises final show's preparation washed over me like a wave. The air was thick with anticipation and the scent of hairspray and stage makeup. It was a familiar chaos, one that somehow managed to soothe the frazzled nerves I'd been nursing all day since the altercation in Nassau. I weaved my way through racks of glittering costumes and busy stagehands, my eyes searching for one person in particular.

I spotted Victor by the dancers' prep area, adjusting his costume with the precision of a seasoned pro. His presence was a calming force amid the whirlwind of activity, always focused, always ready. Despite being far from his home in Russia, he carried a poise that was both reassuring and distinctly grounded.

"Hey, Victor," I called out as I approached, watching his face light up with a mix of relief and welcome.

"Christina! There you are. How you feeling?" his thick Russian accent coloring his words, his eyes held a hint of genuine appreciation.

I admitted "I'm feeling sore and I'm sure it's going to get a lot worse."

Victor nodded as I pulled an envelope from my bag. "Here, I want you to have this." I handed him the envelope, heavier than usual amount I pay him, filled not just with gratitude but with tangible appreciation.

He took it, a questioning raise of his eyebrow giving way to surprise as he peeked inside. His eyes widened slightly as he realized it contained double the usual amount. A broad smile broke across his face, lighting up his features with joy and relief.

"Christina, this–this is too much," he began, but I cut him off with a firm shake of my head.

"No, it's not. You've been more than just an assistant; you've been a lifeline these past few days. Plus, I know this will help with... everything back home."

Victor's smile softened, a warm glow of appreciation in his eyes. "My wife will be thrilled. She's Thai, so you know. This means a lot, Christina, not just to me but to her as well. We're saving to buy bigger apartment, and maybe have baby... this will get us closer."

I nodded, understanding all too well the sacrifices made for family, for love. "I'm glad, Victor. And hey, I might need to lean on you a bit more in the coming days. Things are... well, they're a bit complicated right now."

Victor's expression turned serious, the joviality slipping into a mask of readiness. "You know I here for whatever you need, Christina. There's more going on than just silly little diamond sales, isn't there?"

I hesitated, the weight of trust and the burden of my current troubles balancing on the edge of my confession. "Yeah, there's a lot more," I admitted, lowering my voice even though the din of backstage chatter would likely drown out my words. "It's not just about the shops. There are... complications. With some guests. And maybe some non-guests too."

Victor nodded, his face setting into lines of determination. "Whatever it is, consider me on your side. I take care of things for you. Like KGB." He ends with a wink. I question if that meant more than it should.

"Thank you, Victor," I said, the relief flooding through me so intensely it was almost palpable. "Really, thank you."

He slapped me on the shoulder, a gesture of camaraderie and solidarity. As I turned to join the rest of the performers and crew, I felt at home with each person knowing they were a vital thread in the tapestry of tonight's production.

As I pushed past some heavy curtains, the resonant laughs and applause for the ventriloquist performing echoed back to me, a reassuring sound that the night was off to a great start. I paused, my eyes scanning the darkened space backstage for Camila. There she was, a solitary figure by the wings, her posture tense, her eyes lost in thought. Such a beautiful soul. I walk over.

"Hey, can we talk?" I asked cautiously, the weight of our unresolved past heavy between us.

Camila turned, her expression a mix of resignation and forced cheerfulness. "Yeah. Sorry, I'm in my head right now. I feel foolish for thinking we could pick up where we left off from the last ship."

I sighed, the familiarity of her hurt striking a chord. "Let me explain..."

"No need. I get it. We're done. She's gorgeous. You two look great together and I'm sure whatever you two do naked is amazing," Camila's words spilled out, bitter and tinged with jealousy.

"Camila, stop!" I cut her off, my voice firm yet gentle. "I hate that you feel this way. Emily is only here for the one cruise."

I say, my voice shaky as I finally face her "My Dad died and, Camila, I'm so sorry I ghosted you. I didn't know how to handle everything when it happened. It hit me harder than I expected, like everything just crumbled overnight. I wasn't myself, and I couldn't bring myself to talk to anyone. I felt guilty, angry, and honestly, lost. I didn't want to dump all that on you, so I just... disappeared. But that wasn't fair to you, and I'm sorry."

My voice softened, "I asked Emily for help with something for work and, after tomorrow, she is gone forever. We were great together, Camila, and I really want that again."

The raw honesty seemed to stun her into silence. It even stunned me when I admitted all that. Just then, the production manager handed her a microphone, breaking the moment. She wiped away a tear, possibly of relief, before stepping out onto the stage, leaving me to reflect on our conversation. I question if all of that was the right thing to say.

Meanwhile, out in the audience, the dynamic was shifting in a different drama. Emily and Becca, seated at the back of the theatre, were joined unexpectedly by Kevin. His arrival wasn't welcomed, but it was strategic.

"Hi. I'm Kevin, Christina's boss," he introduced himself, slipping into the seat next to Emily with a sleazy ease.

Emily offered a polite smile, keeping her guard up, watching the show. "So, how is it that you know Christina?" Kevin probed, trying to glean more than was offered.

"I work in sales. After a brief, but memorable, first meeting we thought it would be mutually beneficial to collaborate," Emily responded, her tone neutral but her mind racing. This man was a thread in the tangled web she found herself caught in.

"And your friend?" Kevin leaned out, his gaze sliding past Emily to Becca.

"Becca works in 'entertainment'," Emily replied, her words cloaked in double meanings. She shoots him a 'hard-on' inducing look and Kevin is smitten.

Kevin raised his eyebrows and added "I have no doubt she's really good at whatever she does for 'entertainment'." Emily ignores the sexist comment.

Kevin hands Emily his business card. "I know a lot of people in and around Miami. If you need help finding a new job, let me know."

Emily took the card, tucking it away with a mental note to reconsider her entire career path when she got home. The complications that had unfolded over this cruise made it clear she needed a change.

Back on stage, the atmosphere shifted as Camila invited everyone to join her for a final song. A heartfelt rendition of "That's What Friends Are For". As the singers, dancers, officers, and ship management team gathered, the collective voices filled the theatre, a poignant echo of camaraderie and farewell summed up in a melancholy song.

As the song reached its crescendo, and the entire audience sings along, Camila's glance towards me was filled with something undefinable. It was a look that spoke of potential reconnections and shared pasts, of comfort and simplicity in the chaos that had become my life. Standing there, amidst the melody and the memories, I felt a pull towards her–a yearning for the calm she represented, a stark contrast to the whirlwind Emily had brought.

As the final notes of the song lingered in the air, and the teary-eyed crowd cheered, I pondered my next step. Tomorrow, everything would change. Tonight, I was just me, caught between the echoes of what had been and the whispers of what might be.

Chapter 25

DISEMBARKING DRAMA

Standing at the curb outside the cruise ship terminal, I watched the relentless Miami sun beat down on the crowd, amplifying every sensation–including the sting of the bruises darkening my face. Disembarking had been a drawn-out affair, dragging on in a slow, shuffling procession that seemed to last an eternity.

As usual, the meticulous procedure of leaving the ship, punctuated by endless lines and repetitive security checks, dimmed the glow of the vacation euphoria. Despite the magic of the past week, the tedium of departure was what lingered on every passenger's tongue, a common grievance that united strangers in mutual exasperation.

"So, what do you think? Did you girls have fun?" I asked, trying to lighten the mood as we maneuvered our suitcases along the crowded walkway.

"I had a blast! It was better than expected. I can't wait to thank Bas when I see him," Becca bubbled with genuine enthusiasm, blissfully unaware of the shadows that lurked just beneath the surface of her vacation high.

Emily, on the other hand, carried a weight that was palpable. She managed a smile for Becca's benefit but quickly turned away to capture some selfies, her actions a thin veil for the concern etching deeper lines into her youthful face. "I had a great time. But, I haven't told Becca anything about the guys that were looking for us. What the fuck am I going to do?" she whispered to me, her voice a blend of fear and frustration.

"You really need to tell Becca later today," I murmured back, a sympathetic grimace crossing my features. As Emily nodded,

I watched her turn to Becca, pulling out her phone in a practiced gesture of deception.

"Hey Becca, I just received a text from Dina. Looks like a client you had scheduled, for tonight, cancelled. Listen, you've been working non-stop lately so you should head back home, take the night off, chill in and get some rest. No need to call the office. I'll be heading there after this to get your upcoming schedule," Emily said, her tone convincingly casual.

"Aw, thanks Emily. You're always so good to me," Becca responded, her gratitude shining through her tired smile.

Emily turned back to me, a look of relief fleeting across her face. "That should buy me a little time. Are you going right back onto the ship?"

I shook my head, "No, I've been called into the Shipboard Media office for a meeting. It's in South Beach. I also have to call my mom, too. Something is up with her so I'll need to call her later. Wanna hang for a bit?" I say without thinking and questions why I just said that.

"Actually yeah, I'd like that," Emily replied, her tone hesitant but hopeful.

Becca's phone buzzes, and she glances down at the screen. 'Your UberSUV will arrive in one minute.' She looks up and spots a black SUV pulling up right in front of her.

Thinking the app's just being weird, she shrugs it off and walks over, slipping into the backseat like it's no big deal.

Emily and I casually make our way toward the taxi stand, chatting away, when we see the SUV Becca got into pull off. I don't think twice about it–until, a few seconds later, another identical black Escalade pulls up, this time with an Uber sticker on the window.

The driver hops out, looking around. "Becca?" he calls, clearly confused.

I blink, glancing at Emily. "Uh... did Becca just Uber-hop?" Emily shrugs as the driver pulls closer to us.

214 · SHALLOW DEPTHS

"Are you Becca?" He says through the open passenger window, hoping one of us are the intended ride.

"No, Becca just got in that other UBER Escalade a second ago," I said, pointing to the other black Escalade rapidly disappearing on it's way out of the port area.

"That sucks," the driver muttered, scratching his head.

"Well, we need a ride, can we hop in?" I asked, eager to escape the oppressive heat and the simmering chaos of the terminal.

"Yes, please. Get in," he replied, hoping out and assisting Emily with her luggage.

As the Uber pulled away from the curb, the cool blast of air conditioning was a small relief compared to the storm of emotions brewing inside me. Emily and I sat in awkward silence, each lost in our own tumultuous thoughts.

The drive to South Beach was filled with the kind of tension that comes from knowing something has ended, but not wanting to let go. The heat outside had exacerbated the visibility of my bruises, a stark reminder of the physical and emotional battles I'd endured.

"You know, Camila and I... we're thinking of giving it another shot," I ventured cautiously, "It just makes sense to date someone on the ship since I'm at sea most of my time," I add, watching Emily's reaction closely.

Her smile was sad, tinged with resignation. "I guess some stories are just meant to be chapters, huh? Not whole books."

"Yeah," I sighed, feeling a pang of something like regret. "Sometimes, safety and calm are worth more than... whatever this was," I say, my voice softer now, realizing that sometimes, peace is better than chaos—even when the chaos feels thrilling.

Emily nodded, her gaze drifting out the window. "I need to change things when I get back. Start fresh. Maybe even a new job."

The conversation dwindled as we sped across MacArthur Causeway and approached South Beach, each of us wrapped in our own thoughts. For me, returning to Camila was a safe harbor after the stormy seas of this cruise. For Emily, it was the beginning of an uncertain journey–one that might lead her away from the dangers tied to Bas and whatever lay ahead for Becca.

As the Uber slowed to a stop, I realized that goodbyes were never just about the words spoken. They were about the memories left behind and the silent promises to survive whatever came next.

Standing on the sidewalk outside the Shipboard Media head office, Emily and I shared a moment that felt suspended in time, a pause between the rush of our recent adventures and the reality waiting to engulf us once we walked away from each other. I pointed up at the nondescript office building with a half-hearted smile.

"This is me," I said, pointing up to the 6 story building just off 17th at Michigan, the words feeling heavier than they should.

Emily nodded, her expression a mix of resignation and something more tender. "Nice. I have to admit, I kinda enjoyed the excitement of ship life. And spending time with you. You kinda 'did it' for me, you know." Her smile flickered with mischief. "I haven't stolen anything in days."

Her attempt at lightening the mood did bring a smile to my face, but it was fleeting. "I'm kinda scared to find out what's going to happen with Bas at work," she added, her smile fading into a worried frown.

I glanced around the busy South Beach street, feeling the weight of her situation. "I'd say you and Becca should find another line of work," I suggested, not just to ease her current trouble but as a genuine piece of advice for moving forward.

Just then, Emily's phone buzzed with a FaceTime call. "It's Becca, FaceTime," she said, a hint of relief in her voice as she assumed her friend was just checking in. "She probably misses me already."

"That's my cue," I said, feeling a knot tighten in my stomach. There was so much I wanted to say, about how she'd made an impression on me too, about how I wished things could be different. But instead, I simply added, "Lincoln Road is that way." I pointed south, adding "Anyways, I had a great time. See yah when I see yah." With that, I turned and walked into the building, the finality of the moment settling heavily around me.

As soon as Emily answered the call, the screen filled with a jarring image that sent a chill down her spine. Becca appeared, not with the joyful enthusiasm of a friend calling to say she missed her, but bloodied, bruised, and unmistakably terrified. Becca's face was contorted in pain as she whimpered, her hair clutched cruelly in someone's grip. Then the scene shifted, and Bas's menacing face came into view.

"Emily. You lied to me. You tricked one of my girls to make some money. You are going to repay me every penny you made from my girl Becca, plus fifty thousand more for the trouble," he snarled, his voice cold and ruthless.

A knife suddenly flashed on the screen, pressed against Becca's cheek, causing Emily to gasp in horror. "If I don't get my money in a week, I will cut up Becca's face so she can't work anywhere else ever again," Bas threatened, his tone devoid of any humanity.

The knife's edge glinted ominously under the light, and Emily's heart raced with panic and fear. Becca's eyes, wide with terror, met Emily's through the screen. "HELP!" she cried out, just before the call abruptly ended, leaving the screen dark and Emily frozen in shock.

With her mind racing and terror gripping her heart, Emily snapped into motion. She couldn't leave Becca to such a fate. She couldn't just walk away–not when every second could mean the difference between safety and grave danger for her friend. Without a second thought, Emily darted into the office building after me, her fear for Becca overshadowing her own uncertainty about the future.

As Emily rushed through the sliding doors of the Shipboard Media office, her mind was a whirlwind of fear and desperation. She knew she needed help–my help–and perhaps more than that to save Becca from the gruesome threat Bas had laid out so clearly. Every step was propelled by urgency, her breaths short and sharp as she navigated the sleek, modern lobby. She was painfully aware of every tick of the clock, each one echoing ominously with the potential consequences of her delay.

In that frantic moment, Emily realized the full weight of her entanglement with Bas's dark world. The danger wasn't just a distant threat; it was visceral, immediate, and horrifyingly personal.

Inside the sleek, modern office of Shipboard Media, the tension was noticeable on Emily's face. The office was a perfect reflection of the company's brand: polished chrome surfaces gleaming under soft, ambient lighting, and minimalist furniture that spoke of expensive tastes and corporate power.

While Emily searched the office for me, I was in my bosses office getting an earful from the CEO - Clara Holland.

Where should I start with Clara. At the helm of Shipboard Media sits a force of nature in stilettos. Picture this: crisp white blazer that looks like it's never seen a wrinkle, an immaculate South Beach tan that screams "I brunch with millionaires," and platinum blonde hair in a razor-sharp bob that frames those ice-blue eyes like they could cut glass.

She's the CEO of Shipboard Media now, but trust me, Clara didn't just waltz into that position like some pampered heiress. Oh no, she shagged, clawed, and hustled her way there– literally.

Back in the early '90s, Clara was fresh out of college with that wide-eyed, innocent thing going on, but don't let that fool you. She took one look at the cruise industry and knew exactly how she was going to play the game.

Fresh-faced and eager, she started as a cruise staff, smiling sweetly at guests by day, but by night, well... let's just say she wasn't only hosting a Bingo. It was a different time, okay?

And if there's one thing Clara understood, it was that power doesn't just fall into your lap–you make it happen. And if that meant a few extra hours of "networking" in the captain's quarters, well, Clara wasn't one to shy away from an opportunity.

Male-dominated industry? Please. That was just Clara's playground. She'd bat those perfectly mascaraed lashes, say all the right things, and when the time was right, she'd seal the deal–on her terms. It didn't take long before she moved up the ranks. A couple of well-timed "promotions," and suddenly, Clara found herself as Cruise Director. That's where the real fun began.

Back then, cruise directors weren't just planning talent shows and leading conga lines. No, they were getting kick-backs from all the tours, restaurants, and stores they pushed on passengers in every port. And Clara? She made damn sure she was getting her cut.

She had an instinct for business and a sixth sense for sniffing out profit. It wasn't long before she figured out she didn't need to share the spoils with anyone. Why should the cruise line take the lion's share when she was the one doing the work? That's when Shipboard Media was born.

Clara saw an opportunity and ran with it, faster than most people could blink. She created a network of "Shopping Guides" on just about every cruise line out there, funneling eager tourists into specific stores, tours, and restaurants–all while raking in the cash from the shop owners who were all too happy to pay her for the steady stream of customers. It was brilliant, really. She already had the connections in the ports, and–let's be real–she already had a few flings in high places at the cruise line offices. A well-timed rendezvous here and there, and boom, she had exclusive contracts locked down.

Now, in her fifties, Clara is Pilates-fit and lean, like Gwyneth Paltrow, and still as shaggable as ever, if you ask her. She's built an empire, one perfectly manicured step at a time. And while she may smile sweetly at cocktail parties, don't be fooled– Clara Holland didn't just build her empire. She conquered it.

So, here I was, pleading my case to Clara, trying desperately to hold onto the independence I had cultivated over the years. "You, as a woman, should know how hard this job is," I implored, hoping to strike a chord of solidarity.

"Believe me, I know," Clara replied with a nod that suggested empathy but her tone held a finality that hinted at impending decisions I might not like.

"So I don't need an assistant–" I started, but was abruptly interrupted.

"–I tried to tell her," Kevin chimed in, eager to affirm his stance to Clara and Judy.

I shot Kevin a glare, my frustration boiling over.

"And then there's this fuckin' guy," I muttered under my breath, loud enough for everyone, especially Clara, to hear.

Clara's eyes narrowed slightly at Kevin. "Give us a second here, Kevin," she said, dismissing him with a subtle flick of her wrist. Kevin, looking slightly affronted, backed away and pulled the heavy door until it was almost closed, his retreat allowing us a semblance of privacy, though the glass walls of the office left little to the imagination.

As Kevin exited, a frantic-looking Emily appeared in the open office area, her presence disrupting the typical workflow as she approached Kevin, desperation tinting her voice. "Hey, Emily, right? Are you here to take me up on a job?" Kevin asked, misreading her urgency.

"Where's Christina?" Emily's voice was sharp, her eyes focussed. Without a word, Kevin points down the hall and a frantic Emily bolts toward Clara's office. Kevin followed.

Back in the CEO's office, Judy Tucker, Clara's most trusted VP with a broad Australian accent, thick legs and a no-nonsense demeanor, added her piece.

Straight out of Australia with an accent that could cut glass and legs built for stomping through corporate drama. Judy grew up tough, scrapping her way through life and taking no prisoners. She started at the bottom, working on cruise ships, but her grit and sharp mind quickly got her noticed.

When Clara met Judy, she knew she'd found the perfect partner in crime. While Clara finesses deals, Judy bulldozes through any obstacles. Practical and intimidating in her tailored pants, Judy handles business without excuses or delays. People know better than to cross her, and if they do, they regret it.

Judy Tucker may not be as glamorous as Clara, but make no mistake—she's the backbone of Shipboard Media.

"We have to do what's best for our clients," Judy stated firmly, her robust frame leaning slightly forward over the table.

"It's only going to benefit you in the long run," Clara continued, trying to smooth over the ruffled atmosphere.

I shook my head, the stress of the conversation heightening my resolve. "I don't need the help! I really don't want to share my commissions. I have it all under control," I argued, feeling cornered but defiant.

At that moment, my phone buzzed with a text message, the timing couldn't have been worse. Glancing down, I saw a message that could potentially complicate things further.

The text read "Hey, I'm a friend of Patrick Dumont. He mentioned you can get us five 'Friends' for our cruise next week. GFE. We can do 30k cach. Please confirm." My eyes can't hide the stress this created, and Clara caught the distraction and her expression soured.

"Since it seems your phone is more important than this conversation, and you're not open to working with an assistant, you're fired," Clara declared, her voice cold.

"What? No!" I exclaimed, putting my phone away, my heart sinking as the reality of her words hit me.

That's when Emily burst through the door, her entrance as dramatic as the situation demanded.

"Not so fast, maybe I can help," she announced, drawing the attention of everyone in the room.

Clara raised an eyebrow. "And who are you?"

"My name is Emily, I am a master saleswoman and extremely educated in the finest luxury items," Emily began, her pitch perfect and persuasive. "I know what men, and women, secretly want and how to romance those luxurious items to them. I was onboard, with Christina, this past week, and she had her best sales numbers in years."

Kevin, surprisingly, supported Emily's claim. "It's true. She totally helped," he said, earning yet another scowl from me for these constant antagonisms.

Emily continued, her proposal bold and timely. "It would be a tragedy to fire such a 'seasoned' shopping guide with so many 'years' of experience. That said, she does have a problem asking for, and receiving, help so I'd like to be considered as Christina's assistant. AND, I can start today."

Judy was quick to object, "In case you missed it, Christina doesn't work here anymore, and you can't start today. You haven't done any training," her skepticism clear.

Undeterred, Emily approached Clara and gently picked up her hand, examining the watch on her wrist.

"As I said, I am extremely educated in luxury items. Take this watch, for instance. This is the Omega Seamaster Aqua Terra," she described the watch expertly. "It has a Self-winding movement with Co-Axial escapement. 2 barrels mounted in series, automatic winding in both directions and the power reserve is an impressive 60 hours. Those details are great but only a *Boss*, someone who makes final decisions, would wear a timepiece like this." the words slipping eloquently through her lips.

Turning to Judy with a slight smirk, she added, "I don't see you wearing this watch."

Clara, clearly impressed and perhaps a bit amused by Emily's audacity, made a swift decision. "You're right, it would be a tragedy to fire Christina. And, she needs help." Clara looks at Emily, Kevin, Judy, then to back to me, adding "Christina, you're back on the team and Emily, you're hired."

Judy shook her head in disbelief as Emily hugged Clara and then, with a sleight of hand that was as smooth as her sales pitch, Emily stealthily pocketed a Mont Blanc pen from Clara's desk.

"Thank you, thank you. You won't regret it!" Emily beamed, her relief palpable.

"Christina, count yourself lucky to have a girl like this by your side. I expect big sales numbers this week from you two," Clara concluded, addressing me with a nod that suggested I had indeed just dodged a professional bullet. "Kevin will send Emily's details to the ship's crew purser," she added, then turned to Emily, "*Welcome to Shipboard Media!*"

As Emily and I exited Clara's office, the reality of what just transpired began to settle. I was still reeling from the close call of almost losing my job, and here was Emily, not just saving the day but also joining the fray. The office corridors that had felt constricting before now seemed to promise new beginnings. Whatever came next, it was clear that Emily was someone you wanted by your side, in the boardroom or on the sales floor. And as we stepped back into the bustling environment of Shipboard Media, I felt a renewed sense of purpose and perhaps, against all odds, a spark of excitement for the challenges ahead.

The warmth of the South Beach sun seemed to intensify as Emily and I walked out of the Shipboard Media office, a silence stretching between us, filled only by the distant chatter of tourists and the occasional honk from the bustling street traffic. As we made our way to Lincoln Road, the atmosphere felt charged, the sunlight glaring down as if to spotlight the chaos of my life that had just compounded in the last few hours.

Lincoln Road Promenade was as vibrant and eclectic as ever, a bustling mosaic of locals and tourists mingling amidst the backdrop of art deco architecture and swaying palm trees. Street performers added a layer of lively music to the scene, while couples and families strolled between shops and outdoor cafes, their laughter and conversations creating a tapestry of everyday joy that felt worlds away from the turmoil Emily and I were navigating.

We found a bench outside the GAP, its metal surface hot from the sun, forcing us to shift uncomfortably as we settled down. For a moment, we just watched the world go by, a brief respite before diving back into our realities. I turned to Emily suddenly, pulling her in for a hug that was both a thank you and a plea for the normalcy we both craved.

"Thank you for saving my job. You have no idea how much I need this job right now and how much that means to me," I started, my voice thick with emotion. "It's crystal clear to me now that I do need help. I've struggled all my life to do things on my own only to get so far. You've helped me accept that, I know now I could never do this on my own."

Then, as reality seeped back in, I frowned, "Now, what the fuck was that? We're working together now? What about your job and your classes?"

Emily's expression darkened with worry as she slid off the bench and knelt in front of me, her eyes earnest and scared. "Christina, I can explain," she began, her voice trembling slightly. "I have a terrible trait of lying. I get away with it 99% of the time, but when I get caught, I really get caught in a big lie." Emily exhales like a huge weight has finally been lifted off her chest, her shoulders dropping as if she's been carrying the world on them.

Emily continues. "I lied to you, telling you my boss let me take vacation time. I also lied to my boss about being sick then taking a vacation with Becca. He found out what I did. What WE did. You know I lied to Becca too and told her Bas approved, and paid for, the trip. Because of my lies, Bas kidnapped Becca and he wants all the money she made on the trip, plus $50,000, returned ASAP or he'll disfigure her so she doesn't work again. I need your help. I can't go back to work, or my apartment, since I'm roommates with Becca. I have no savings and have no one else to turn to. I'm so sorry for all of this. You're my only hope. I know together we can pay back Bas before Becca gets hurt."

The weight of her confession hit me like a physical blow, my mind racing as I ran my hands through my hair, feeling the heat of the sun and the weight of the world all at once.

"Holy Fuck, you suck. Let me think," I vented, then sighed deeply. "Ok, I can borrow some money to pay Bas back, but then I need to pay 'that' person back. Which brings us back to square one."

Just then, my phone buzzed with another text from Patrick's colleague, asking for confirmation on five escorts for the next cruise. "So, are we good for the GFE's? Please confirm!" it read.

"We also need to find 5 girls before next cruise," I share with Emily, texting Patrick's colleague back, "5 GFE's confirmed. See you next week."

I continued, feeling the enormity of our predicament, "Since we can't use any girls from your old job, I only know one other person I trust who can make that impossible task, of getting 5 escorts who have time off to take a cruise, happen."

I scrolled through my phone and dialed a number on speakerphone. The display read: "Sister Laura Delgado."

As the phone rang, chaos unfolded in front of us. A shuttle bus emblazoned with "Evergreen Nursing Home" screeched to a halt, one wheel on the curb right in front of us. The doors flung open, and my mom, Martina, stumbled out and crashed to the ground. Handing my phone to Emily, I rushed over to help my mom.

"Christina, there you are! I knew your office was around here someplace. Got to love Google maps," my Mom exclaimed, somewhat disoriented.

My sister Laura's voice echoed from the speaker phone. "Mom, is that you? Are you with Christina?"

Martina shot back, her voice loud and filled with a mix of irritation and relief, "Laura, oh my god, it's been so long, I didn't know you knew how to use a phone SINCE YOU NEVER FUCKING CALL ME?"

As police sirens wailed closer, leading to a patrol car pulling up next to us, the situation spiraled even further. "Fuck you, Mom! What do you want, Christina?" Laura's voice crackled through the speaker.

I grabbed the phone back from Emily, tension knotting my stomach as I tried to process the unfolding drama. "Hey Laura, thanks for taking my call. It's a little crazy right now but I have a huge favor to ask. But first, hang on a second," I said, then turned to Emily, "The police have arrived so you need to get outta here! Get back to the port and sign yourself on the ship using the crew gangway. Kevin is sending all of your details to the ship's crew purser so you should have no problem getting on board. I'll figure out all of this craziness and meet you back on board. Hopefully alone, but more than likely, by the sounds of it, with my mom. Sorry."

"No, it's OK. I'm sorry, All of this is happening so fast, I just want to let you know I really like you, I like *this* and I don't want you to get back with Camila. I want you all for myself," she confessed breathlessly.

"I...I was thinking the same thing. I loved hanging with you this week, being with you felt...like the right thing. I was just too scared to admit it earlier," I replied, feeling a surge of hope amidst the madness.

As we said our hurried goodbyes, Emily leaned in and kissed me, a moment of sweet amidst the chaos.

The moment seemed to pause around us, the usual bustle of Lincoln Road fading into a soft blur as Emily stood and closed the distance between us. Her movements were hesitant yet determined, a contrast to the decisive, almost brash way she had navigated the chaos of the past few days. The afternoon sun cast a warm glow around us, illuminating her features with a soft light that seemed to highlight the earnestness in her eyes.

As she leaned in, the world seemed to slow, the noise of chattering tourists and distant street music dwindling into silence. Her hand reached up tentatively to cup my cheek, her touch gentle but firm, grounding me in the reality of what was happening. There was a brief moment where our eyes locked– a silent question in hers, seeking permission, an affirmation that this was okay, that this was wanted.

I could feel the heat of the sun, hotter and more intense as if mirroring the heat between us. Then, as her lips finally met mine, the sensation was soft and warm, a gentle pressure that was explorative at first but quickly deepened with an intensity that took my breath away.

Emily kissed with a passion that conveyed both urgency and a deep-seated fear of not having another chance. Her lips moved against mine with a fervor that spoke of raw emotions, of days filled with tension and nights filled with longing. The kiss was a confession, a promise, and a desperate plea all at once. It was as if she was trying to communicate everything she felt, everything she feared, and everything she hoped for in that one act.

The world around us resumed its pace, but for those few seconds, everything had stood still. The heat of the sun, the sounds of the city, the weight of our troubles–all of it melted away, leaving nothing but the sensation of her lips on mine, soft yet insistent, gentle yet demanding.

As we pulled apart, the cool breeze that followed felt stark against the warmth of our lips, a reminder of the reality we were about to face. But for a moment, none of that mattered. For a moment, it was just Emily and me, and a kiss that felt like it could change everything.

As Emily walked away, Martina, managed to drop her jaw in shock. "What? Are, are you *a* gay?" she blurted out, causing both the police officers and me to turn her way.

"Who's gay? Christina, what's going on there? I heard sirens," Laura's voice demanded attention from the phone.

One policeman helped steady Martina on her feet, while the other approached me. "Alright, who wants to start explaining this shit-show?" he asked, his tone exasperated yet expectant.

Grabbing the phone, I sighed, "Laura, I think I'm gonna have to call you back."

ABOUT THE AUTHOR

As fresh as Ryan Reynolds' toupée and busier than Diddy's defence lawyers, Milan Skrecek's distinctive voice and knack for crafting evocative, compelling stories have earned him multiple awards for both writing and directing.

Along with his writing and directing credits, Milan has worked on projects for global heavyweights NIKE, Nintendo, Royal Caribbean, Celebrity Cruises, Cheech & Chong, LVMH, EFFY Jewelry, MuchMusic, Epic Rights, and rock legends KISS. Yup, you read that right–KISS.

Milan heads Ketchum, Killum Wynn Studios, LLC, a dynamic production studio based in Tampa, Florida, where he's spearheading a slate of exciting film and TV projects. From the gripping thriller 'Shallow Depths' to the holiday rom-com 'A Caliente Christmas', Milan's creative vision knows no bounds. He's even got the wildly imaginative horror 'Betty White Kills Zombies' in the pipeline. And let's not forget 'Light It Up!', a vibrant, high-energy Christmas rom-com, starring locator wrestlers, that promises to be a hit. Milan's studio is quickly becoming a hub for bold, diverse storytelling with plenty of surprises on the horizon.

Manufactured by Amazon.ca
Acheson, AB